I0582752

THE NAMELESS

STUART WHITE

PENOBI PRESS

To the teenager who needed to escape and learn his true identity

INTRODUCTION

The Nameless is a young adult dystopian novel set in a fictional, futuristic world. It contains scenes of violence, torture, and cannibalism, as well occasional bad language.

It is born from my love of dystopia, from Brave New World and 1984 in my childhood, to The Hunger Games, Divergent, and The Maze Runner when I was a young adult.

I've drawn much inspiration from the energy, tension, and darkness of those worlds, and I hope this is a tale that will sit alongside those novels in your mind as the reader.

PART I
THE GREENHORN

CHAPTER 1
SEVEN

Realm Rule ɪ:
Honour thy Autokratōr and esteem thy Realm. Both come before thyself.

Today is the biggest day of my life. I will find out my name.

'It'll be fine, Seven. You're going to ace it,' whispers Six. I tilt my head closer as her voice tickles my ear.

I turn my head to face her, and frown, lost in her dilated pupils. The impending Caste Test is forgotten for that second. 'Maybe.'

I'm soaked and sticky, surrounded by twenty fellow Greenhorns from our training camp. Well, at least we're Greenies for one more day...after this, we'll either be someone else or no-one. Named or Nameless.

The smell of damp, old sweat, and urine fills the back of the truck. Twelve wears a permanent scowl, One bites his nails, and Nine's hands shake on her tapping legs. The road out of camp is bumpy and the rain outside thumps on the canvas roof.

The Guardian stares at me. Smiler, I call him. He's never seen a fluoride bar in his life and his teeth are rotting, black shards of obsidian. He must've heard something but can't be sure I spoke otherwise he'd smack me over the head with his rifle.

'Silence. 'Specially you, Seven. And you, Six.' He gnashes his decaying teeth, glowering at me, then her.

I stare down, rubbing my scarred back. My stomach howls in hunger. I didn't eat the meal they gave us last night. Nerves kicked in big style. The prospect of finding out my real name sent my guts jumping like an angry snake was lodged in there.

When we're alone my foster mum, Cherish, calls me Cas.

But it can't compare to a real name.

A name will make me human.

And closer to discovering my real family.

Part of the Realm.

It's all I've wanted for as long as I can remember.

Six chews her nails, then stares at them. A fly crawls through her matted, blonde hair. At least, it would be blonde if it were clean. Mud and dust make it sludge brown. If we get assigned to Military, I heard we'd get to shower any time we want.

The truck turns hard, and I'm pressed against Six. The bare skin of our arms touch. I keep mine there for much longer than I should. I close my eyes. Then it's gone and my skin is cold once more.

I rub my arms to heat up, but it's useless, so instead I rub the tattoo on my triceps. E820907. It gets lasered off when we graduate. If we graduate.

Every Greenie in our camp wears the same thing - a sleeveless grey top, with calf-length trousers in the same colour. No shoes, of course. The Guardians swagger around in their worn boots all day, thinking they're big shots. Yes, shoes would be real good.

I assess the twenty Greenhorns around me. Some have stern, focused looks. Those are the ones who'll pass the Caste Test, get assigned to their role and find out their names. But some have pale, panicked faces. Those will fail. Especially Three. His round, colourless face is sodden. His fear makes me angry. He's given up. I want to shake him, but it wouldn't do any good. He used to be decent, maybe even one of the better ones, but now he's done for.

I shiver at the thought. We all know what happens if you don't pass.

The truck stops and a Guardian opens the back door.

'Out. Single file.'

We form a straight line, facing a large criss-cross wire gate. All that metal makes me shudder.

Rain splashes down hard, creating a mud bath at my feet. I squeeze my toes into it, releasing some of my nerves. Floodlights surround us, chasing away the timid night.

'Scary, huh?' whispers Six.

Smiler's on us in an instant. 'Who spoke? I heard something. One of you spoke.'

The group of Greenies remains silent. Smiler prowls. He slides his hood back and eyes us all, one-by-one. As his hair gets wetter, his frown gets deeper.

'It was her,' says Twelve, pointing at Six.

Smiler licks his lips as he approaches Six. 'Ah, the pretty little Alpha. Not sure I've lashed you before. Down on the ground. Lift your top...'

Six leans away, her hands trembling as she grips the bottom of her shirt. She's always in-line. She's never been in trouble before.

'It was me,' I say, my jaw tightening.

Smiler turns his ugly head.

'No,' says Six.

'It was me. I said it.' I nod to Six, who shakes her head. Her eyes are wide.

Smiler's smirk capsizes. 'Down. Top up. Three lashes.'

I fall onto the ground and slide my top up. My stomach squelches against the soft mud, my back exposed to the rain.

Smiler hands me the wooden stick, covered in deep bite marks. Probably half of them are mine. I place it between my teeth and wait. The whip snaps through the night air as he gets ready. An earthworm slides and burrows through the wet mud, struggling to survive.

5

Smiler's foot pushes my head further into the sludge.

CRACK.

My teeth bite down into the wood, a splinter piercing my gum. My eyes scrunch closed to better hide the tears. My back arches as a reflex to the lash.

'Flat on the ground, Seven. This's good for you. Embeds discipline and respec', yes it does.' And some nasty scars to remind you of both.'

CRACK.

The leather slices through the skin still raw from the first lash. My fists ball and bury into the mud. I force my face further into the sludge, trying to disappear, hoping it's over soon. Maybe the worm has it right. My teeth are now embedded in the wood, my mouth almost numb. But I know there's one more to come.

I hold my breath.

CRACK.

It's the worst. The end of the whip catches my cheek, right up to the corner of my eye. The blood flows down my face as I freeze, unable to unclench. My back is on fire, but my face is worse, like a knife carved right through it. I lay it on the cold, wet ground, hoping the temperature will soothe it, but it only stings more.

I breathe.

Rough hands pull me to my feet. 'Good, Seven. Took it like a Guardian. No crying or whimpering. You might have a future, yet.' Smiler gives me a broad grin, showing every one of his five decaying teeth, and moves to the front of the group. He indicates for us to follow.

I pull my top down over my bleeding, stinging back. That sure isn't going to help during the Test. But I would never be able to watch Six get lashed.

I try to use the emotional shutdown technique. Imagine the blank, white wall. Close eyes. Relax muscles. Slow breathing. But it's not working. Every movement, every breath is a continuum of agony.

6

A small hand from behind brushes mine. I turn as much as I dare and see Six. She nods but doesn't risk talking. I nod back and walk on, the pain softening.

Our group marches, silent and in sync, towards a low, square building, unlike anything back at camp. The gutters around the flat roof overflow and cascading waterfalls give the metallic walls a shiny, cold look.

A barbed wire fence claws twenty feet into the air. From two towers, men with large rifles watch us. One of them fixes me with a frosty stare. I turn away and scold myself for losing focus again.

As we pass the front doors, a yellow laser drifts through the air, scanning our tattoos. The number E820907 appears on a screen to the left. My number. My name.

For now.

A plastic frame beeps as we march beneath it. They could be metal detectors, which they had at the old A-reports. I want to ask, but Realm Rule gigabillion, or whatever; think, but don't speak out of turn. Crap, I can't even remember the Rules.

Breathe, Seven. You know this. It's Rule 16, isn't it? This is what happens when you lose focus. Loss of focus leads to confusion, which leads to frustration, and ultimately to indiscipline. Nobody wants that. Not the Autokratōr. Not the Realm. Not me.

We stand for a moment in a long corridor. Cold, sterile, and white. I feel cleaner just being here. Once everyone passes the detector we begin moving again, deeper into the station. Six's eyes are wide, taking in every detail.

At the end of the atrium, there are two doors, one labelled female and the other male. Three new adults scrutinise us. I wonder if they've started assessing us already.

'Welcome, Greenhorns.'

A lady, tall and thin, pushes a strand of dark hair from her stretched face, and holds out her skinny arms. She's dressed in white, like everybody who serves the Realm. I can't wait for my own whites. My bones ache at the thought of belonging.

'I'm Serra. The Chief Tester for this centre. Today's a big day for you all. If you perform well enough, you get assigned a role and serve our noble Autokratōr Tyndareus. *Hail the Autokratōr. Serve the Realm.*'

Everyone mimics her, in unison. It's strange but I don't want to say the memorised words. I've never hesitated before. I pause, glancing at Six, but finally murmur it, just a second after the others. Serra doesn't notice. She smiles and walks through an unmarked door.

I know I should respect her because she works for the Realm, but I don't trust her forced smile as she turns away. I've seen that fake smile before, when that scientist from Circle City came and took my blood. 'It's just a little sample we take from everyone,' he said. He lied. Broke Rule 5. Nobody else had blood taken.

Several Guardians, who'd been waiting behind us, now stand beside the marked doors.

'Greenhorn males through here, and females through there. Time to get cleaned up.'

Six gives me a small smile before disappearing.

Inside the changing room, my bare feet trace dimpled cream tiles. Rows and rows of white sleeveless shirts and three-quarter length trousers hang from pegs all around the room. In the centre are showers.

'Remove your dirty clothes and place them into this garbage chute,' shouts a squat, dark-haired Guardian. 'Then shower, *properly*. The Testers don't want to deal with filthy Greenhorns. Dry yourselves with towels from the shelf in the back, then put on a set of whites. There will be one that fits you. Find it.'

The Guardians exit the room through a second door at the back. We're alone.

I stare at the boys from my training camp. They don't speak to me usually, unless it's to throw an insult, so I look for a spot to change, imagining life in the City. I've seen incredible pictures.

The Realm covers all Europa, but I only care about The Hall of Ancestral Records.

'What do you think will be in the Test, Rex?' asks Thirteen.

'It changes each year to make sure we can't prepare for it,' says Twelve. His fan club calls him Rex. Thinks he's better than all of us and can get a name without earning it. He's the biggest grub around here.

My body tenses as I approach him. 'Why'd you tell Smiler it was Six?'

Two of his groupies stand in my way.

'She'll have enjoyed your little hero act. Pity you'll always know I've been there first.'

Twelve laughs and his fans copy. I surge for him, try to fight my way past Thirteen and One to hit him. Hard. With anything. My arms, legs and head jerk back and forth, but four of them have me held tight-like.

'Always the hot head, Seven. That's why you'll never make it in the Realm. I'll need to speak to Father about getting you a nice Guardian job back here at camp. You and Smiler can be Gutters together.'

I continue to wriggle but I'm wedged in. My back's agony, wet blood sticking my shirt to my skin.

'Leave him.' It's One.

'What's it to you?' asks Twelve.

'It's not a fair contest, four on one. Let him go, he's been through enough already, no?'

I turn to One. He towers over the rest of us, staring at Twelve.

'Leave him, boys. Not worth it,' says Twelve, turning back to his shower.

They let me go and move into the water.

Nobody messes with an Enhanced. And One is clearly that. He's what the Realm is all about: honesty, integrity, and fair play. Unlike Twelve or Smiler.

'Thanks,' I say.

He nods then heads to a shower at the far end of the room, alone.

I remove my bloody, wet, and muddy shirt with care and step into the hot water.

Wisps of steam circulate the room as I enjoy the first warm shower I've ever had. My earliest memories are of life in camp and one or two snippets of time when Cherish first took me in. She's always been there for me; sneaking extra food or clean clothes, even when I haven't earned them. Those other Greenies hate it, but it saved me. Plus, the Guardians love her, so she gets away with it.

My skin turns red, and I push my muddy hair off my face. The water stings the bleeding flesh on my back, but I force myself to stay under. I won't give anyone the satisfaction of seeing me in pain. Turning for relief, the water running down my chest, I close my eyes and enjoy the pulses of the shower. I want to stay under here forever.

I wriggle my toes in the rust-coloured liquid pooling at my feet. I'll get a shower every morning in Military training. And probably clean clothes, too. And I'll be with a group that like me. Maybe.

'What you hoping for, Rex?' Thirteen asks.

'Military or Academics. As long as I don't get exiled. I'd rather be killed than take that shame.'

'Really? You'd rather die than be exiled?'

'Absolutely. Living off next to nothing, fighting and killing each other for scraps of food. Nothing but the rags on their backs. And worst of all, they don't even have a name. I'd never live like that.'

'And cannibals,' adds Thirteen. 'I heard some of them are scutting cannibals. Leeches, they call them.'

'Wouldn't surprise me,' says Twelve. 'Anyway, Father says he'll talk to the Autokratōr himself if my score is high enough. I might even get assigned to the Black Knights. Father used to serve with them on the front line of the Eurasian border.'

The Greenhorns surrounding him give gasps of awe. He's told

everyone this story, a million times, but they always lap it up. Black Knights, what crunk. I'll still hammer him in the Physical Test.

'Did you hear about that new Black Knight, Rex? The tele-screen showed him in a training drill last night. He was so good, they promoted him right up. That could be you!' It's Thirteen. Sniveller.

'He's no big deal. He's not even been in combat yet. Father served for twenty years.'

Here we go again. His Father is some kind of big deal, apparently. It's why he gets to see and know his parents, while the rest of us runts must fight and scrape for any kind of identity.

'Are your parents coming to the Destination ceremony?' asks Thirteen.

'No, it would be beneath them to travel to such a place.' Twelve turns to me. 'Only muck like Seven's wet-nurse will be there. Can't believe he took lashes for his girlfriend, the big sog.'

My eyes blaze. My fists clench. I take two steps forward. 'Shut your mouth or I'll break it.' The words spit out angrier than the wounds on my back.

He takes a step forward, a mammoth grin on his face.

I swing for him, but my feet slide on the soaked tiles, and I fall hard. On my back.

Seconds pass where I hear, see, smell nothing. The pain plummets me into an abyss, which I don't want to come out of.

A kick to my stomach brings me back around. As I double-up, the wounds open further on my back. Twelve laughs, echoed by several others. An almighty punch lands on my right thigh. The tissue throbs and I struggle to move my leg.

Lying on the floor, lashed, beaten, and naked, the thought of destroying Twelve in the Tests consumes me. I want to pass for me. But even more, I want to pass with a better score than Twelve, just so I can see that smug face fall.

I stand up and Twelve stares at me, expecting a backlash. My muscles contract, my fists close.

Smiler walks into the changing room. 'Two minutes, Greenies.'

I turn away, exhaling to blow out the hatred. I'll wait for my chance.

Closing down my feelings like they taught us, I'm in the zone. Concentrating on what's to come. If I blow this, I'll never discover who my real family are. A mum or dad, perhaps a brother or sister.

I must pass the Caste Test.

I must become a citizen of the Realm.

I must find my name.

CHAPTER 2
PHYSICAL

Realm Rule 2:
Respect fellow Realm citizens like you respect thyself.

I exit the shower room in my fresh, clean clothes and we gather in a small, white waiting room. I wait, stretch, and concentrate on my controlled breathing. The sweet soap smell fills my nostrils. I inhale and use it for stimulation. My heart beats quicker. Sounds are sharper, scents are stronger.

'You'll be separated into your Test groups according to your current training rankings,' Smiler says, reading from a script.

I'm surprised he *can* read. He's hardly the élite of the Guardians. None of the ones they station out here are.

'Alpha to Theta, you're doing Physical first,' he adds.

Six is the Alpha, of course. I'm the Delta. The six others include the king of grubs, *Rex*. Ugh, it's hurts me to even think that name. Twelve. The Beta. Man, it frustrates the crunk out of me that he's above me. Just because he's better at all that Realm history stuff.

'Iota to Pi, you're on Mental. Rho to Omega, Genetics.'

My group moves through a dark, stuffy corridor, so low I have to bend my neck. When we emerge into the biggest room I've ever seen, I gasp.

It must be at least two hundred metres in length and width. A red running track with white lines encompasses a large grass field. The grass looks strange—it's all one length, and short, like it's been cut, shorn like hair. None of my training has prepared me for this.

The Guardians who escorted us here move to the side of the hall, and a man with curly, dark hair stands in front of us. He wears the same clothes as us but fills them much better. I look at my own skinny legs, swamped by my white three-quarter lengths. Why doesn't he wear the normal whites of the Realm?

'I'm Saull. Welcome to your Physical Test. Over the next few hours, I'll be assessing physical components important to the Realm in its recruitment of Military personnel. I did this same Test five years ago, so I know what you're going through. I know you're nervous. Relax and do your best. Your scores are cumulative, so the better you do here, the better chance you have of making the cut.'

I move closer to Saull as he speaks. His long hair falls over his face, and his top two buttons are undone. His stance relaxed and informal, unlike the erect, rigid posture of most others from the Realm.

Three stands next to me, his belly hanging below his shirt line. He's shaking, and I don't blame him. He never did extras after our physical sessions, back at camp, and should have worked harder. He's not Realm material. I can only imagine his Mental scores put him in the top eight with us.

Six is in much better shape than Three, and as we move towards the track, there's a confident bounce in her light step. Her hair's much brighter now that it's washed, and I'm reminded she has freckles, now uncovered from under layers of dirt. She looks...different...

She's quick, and so is Twelve, but he's not even my main competition.

'Ready for this, sog?' he mutters to me. 'I'm gonna get you this time.'

'Keep your mouth shut,' I say. 'Or you'll choke on my dust.'

I look to the right. One is in the starting position already. Crouched and intense. He's my rival. That grub beat me back at camp loads of times.

This is about me. The Caste Test will define my whole life. This is my chance to get the first clue to finding my family. I can't... I won't mess it up.

I stand on the white line at the start of the 100-metre sprint and examine my competition once more, determined that none of them will beat me. I need to make Cherish proud. I want that moment where she looks at me, when I graduate, and she is glad she made all those sacrifices for me.

'Remember, it's time, not position, which decides your score in this one. You're not in direct competition, so stay in your lanes. Do not interfere with the other runners,' says Saull. 'You'll go when I blow the whistle.'

The whistle shrieks and I'm off; forcing my legs forward, pumping my arms, remembering the technical training we got in camp. Plyometrics, the instructor called it. I run as hard as I can. My heart thumps and my feet pound the track with every stride.

Then I feel it – my bruised thigh screams at me. Every stride makes it worse, but I force it out of my mind.

I glance left, out the corner of my eye. No one. I glance right and One's there. I dig in, ignoring my tight lungs. Halfway. A second glance and he's just behind me. I force myself forward, giving everything. *I will be assigned. I want my name.* I repeat it over and over.

A surge of energy and clarity flows through me. Perhaps it's my adrenal glands, perhaps it's the training. Keep running. Keep breathing. Keep the pins pumping. No matter that the lacerations on my back sting.

The finish line approaches, my legs fiery with fatigue. I check over my shoulder, and I've five metres on One. How? But as I turn back, I lose my balance, my ankle twists, and I smash down onto the hard track.

All I've worked for all these years, gone.

I've lost.

I've failed.

I'll never earn my name.

'Get up, Seven...' Six's voice brings me back to life. I leap up and sprint over the line.

I wasn't last, but I've blown one of my best events, and my thigh's screeching. I massage it as the others finish...

Three ambles over the line last, at least ten seconds after me. He also collapses. He catches my eye, and I push my urge to help him to the back of my mind. My Gurus at camp would say it's pointless to help the weak, that we should be weeding them out, not helping them.

'Two minutes until the next Test. Let's go.' Saull lifts Three and pushes him towards the field. I notice his breathing has returned to normal, way too fast. Is he really not pushing himself.

Focus, Seven. This is all about you.

The rest of physical goes pretty well, although I struggle with flexibility. I win all the other races, determined to make up for my failure – 200 metres all the way up to 3000 metres. And I perform well in the strength Tests – squatted 120 kilograms – that's 20 kilos less than One. I'm buzzing that all those extra hours of training have paid off. But the toughest bit is still to come. I can't expect to be the best in everything; no matter how hard I try.

And my thigh stings but no worse than my tortured back.

'The last part of Physical is combat,' says Saull, bouncing on the balls of his feet.

We approach the ring in the centre of the field. At the side are two sets of boxing gloves, two quarterstaves, and a pair of blunted claustroBlades. We've all practised with this equipment, but I was never the best with a quarterstaff. It's too long for precision. Fingers crossed I get someone easy for that duel.

'Sit around the edges of the ring, please.' Saull instructs. 'Each of you will fight several times, against different opponents, in each of the three forms selected for today: boxing, close combat, and stick fighting. The rules are simple: first to strike an opponent's body five times wins. Best of luck.'

I'm not up first, which I'm glad about. It's One against Three, boxing, and over in seconds. Three falls to the ground before he's even hit.

'Three, you need to swing back,' says Saull, after he hits the deck for the third time.

'I won't hit him,' mutters Three. 'Don't believe in fighting.' He avoids eye contact with Saull as he stands up and takes another jab to the face. Saull shakes his head, clearly thinking the same as me. What's made him like this? It's weird, but his defiance makes me warm to him...well, a little. And you gotta be tough as lead to take punches like that, especially from One.

It finishes 5-0. A walkover. Why didn't I get such an easy opponent? Duel after duel, I concentrate on the movements of each fighter to help me when I take them on.

My first is against Twelve. I refuse to call him Rex. He isn't a king over me. His little fan club sits straighter, eager to see him win. Time to demolish him and shut them all up.

He annihilated Sixteen, the Epsilon, at boxing, so I know he's on form today. We're given the quarterstaves. As we exchange the first few neutral blows, I see he favours his right side, leaning back on his left. A weakness, maybe?

Our sticks clash, wood upon wood, vibrations jarring my arms. I feint to hit him on the right shoulder, spring left, and jab his leg, sweeping my quarterstaff and flooring him.

Yes!

He gets up, livid. Teeth bared, he charges me. I duck his wild swing and jab him in the ribs. He's so angry now; I spend the next few assaults avoiding the feral sweeps of his staff. And twice I get him when he's swinging, so hard that he falls off balance.

I finally win with a shot to the jaw, which draws blood from his mouth.

His face is angry red, and he runs at me again, but Saull stands between us, calming Twelve down and telling him to return to the edge. It's over. His eyes never leave me, even as the next duel starts, between Six and Three. I try to focus on the new fight.

It's close combat, and Six gets the first strikes in. I edge closer with each blow. Three moves like a snail, while Six's nimble movements are a blur. She moves the claustroBlade so deftly, I hope I don't have to face her. But it's also clear Three isn't trying.

'Haha, Three's getting battered by a girl.'

I don't think she hears. Lucky for that grub. She'd kick all their asses with a claustroBlade. But they're right; Three's getting beaten real bad. He better ace his mental or he's in trouble.

Six gives me a nod as she wins and takes her place at the edge. I feel my cheeks flushing and put on my helmet to cover it, before standing to fight.

I quickly beat Thirteen, 5-1, in close combat and scrape a win over One, 5-4, to take my third victory.

My muscles are aching now, and I'm hungry, dehydrated, and tired, but I've got one more fight to go.

'Six versus Seven. Boxing.'

Blood drains from my brain, leaving me light-headed and faint. I don't want to fight Six. I'm a better boxer, but I want her to get another win. She's lost once (to One with the quarterstaves) and won two, but three wins would help her score.

She jumps up, unruffled, and throws me a set of gloves. 'Come on then, *Seven*. Let's see what you're made of.'

I get an early point, when I block her first jab and give her a light punch on the ribs. She winces but isn't seriously hurt. She comes back at me and gets a punch through my guard, smacking my jaw. I taste iron.

I get another point by dodging her next hook and catching her on the side of the head guard. These things are so well cushioned, I know I won't have hurt her. Well, not physically. Sweat drips from her forehead, her face scrunched.

'Don't go easy on me,' she shouts, then launches a jab, faster than her previous one. This one flies through my guard and thumps me on the cheek. I stumble backwards. All I can see are spots. That was some hit.

'I'm not taking it easy,' I say, honestly. My vision's still blurry. I swallow blood.

'Seven, if I think you're not trying, I'll report you.' Saull looks intense, like the Gurus at camp before they dole out punishment.

'Yes, sir.' I get up gingerly and try to focus, but I'm still dazed. The ferrous flavour won't leave.

Six launches another attack, but I block her and stumble backwards. My arms feel heavy, so I should finish this quickly, if I can. If these scutting spots would disappear.

I send off three quick punches, and she's on the deck, her mouth bleeding. If it was anyone else, I'd be happy.

I throw off my gloves and kneel next to her. 'You okay?'

She looks up and gives me a bloody smile, her teeth red. 'I got you good on the cheek, huh?'

I nod and pull her to her feet. We take our places around the edge of the ring.

'Seven wins 5-2.' Saull returns to the middle. 'That's it. Physical is over. I was very impressed with some of you.' He looks at One and then Six. 'Not so impressed with others.' His gaze lingers on Three. 'Go get your lunch. You have Mental afterwards.'

We walk away, but Saull calls me back. My head's banging and the lash wounds sting like hell, so it better be quick.

He waits until we stand alone, the last of the group disappearing through the corridor.

'About your Test...'

'I wasn't going easy on her. Well, not really,' I say, a little too angrily. More blood trickles down my throat. It makes me shiver.

Saull narrows his eyes. 'No, it's not that. Your Physical score looks like it's going to be high.'

'Really?' A flutter of excitement swashes through me, mixed with confusion and doubt. Why's he telling me this? Is this a test?

He nods, giving me the smallest of smiles.

'Like the best in the group? Could I get Alpha?' I probably shouldn't ask, but I can't help it.

'No, not the best in the group.'

My stomach plummets. Well, as long as Twelve isn't the Alpha, I can probably deal with it.

'But it is excellent. If I take out the mishap in the 100.'

I gape at Saull. I knew I'd done well, and I'm better at the physical stuff than most of the others. But for someone to single me out like this. That never happens.

'When I process these results, it will open eyes. You're likely to be put forward for a high-ranking Military position, providing your genetics check out. Commander training probably, depending on your mental score. Perhaps even the Black Knights. Though the Autokratōr picks them personally.'

Commander training? At my age, I was just hoping to get assigned to the Military. And the Black Knights...the best of the best. Something isn't right. I want to believe it, but it doesn't add up. No one's ever mentioned this kind of thing before. My Gurus thought I had potential, but they never raved about me.

My head whirling, I limp after the other Greenies, saturated with daydreams of fighting on the Eurasian border alongside the legendary Grand Guardian Sharan.

But I'm also confused – why did he single me out and tell me all that stuff? There are other strong ones in the group - One and, it makes me vomit to say it, Twelve, too.

What if this is a test? A test within the test, designed to distract me for Mental?

No, it's not that, but something isn't right.

As I leave the field, I notice a swivelling camera following me, like a snake eyeing up its prey, ready to strike.

I wonder if *they* heard all that, and if they'd approve of what Saull told me. I'm not sure I should be getting informed of my results yet. Feels like it's against at least one Realm Rule.

And I wonder who *they* are, always watching and listening in here. Are *they* part of the test, too?

CHAPTER 3
DESTINATION

Realm Rule 3:
Every citizen must work for and serve the Realm.

'He really said that?' Six beams at me. 'Well done, Seven.' My brain swirls.

Our lunch is bread, rice, and vegetables. The best I've ever tasted. One is munching down his third portion and no wonder. We usually get gruel at camp.

Six plays with her rice. She glances back at me and smiles. I look down, buzzing inside. Not sure if it's the look or the caffe-Boost they've given us. I take another sip.

It's years since I've felt this alive, this free. Not since I was locked up in the Cage with no food for days. I didn't 'fess that time and they let me out eventually. During those days in the darkness, I cried for the only time in my life. I wasn't sad or upset, I just did it because I could. It was then I realised it's the food that suppresses our emotions. Without it I could express anything: hate, anger, joy, even love.

Ever since, I've been skipping meals or only eating small amounts. But I reckon today's is drug-free. It isn't mushed up, and I can see the effect on the other Greenies. Grins, mmm's, slurps and happiness. Not the conditioned happiness we've been used to. Real happiness that makes you smile despite an imminent, life-determining Caste Test.

Three walks past our table, having been last to get his lunch.

'Hey, Three. Come sit with us,' Six says, patting the empty seat next to her.

He looks at me, then at One who's taking up two seats. Finally, he shakes his head and moves to a table on his own.

'What's his deal?' I ask Six. 'Why didn't he try in Physical?'

She stares at him for a moment, then turns to me. 'I don't know, but I like it.'

'You like what? Him? Since when?' My chest feels hollow.

'Yes. He's weird, sure, but don't you remember what he used to be like? He could ace these Tests if he wanted to. But he's doing what he thinks is right, not just doing what he's told. I respect that.'

'You respect him failing his Test? He'll become an Exile. How can you respect that?'

'I like people who dare to think their own thoughts and don't always follow. That's why I like you, Seven.'

'Not sure that's always true.' My chest inflates. 'And I'm not sure the Autokratōr would love to hear you say that.' I glance around for any sign of a Guardian, or a little grunt like Twelve.

'Listen, I like and respect him, but I'm not stupid. His defiance is pointless in such a small environment. What impact can a stubborn Greenie make?' She notices One staring at us. 'Anyway, eat your lunch, you'll need it for the next Test.'

After lunch, we move on to Mental, a two-hour multiple-choice test on topics from advanced genomics to Realm history and warfare strategy, as well as morals and ethics. Those are the questions I find the toughest, and I wonder how they'll grade my responses.

Do you agree with genetic segregation?

I should, knowing from our Realm studies class that it's probably what they want to hear. Only a couple of months ago, I would've believed it, too. Until I had a long talk with Cherish. My pencil hovers over the paper in the motion of writing *no*. I look up and see a Guardian in the corner, tall and proud. Happy serving the Realm, like I could be. Keep it together and do the right thing.

Hell, do I have to agree with everything about the Realm? A small voice whispers *yes*. I only half answer some of the other questions.

1. *Label the diagram of the world, below, stating the names of the different realms in the appropriate section and clearly highlighting the borders.*
2. *In which year was the New London wall built, prompting the new name Circle City?*
3. *Explain clearly, with the aid of a diagram, the process of genetic engineering using human embryos.*
4. *State the name of the fourth Autokratōr of Europa.*

I'm really worried about getting that last one wrong. They'll probably kill me if it's not Autokratōr Redman. Bet that twerp Twelve got it.

I glance at Six. I guarantee she has every one correct. Her little Alpha hand scribbles away, moving even faster than when she punched me.

'Time's up.'

That was awful. I can't stop thinking about what Saull said. Did he make a mistake? Or are they up to something else? Trying to see how I respond, perhaps. I just want this Test to be over now.

Still, two down, one to go.

. . .

My skin stings from the electronic bracelet on my wrist. A wire extends from the bracelet back towards a screen, where lots of letters zip across. Genetics is pretty much what I thought. They're taking a sample of our DNA. What they're going to test it for, I've no idea. I know about basic genomics but I'm not an academic like Six, so I'm not going to worry about it too much.

Three is grimacing, his nose scrunched. I hope he did better in Mental than Physical. I cross my fingers, wishing none of these Greenies get exiled. Except Twelve.

The device on my wrist clicks off. I rub the area where loads of red circles mark my skin.

'Off you go,' says the lady in the long white coat. I look down at my own clothes, wondering if these sogs ever wear colours. Right now, it's too much white. I can't believe I dreamed of whites for so long. I'd love to put on a cherry red t-shirt right now. And yellow trousers. Yeah, that would mess up the conformity.

'Pass through here once your Genetic Test's over,' shouts a Guardian, opening a door at the far end of the very clean, and very white, room.

I follow the group into the new room. No chairs. No anything. The walls are, guess what... WHITE! It's driving me crazy. I want to get some black paint and throw it all over this place.

Breathe. Relax. Tuck that feeling away.

Need to stop these emotion tsunamis before one of them spills over. Can't blow this. So close.

I pace the room, silent and alert, and wait for others to finish their Tests. All these feelings are overwhelming. Not to mention what Saull said.

Did my Physical really go so well? It's so un-Realm-like for someone to confide in me. They're usually so focussed and professional. Usually. Smiler's hardly a model Realmer. He's still trying to earn back his name, so he must've messed up bad.

No one ever talks to me like Saull did, except Cherish. But that's making me even more suspicious. Why would he tell me? He could be lying. Actually, I'm sure he is. This is me. I'm decent, top two in my group at Physical, but I'm no standout. No chance.

Or is it another part of the Test?

Ten minutes pass without a word, and finally the last person's finished. It's Three. No surprise there. Even his DNA is slow.

The Guardian leads us along a hot, compact corridor with no windows. Sweat slides down my back and stings my slashes. I've decided that when I graduate from Military Academy, I'll come back here and smack Smiler on the face for all those lashes. Knock a few more of those decaying teeth out.

We walk single-file, and the corridor seems to go on forever. I just want to sit down; don't they know how tiring the Tests are?

We're led into a wide room with folding metal chairs and a huge screen, like the ones that display the news and education programmes back in camp.

'You will remain here until called. You may talk. The telescreen will offer those of you who wish to remain silent wise words of the Autokratōr.'

He switches the screen on, and the symbol of the Realm is emblazoned upon a blue background.

Talking erupts at once.

'Can you believe that genomics question?'
'The long run was nails. And I got gubbed with the claustroBlades.'
'What was that Genetics Test all about? How are they going to score that?'
'Reckon you're still on for Academics, Nineteen?'

I listen to the chatter, sitting on a chair in the corner. Six remains reticent, next to me, chewing her nails then biting her lower lip. I don't disturb her thoughts.

It's surprising they've left us alone. Maybe they think we've earned it. We're almost adults, fully-fledged citizens of the Realm, destined for our roles. Six always says us Greenies are a bit like the stem cells we learn about. Undifferentiated, unspecialised, until we're assigned. Then we all become different, divided to unconnected parts of the Realm, doing our specific responsibilities until we're renewed with younger, newer Greenies.

One sits alone in a corner. We also learned about the Enhanced in Bio. Twelve calls them 'tubers'. But we all know he's a scut. None of us are truly natural anymore, but at least we all have parents. Somewhere. But One's an orphan, engineered by the Realm for one purpose.

The War.

He won't even get a name. He has nothing to earn. He will die for a Realm that will only give him a number.

Over the rabble, the smooth, even voice of our ruler: *'Mastery of one's emotions is mastery of one's actions'.* Well, having no emotions does make life easier. I frown at Six. What if we're not together after this? I decide to close off *that* feeling for now.

The waiting is worse than the actual Test. I rock back and forth. Six stares at the ceiling, her brow furrowed. I want to know what lies in store for us both. But I know I did my best and if Saull was right, and a small part of me doubts it, I've definitely aced my Physical.

'You worried?' I ask. 'I'm sure you did amazing.'

I want to place my arm around her shoulders, and inch it closer and closer. When it's nearly there, she slides against me and puts her head on my chest. I hope she can't feel my heart beating faster. I slowly settle my arm against her the rest of the way.

'It's so easy for you, Seven. You're good at Physical. I was terrible. Got my butt handed to me during combat.'

'No, you didn't. Look.' I turn her head and point at my cheek. 'That was you. Nobody else got a head shot on me. Plus, I'm sure you aced the Mental. You're a dead cert for Academics. Chin up, Six.' I lift her chin and she gives me a teary smile. I've never seen her cry. Emotion is weakness, they say.

But I like it on her.

We sit for a long time in this position. I don't want it to end, despite how sore it is on my back, because when it does, when we get our results, I must say goodbye to Six. And Cherish, who's already told me she can't come to whatever base I'm assigned to. Life without both will be tough.

As we wait, I stroke Six's blonde hair and watch the telescreen.

'Good morning, citizens. Welcome to Roundup, the latest Realm news brought to you as it happens. It's Saturday 17th March 2091 and I am Ged Geddes.

War continues at the Europa/Eurasian border. Eurasian Realm casualties have reached the one million mark in Autokratōr Tyndareus' latest campaign. We are winning the war, but we still need more of our young Greenhorns to be assigned to the Military. Grand Guardian Sharan continues to inspire us all with her efforts. Reports suggest she has almost singlehandedly forced the Eurasians deep into Russian territory.'

That could be me. In just a few months I could be through basic training and into the war, fighting alongside Sharan. I might even get a mention on the telescreen. Cherish would be proud. I wonder if Six would be? I know she'll do many great things, and I'll be proud of each and every one of them.

'The Autokratōr released a statement today. It read, 'This war is not about territory or financial gain, nor is it about power. No, this is about expanding our irrefutably efficacious ways to the rest of the world. Our society has been immensely successful at all levels, and it's vitally important that everyone in the other Realms gets the same opportunities that the people of Europa do.'

I wonder if they have Greenies in other Realms. There's probably one just like me in Eurasia, sitting petrified, awaiting his result. Perhaps he's with a girl, too. Perhaps he's actually telling her he likes her.

'Closer to home we're going live to Westmine, where Hick is waiting to update us on the latest news from the Vanadium mines...'
'Yes, thank you Ged. I'm standing here at the entrance to Westmine, home to the largest population and working force outside the cities, where our lucky Exiles get a second chance to contribute to the Realm. It appears there has just been an extraordinary find, not of Vanadium, the metal they usually mine for, but of Generium, the newly discovered element that is key in modern genetic engineering processes. As most of you know, Generium allows our renewable energy creation to be amplified, and therefore allows our G.E. processes to work much faster. It was the discovery of this element thirty years ago that led to the first safe human modifications, and the cure for genetic disorders such as Cystic Fibrosis and Muscular Dystrophy. Stores have been low and modification work has been limited recently, but this discovery should aid the Academics' efforts in finding the key to improving us and finally ridding the Realm of all genetic imperfection. Back to you, Ged.'

'Did you hear that, Six?' I ask.

'Yes.'

'Aren't you excited?'

She shrugs. 'Not really.'

'But isn't that the kind of thing you want to study?'

'I want to use knowledge and research to improve the lives of everyone in the Realm, not just improve *some* people in the Realm. What's wrong with us the way we are? Why do we have to be improved? In fact—'

'Shhhh.' I nod towards the camera, directed straight at us.

We become silent for a moment, watching it. Finally, it starts to swivel around the room.

'Be careful,' I whisper.

'Yeah, sorry. That was silly.' She snuggles back into my chest.

I hope they didn't hear her.

'And finally, the rebel Exile group calling themselves the Orphans of Thasos no longer exists. A team of Black Knights stormed their headquarters yesterday and have captured the separatist leaders. All Realm citizens can now rest assured that the Autokratōr has stamped out those who rally against his plans for peace. This ends the Orphans of Thasos as a topic of conversation and any discussion of this will lead to arrest and trial for treason.'

The telescreen goes black.

CHAPTER 4
TREASON

Realm Rule 4:
Serve the Realm dutifully and diligently.

The first Guardian opens a door at the side of the room and holds up a small piece of paper. 'Some parents have arrived. The following Greenhorns will come with me. E820904, E820907, E820909.' He scrunches up the paper and puts it in his pocket.

Four, Nine and I follow the Guardian through the door into a long, white walled corridor, with many doors on either side. The Guardian sends us through three different doors.

I open the door and see Cherish sitting on a metal chair. Her long curly hair looks even wilder than usual. Her dark skin is paler.

'Hey.' She looks at me, curling her hair round her right index finger.

'Hey.' I move round the table that separates us.

She stands and pulls me tight into a deep, warm hug. My shoulders relax and the nerves of moments before scatter.

As she pulls away, she holds my wrists with her hands and looks at me, right in the eyes, for several, uncomfortable seconds.

'What's up?'

Her eyebrows are squashed together. 'It's just strange, seeing you all grown up, finishing your Caste Test.'

'Yeah, I can't believe it's all done as well.'

'You did well, though, yes?' She pushes a curling strand of hair behind her ear with a shaking hand.

'Yeah, I think so. Physical was good.'

'Great...I am so, so happy for you...regardless of what happens in the future, I am incredibly proud of you, Cas. Incredibly.'

I smile at Cherish, seeing a tear in her eyes. 'Thanks.'

She grasps my hand and squeezes it tightly with her own, tilting her head to the side. She wants to say more, but I see a small camera swivelling in the corner. Instead, she puts her other hand on my neck and pulls my head down to rest upon hers.

We remain close, silent, for about a minute. A slideshow of images flicker through my mind, snippets of my childhood with Cherish; a wiped tear, a grazed knee cleaned, juice squirting from a stolen peach.

But one pushes into the foreground, more prominent than all the others. A birthday present, an old tradition she told me. She handed me a rag, with a map drawn on it. She wouldn't tell me where, or what, or why. She simply said, 'memorise this, Cas. Memorise this, it will be useful one day, I hope.'

I kept that rag with me every day since. Most of the map has now faded, I've memorised it anyway, but I keep the tattered rag. My first and only birthday present.

I return to the waiting room and take my seat next to Six, who gives my hand a squeeze before resuming her nail nibbling.

Serra enters. 'It's time. Follow me.' Her face is cold and expressionless. Realm efficiency exemplified. Her glacial expression looks more natural than her smiles.

We follow her along another sterile corridor and down two flights of cold, steel steps, each descent darker. Six shivers next to me as my teeth chatter. The stairs echo as our bare feet trample after Serra.

She stops outside a wide door.

'The Destination ceremony is about to begin. You will be called in order of your numbers. If you have been assigned, you will be told your name and role. If you have failed, exile awaits you. You will be transported to a Nameless settlement.'

Her eyes narrow.

'If you are deemed genetically unfit, in collaboration with a poor Physical and Mental Test score, you will be taken away for re-evaluation – where you will...have a procedure to ensure sterility before you're exiled. The Realm must only promote the strongest genes and abilities.'

She says every word evenly, no hint of distress or emotion in the last few words. Our fates mean nothing to her. Just another set of numbers...being assigned or not...

I stare at my feet, steadying my breath. Life was tough back at camp, but exile would be worse. I just hope I'm not taken away for 're-evaluation'.

I look at Three and hate myself for it.

'Please sit here.' Serra indicates four rows of metal chairs, which face a raised wooden platform in an otherwise empty room. There are four other doors, each with a huge black letter: M, A, R, or E.

M for Military. A for Academics. R for Re-evaluation. E for... Exile? Probably. Why do they have separate doors? My stomach stirs.

I spot Cherish and a few other parents. Not many of them have come, as Twelve predicted. I beam at her, and she gives me a small wink, while blotting the sides of her eyes with a tissue. I walk taller, my strides longer, and take my seat with a grin. Next to Six. To my right is Eight, waving to her mum.

Serra walks to the top of the platform, stands at the lectern five feet above us and calls the first number.

'E820901, please come forward.'

One bounces up. He did well in the Physical. He'll be assigned Military...probably. He reaches a white circle in front of the platform and stops.

'You passed the Caste Test. Highly commended score in Physical. You are the group Gamma,' Serra says. 'Your name is Cyril Yensen. You will be assigned to Military. Enter the door marked with the 'M' and follow the instructions you receive through there.'

I knew it. And I did better than him in Physical. Surely, I must be in Military now. My feet are tapping incessantly, my fingers twitching.

One nods, smiles and swaggers to the door.

'E820901, you might have passed, but maintain an appropriate walking gait.' Serra's scold has an instant effect as he tenses and marches out, Military-style.

I might have to train with that arse. But I can always call him Cyril to wind him up. What a ridiculous name. I hope mine is a bit cooler than that. Well, if I get one at all...

'E820902, please come forward.'

Two approaches the circle. She's a tall, athletic girl. Doesn't speak to anyone. I kissed her once. Six didn't speak to me for a month after. I didn't kiss her again.

'You passed the Caste Test. You maintained your predicted levels. You are the group Lambda. Your name is Felicia Johnson. You'll be assigned to Academics.' Two gives a little fist pump. Serra raises her eyebrows and Two immediately lowers her arm, becoming as still as a statue of the Autokratōr.

'Enter the door marked with the 'A' and await instructions.'

She nods and walks to her door, blank and unreadable. And I had my guess on Military. At least I won't have to endure her awkward silences in future.

Well, at least I know for sure what two of the doors are for.

'E820983, please come forward.'

Three stands in the circle, shaking.

'You have failed the Caste Test. Your scores were too far below your predicted level. You are the new group Omega. You will not be assigned.'

He remains mostly unmoved, but his silence belies his shaking hands.

Murmurs circulate the room. Six shakes her head slowly. Poor Three.

Twelve sniggers. Man, I wanna smack that scut.

Serra continues like nothing has happened, ignoring the noises that would normally get us a punishment. They must be more lenient because it's such a huge deal for us. 'You will therefore be exiled and remain nameless. Go through the door marked 'E' and await instructions.'

A Guardian grabs Three, who mumbles as he's pushed away. I try to catch his words, but Serra stares at me wide-eyed, so I avert my gaze.

Coward.

Something acidic is building up in my throat. I press my trembling lips together. Hard.

Four gets Academics. Five, Military. My feet are tapping incessantly, my fingers twitching.

It's Six next, and my stomach jolts. Please, please let her get Academics.

'E820906, come forward.'

She smiles at me and brushes my hand as she walks away. Her clean, blonde hair floats behind her. Please, Academics. Please, Academics. She stands in the white circle.

'You passed the Caste Test. You are the group Alpha, as predicted.'

She turns to me and smiles. I nod back, my shoulders relaxing.

A door flies open. One of the Testers runs in. It's the lady who took my sample in Genetics. She rushes towards Serra.

'What is the meaning of this?' Serra's voice echoes through the room. 'We are in the middle of a Destination ceremony.'

'I'm sorry,' says the Tester, surging past us. She steps onto the stage, cowers, and whispers something to Serra.

Six remains frozen in the white circle.

'It appears...' begins Serra, motioning the Tester to leave, 'that we will have to stop the Destination ceremony for a short while. There is an issue that must be taken care of. Immediately.'

Serra leaves the stage, strides over to one of the Guardians and whispers something in his ear. She leaves the room, through the R door.

The parents begin whispering. All except Cherish. She stares at me, a sad smile penetrating me. The other Greenies are watching the parents and the Guardians with bewildered expressions.

A Guardian speaks to us. 'All remaining Greenhorns are to return to the waiting room. Except E820907. You will follow me. Adults, remain seated.'

My body becomes rigid. The artery in my neck throbs. Questions circle in my head. What have I done? Do they know what Saull said to me? Did I do something wrong in my Test?

The Greenies shuffle out of the room, still glancing around. Twelve gives me a colossal grin.

Six's brow furrows. She's looking so worried that my hands begin to shake. She mouths, 'What's happening?'

I shrug as she exits.

When Six is gone, I look to Cherish, who remains seated.

'E820907, move,' orders the Guardian that Serra spoke to.

I follow him to the R door.

'You, too.' He points to Cherish.

What's she done? I'd never forgive myself if she got punished because of me. Guilt worms squirm through me. I want to ask her, but I daren't speak.

We follow the Guardian through the door. A long, white

corridor with many doors on either side appears. We enter the second door on the right. Serra is seated at a large, metallic table. Two empty chairs are opposite her.

'Sit,' she says.

We sit. Cherish grasps my hand and it shakes even worse than mine. Her dark skin has turned to a deathly shade.

'We have an *irregularity* in a gene sample. I have been informed there has been some *tampering*. Some long-term tampering. In sample E820907.' Serra stares at me.

My tongue is glued to the roof of my mouth. My neck frozen.

Me? How?

'But not by you. Oh no, you are too well trained for that.' Serra fake-smiles. 'No, the culprit is an adult. A traitor. In this room.' She turns her face to Cherish.

I gasp. What happened? Cherish's face is stone. A single tear begins to form and fall.

'What have you done?' I say.

She gazes at me, her eyes shining with sorrow. 'I'm sorry.'

'For what? Tell me!'

'Nurse Cherish has been hiding your identity for years. Providing false DNA samples by the looks of it. But today, we took a sample of your DNA, and it didn't match your records. My colleagues checked the log and Nurse Cherish has managed to be present at each one of your previous medicals.'

'So, it could have been someone else. A mistake...'

'No, Seven. There is no mistake. Your DNA is interesting, and we need to discuss this peculiar situation. But we should do it away from the traitor.'

Serra turns to Cherish. 'Guardians. Take away Nurse Cherish. Gene sample manipulation cannot be tolerated.'

A Guardian grabs her left arm and drags her to the door. I'm still paralysed. What do I do? What can I do?

Her eyes meet mine, connecting in a way words could not.

I stand, uncertain.

'E820907, sit down.'

Cherish thrashes and pulls at the Guardian. Fury creeps up into my chest.

I want to help her, to save her, but I'm so close. I'm just about to find out my name. And so is Six.

'Cas, I'm sorry. I just wanted...you to have...a normal life,' Cherish cries.

Rage swells in every part of me. My knuckles tighten, my jaw rigid. How can they do this? How can she do this? I'm so close.

She struggles to get back to me. I hold out my hand to touch hers.

The Guardian hits her across the face with a curled fist and her nose erupts with blood.

Scut it.

My arms and legs fly at the Guardian, my muscles contracting more powerfully than ever before. The contact, the crunch, the splitting of skin. I connect many times, fury flooding inside me.

'Stop it, Cas! This won't help.'

I stop and turn to Cherish, lying on the floor, blood pouring. She shakes her head.

'GUARDIANS!' Serra's cold voice has boiled.

I share a glance with Cherish, before other Guardians run in, and I'm overwhelmed.

I close my eyes as I'm slammed to the ground and fists and feet slam into me repeatedly.

CHAPTER 5
STRENGTH

Realm Rule 5:
Science is the only way to improve our Realm.

My left eye is glued shut with congealed blood. With my right eye, I scan my cell – a steel box. With a *tiny* bed. I lie with my legs hanging off the end and touching the floor. My back is on fire, like the wrath of hell is burning through it. Damn you, Smiler!

The door flies open. My ribs ache as I sit up.

It's Saull. His face is red.

'You're an idiot!' he shouts, slamming the door behind him.

I lower my head.

'I stuck my neck out and convinced Serra you were ready to be a Captain, even a Black Knight, and she was just about to assign you, when you start attacking Guardians. What did you do that for?'

'They were taking away Cherish! They called her a traitor. They were going to execute her.' I stand up, fists clenched, but the earlier head blows make me unsteady.

'They will still execute her, despite your little hero effort. What were you trying to do? Save her?'

'I don't know.' I massage my right temple, trying to relieve the headache. I was willing to give my life for the Realm. Serve like everyone else. But how can I now?

'I can't let them kill her. After all she's done for me. I was scared, alright.'

'But they will anyway, Seven. Don't you get it? It's the Realm's law. And neither you, nor I, can do anything about that.' Did he just wink at me?

He paces my cell, breathing heavily. He comes so close at one point that I can smell his caffeBoost breath.

I sit down and put my bruised and battered head into my hands. When I look back up, Saull is rolling his eyes to the right. A camera swivels in the corner. I look at him, then the camera again.

'I'll do what I can, Seven.' He turns to the door. 'But I doubt it will be much. You assaulted Guardians. They'll probably execute you if they think you are no longer loyal to the Realm.'

He leaves. The door smashes shut. The metallic vibrations rupture the quiet. It's suddenly cooler, so I rub my arms.

Maybe I am an idiot. Maybe I shouldn't have done it. But I'm proud of what I did. I know the Gurus would shake their heads at me, but it was the 'correct emotional response'. I'm not a robot, like some of them. I stare at the camera and slam my fist down upon the bed.

Images of Cherish, ashen-faced and lifeless, circulate in my mind. I think about dying and how it might feel. Would it matter if I did? And what would I live for if I can't be part of the Realm? But I imagine what Cherish would say if she heard that. She'd be angry with me for giving up on life. The life she worked so hard to make worthwhile. The life she has now exchanged for her own. If only I knew why? If only she had told me everything.

I just wish I could see Cherish now. Spend some time with her, even if she wouldn't explain things. She would sing to me, like she used to, comfort me, and assure me that everything would be okay. Instead, I lie alone, beaten, tired, a traitor by association and absolutely nameless. I really hope they haven't hurt her because of me.

But I know it's useless to think about what's happening to her now. Saull was right, the law is clear about traitors. We're both going to die.

The door bangs open. Again.

I turn around, expecting to see Saull.

Two Guardians approach me, one slow step at a time. Two others stand in the doorway, rifles aimed at my head.

'Come with us. Do not resist,' says one of the rifle-carrying Guardians.

I hold my fist to my chest to indicate I'm not going to fight.

For now.

They cuff me so tight, my wrists bleed. They lead me out and down the corridor past many other cells, which appear to be identical to my own. I wonder who else is in there? And why they need so many cells in a Greenie Testing centre?

We pass through a series of duplicate doors and white corridors. I am counting the turns and trying to draw a mental map.

We stop beside an open door and two Guardians push me inside, while the other two remain in the corridor. The room has a large window on the wall to my immediate right, showing the corridor. No furniture, no other windows, white walls. One person.

'E820907, I trust you have had time to amend your emotional state?' asks Serra.

I nod.

'Good. Our merciful Autokratōr wishes to extend to you a second chance. You made a mistake. One born from the poor choices of another. Therefore, it is not your fault. If you can prove your loyalty and obedience to the Autokratōr, you will be given the opportunity to commence your career within the Realm. Your criminal record will be wiped.'

A small fire of hope ignites within me. My name.

'What would I have to do?' I ask, glancing around the empty room.

She steps forward, holding a small pistol. 'There is one bullet in this gun. You will execute a traitor and the Realm will forgive you. A second chance for a fine, young prodigy. Once you have displayed your loyalty, we will discuss your heritage and the next step.'

She places the gun in my hand, steps out of the room, and stands behind the transparent window that looks in from the corridor. I look round, frowning. My heritage? Does she mean my parents? *Shit, I'm holding a gun.*

'Where is she?' I say.

'Just a moment,' replies Serra, her voice ethereal, as it passes through a tiny comms speaker in the ceiling.

The cold metal sits lifeless in my hand. I manoeuvre it into position, gripping the handle, fingering the trigger. I've never shot a person before, only inanimate targets. But it's all a show, buying some time, trying to work out what the scut to do. It's much heavier than our practice ones, weighing me down like the decision I need to make.

The door opens, but I don't turn. I know who it will be. No need to look. The door shuts again, and I'm left with the person I'm supposed to shoot. Execute. Murder. I stare at the gun, stroking the trigger with my right index finger.

'Do you know what they want me to do, Cherish?'

'Yes.' Her voice is strong.

'I won't.'

'You will.'

I turn around and look at Cherish. She has bruises all over her face, her nose clearly broken. Clotted blood blocks one nostril, her eyes puffy. Her bare arms are covered in incisions; precise cuts, deliberate. A cruel torture for a kind traitor. Her top is damp with sweat and her hands shake as they hold her ribs. She's about to fall. A thick bead of blood drops from her chin.

Serra watches us, her face close to the window.

'E820907. Execute the traitor and you will be given back the life you have earned. Being in the Military involves killing. If you can't do this, what use are you to us?'

'SHE'S MY MUM, NOT AN ENEMY!'

'E820907, control your emotions. We want a cold killer, not a hot-headed boy. Oh, and she is not your mum...she is just a traitor to the Realm...she is now your enemy.'

Cherish nods. 'Do it. Please. They'll kill me anyway, and you'll lose everything...I only did it to protect you. But I can't protect you anymore...this is the last thing I can do for you. Kill me...please.' She stumbles forward and I move away. I fight my instincts to cradle her, to hold her. If I hug her, how will I have the strength to do what I must?

I won't pull this trigger.

'Protect me from what?'

She shakes her head, but her focus remains on me.

I lean against the wall, looking into the deep, grey eyes that mothered me from infancy, the soft hands that held me, the tough love that moulded me. She takes a step closer and the stench of vomit hits me. Her clothes are stained with it.

'Stay away, I can't. Even for my name.' I slide further along the cold wall.

'No point fighting it. You need to do this. You can do more alive than dead. Which is what you'll be if you don't do it.' She falls forward onto her knees and moans.

I place the gun down and drop onto the floor next to her. I cup her chin in my hands and raise her head to look at me. Inches apart, I gaze at her. Her tortured eyes give me the message. I must do this.

'I don't...I can't...'

'Shhh, shhh...it's okay.' She pulls my head onto her chest and whispers in my ear. 'You will kill me, and then you will do something memorable with your life. Make it meaningful.' She pushes my head up, searching my eyes for acknowledgement. 'You understand?'

I nod slowly. I collect the gun and get back to my feet. My shaking hand rises, finger on the trigger, forearm straightened, taking aim. She nods and smiles, encouraging me.

My name. My parents. My life.

I tighten my finger on the trigger.

My name. My parents. My life.

Then I breathe out, long and slow, and lower my arm.

'Sorry.' I shake my head.

I put the gun to my temple. The cold metal rests on my damp skin.

'No, Cas.' Cherish grabs my other arm, but I shake her off.

This is for her.

I walk towards the window, my finger resting on the trigger.

'You want loyalty? This is loyalty.' I begin to squeeze the trigger.

'I thought this might happen.' Serra's voice echoes around the white room. 'So, I have something that might help remind you just how loyal you are.'

It's Six. With a gun to her head. She's shaking, teeth biting into her lip.

My heart stops, my lungs empty. I lower my gun.

'You have one minute.' Serra smiles, not the fake smile from earlier, but one filled with wicked glee, every one of her shining white teeth showing.

My arms tremble, my teeth grind. My body shudders as my right arm comes up.

Cherish nods again, still on her knees. 'Six is worth a thousand of me.'

I shake my head. I can't do it. I turn back to the window. Serra has the gun aimed at Six. Serra raises an eyebrow.

I fall to my knees in front of Cherish. I move closer.

'I don't think I can do it.' But the thought of what will happen to Six if I don't is ripping my soul.

Cherish holds out her shaky hand. 'Let me help.'

She pulls me closer to her, moves my hand, holding the gun, against her chest, directly over the heart. 'Remember I love you. Remember it was all for you. Everything I did, it was for you.'

She moves her trembling finger to cover mine. We both start crying, but I try to hold it in. I try to be stronger, but really, she's the strong one.

'There are other people in this world who are good. Remember that, Cas. Remember everything I've told you. Everything we've discussed. There is more to live for...than this.'

She releases her finger. Now, only mine traces the trigger. Slowly...I never take my eyes off hers. Slowly...her lips quiver.

'Be strong, Cas...live for more than the Realm...or a name...live for a better tomorrow...and find your true identity...it's more than a name. And most importantly, be happy...remember me...'

Slowly...BANG.

Her body falls back. Blood sprays onto my face and down my front. Small drifts of smoke rise from the end of the gun, and the smell stings. My arm still holds the metal herald of death. My eyes move slowly to Cherish, on her back, taking her last, rapid breaths, peering at me through the pain. A small line of blood slides from her mouth as she takes her final breath.

From the speaker, I hear Serra's words. *Hail the Autokratōr. Serve the Realm.*

I didn't know how long it took for a person to die after being shot in the heart. Now I do. Eight seconds.

Eight seconds to watch my mother die. From a bullet...I shot... through her heart.

Twelve hours. That's how long they have kept me in the room with her.

I have watched her body stiffen. Her red lips turn blue. I felt her skin get colder and colder. I smelt faeces and urine, both growing stronger and stronger. I tasted salty tears, sometimes in drips and other times in floods. I stared for hours at the large pool of blood lying beneath her body, watching her life force drain.

I closed her eyes after a while. I couldn't look at those eyes any longer. Eyes that always watched over me. The same eyes that pleaded for death. Pleaded for death to save me. To save me for what? A Military career with the Realm.

I won't kill for the Realm.

I will kill the Realm.

After Serra had lowered her gun, she took Six away from the window and no one has appeared since. I thumped on the window. Then the door. They ignored me. Left me alone to watch the sunshine of my life dull to a pale corpse.

I picked up the gun and pulled the trigger time after time, but Serra was true to her word. One bullet.

When they finally came and took me away, I was numb. I had cried out all the emotion: the small light that glowed in my chest, illuminated by years of love from Cherish, was extinguished. Left was an abyss, filled with the echoes of hate, revenge and death.

Now, as I march away from her murdered body, I say goodbye to the Realm as it is, to the young Greenie that I was, and to the incredible person that Cherish will always be.

CHAPTER 6
RUN

Realm Rule 6:
Strive for the betterment of our glorious Realm.

The Guardians push me into a room packed with Greenies.

'Stay in here for now. The Destination Ceremony will resume in the morning.'

'Why not now?' Twelve strides forward. 'I demand to know why we are being held like prisoners, rather than allowed to graduate into our roles within the Realm, right now?

'Sit tight. Trust us, you'll be safer in here.' The Guardian turns and leaves, locking the door after him.

Eyes drill into me. They must spot the blood covering my clothes.

None of them are covered in blood. None of them had to kill their mothers.

'This is your fault, isn't it? You and that pathetic wet-nurse of yours...'

My clenched fist crunches Twelve's nose. Every atom is alight with emotions; guilt, anger, confusion.

'You speak of her again and I will end you.'

He pushes himself up quickly, but he decides not to retaliate.

His groupies follow behind as he retreats to the large table at the far side of the room.

The near side of the room contains twenty bunks, so Six and I slouch off and sit on one of those. The mattress is super soft, seducing me to lie down and sleep.

Six is silent but wraps her arms around me. I don't even mind the pain from my wounds. It's good to feel something else.

'That was...beyond evil...' she whispers into my ear. But I have no words.

We hold each other for a long time.

I drift off on her shoulder but wake suddenly to a loud siren. The room's bright lights have been killed, replaced by a dull red glow.

'Emergency lighting,' Six whispers. 'That means we're under attack.'

The telescreen plays the audio, but no picture. Weird.

Greenhorns, please remain calm and listen to the following instructions. We are under attack. But the exiles will not be able to get past our defences. You will all follow the Guardians when they arrive. They will take you to an individual, sealed cell. This is for your safety, as a precaution. I repeat, do not panic, our defences are strong.

The audio finishes and Greenies burst into voice.

'She *really* wanted to reassure us we'd be safe, huh?' Six says, frowning.

I rub my eyes and stretch my aching body.

'The way I'm feeling right now, I'd happily see the exiles get in here and kill Serra.'

'You don't mean that, do you?' She puts her hand on my leg, as she speaks. Perhaps trying to draw me back to her, up and out of this abyss I'm wedged deep within.

'You hear that, boys?' Twelve moves closer. His nose and face have swollen, his eyes purple-ringed. 'Got a little Realm traitor here, do we? That what they got Cherish for?'

Six squeezes my leg.

She's trying to calm me, but a promise is a promise. I'm going to end him.

But before I even stand, One has Twelve by the throat. He lifts him off his feet and slams him against the wall.

'Enough. You will not talk to Seven, yes?'

Twelve nods, his wide eyes streaming.

One dumps him to the ground. 'Seven, you will leave him. Everyone else listen. You are no longer children. No longer Greenies. We are under attack. We will work together and do as we are instructed.'

Nobody argues, retreating to their corners of the room.

'Can the exiles get past the defences?' I ask Six.

'I doubt it. When any Realm building goes into red alert, everything seals. Nobody without top clearance is getting near us. Unless someone helps them from the inside...then it would be straightforward.' She moves her hand away and her head closer. 'What they did to you and Cherish back there was beyond redemption. Serra is the devil.'

'They did it to you, too.' I clasp my hands tightly together.

'How much does your name mean to you?'

'It means everything, Six. Everything. I must know who I am. Who my family are. Where I came from. You know?'

She puts her hands over my clasped ones. 'I understand. But is it really worth this? Killing people for no good reason. Remaining loyal to sickos?'

I shake my head and punch the mattress. The image, the feeling of Cherish's cold, dead body is still raw and clear. 'I don't know. But if I don't find out my name, did Cherish die for nothing?'

The door opens and several Guardians wait in the hall. 'Follow us to your cells. For your protection. Now.'

When I reach my cell, I file in, spot the single bed and collapse on it.

. . .

In the dull red glow, I can just make out the outline of the door.

A note slides under it.

I look at it, wondering if I'm hallucinating.

'Hello?'

No one responds.

I approach the door cautiously, pretend to touch my toes for the camera, then pick up the small, folded white paper. Hopefully they didn't notice the note sliding in. I fall into press up position slipping the note beneath my body. I push up and down, opening it on the down motion. Pain shears across my back.

In 5 minutes, your door will unlock.

It's anonymous.

I slip the paper down my trousers and get up.

Saull? Who else could it be? He's not like the others. The way he shows his emotions. He was so angry with me. That's so unRealm-like. But why would he help me?

I pace the cell. The five minutes are an epoch. The Cherish image reel goes round and round and round. I bite my lip to stop the tears.

The time is close. I stand beside the door, waiting, ready to get the hell out of here, or die trying.

The lock clicks. The door moves an inch inwards.

Silence.

I peek out into the long corridor. On both sides, doors open. Greenies emerge.

'Six?' I run towards her. 'What's happening?'

'No idea...maybe a power cut?' She grabs me in a tight hug, her squeeze on my back excruciating. I bury my nose in her hair, trying to hide my pain.

'Who was it?' It's Smiler. He points his rifle at us. 'If one of you opened these doors you will be *severely* punished.' He licks his lips.

For several seconds, everyone freezes. No one knows what to do.

'Move it. Into your cells,' he repeats. 'Must be the stupid 'lectrics failing again. Lucky Smiler's here to keep an eye on things.' His wide grin reveals his horrid teeth.

I grab Six's hand and pull her away. The other Greenies are also moving back.

The lights go out. There are gasps and whispers.

'Right. Don't move,' Smiler instructs us.

But I do. No point waiting 'til the lights come on, so I can get put back in my cell. Holding Six's hand, I tiptoe down the corridor, away from Smiler.

'I said don't move!'

But people are moving around all over the place. We bump into several other Greenies.

'Oi, watch it. You stood on my toes.'

'Stop moving around. We were told to stay still.'

'Aaaah. You knocked me over.'

A flare lights at the far end of the corridor. We're now twenty metres away from a glowing Smiler. His rifle is raised again. 'I told you not to move.'

Six and I become statues. It's still dark enough down our end that he won't spot us. As long as we don't make any sudden movements.

'Where's E820907 gone? Seven? Don't you go wandering? I've to keep an eye on you, 'specially.'

Smiler walks down the corridor pointing his rifle in the Greenies' faces, looking for me. 'Where are you?' He stops halfway along the passage. 'A strip of Toffalate for whichever Greenie finds me Seven.'

Six pushes me back into the nearest cell. She edges the door almost shut. A slither of red projects into the room. Greenies move around outside, looking for me. The lure of Toffalate and the innate sense of obedience must be hard for them to resist.

'Get behind the door. I'll try to distract him,' Six whispers.

'Get out. This is my cell.' A boy's voice comes from behind us.

'Who's there?' asks Six.

'Nobody important. Just get out my cell. I want to be alone.'

'Three?' I ask.

'They're looking for you out there. I heard Smiler. Get out or I'll shout for him.' Definitely Three. His timid mousy voice is clearer in the darkness.

'Shhh,' whispers Six.

The cell door crashes open. Red light illuminates the middle third of the room.

'Who's in here?' It's *Twelve*, the grub.

'It's just Three and me.' Six moves into the light.

I drift backwards, towards the shadowy corner. It's against all my instincts. All I want to do right now is pound Twelve's face in, until there's nothing left.

Three's beady eyes follow me. He looks like he wants to say something, but nothing comes out. I almost want him to, so I can thump him, too.

'I don't believe you, Six. You always did lie to me. Let me check.' Twelve pushes her out the way.

That's not happening. I surge forward, my arms outstretched, ready to hit him.

BANG.

We all hit the ground instinctively. Smiler's fired his rifle. I hope that isn't a Greenie he's shot. I glance across at Six, lying to my right, then to Twelve, lying a metre in front of me. I master the urge to hit him with the thought of getting out of here. Six pushes me towards the darker side of the cell, while Twelve stares back into the corridor.

We wait in the dark silence. Her arm rests on my back. Shallow breaths. Quiet consumes the cell and the corridor beyond. No one dares move or speak.

'Smiler?' It's Twelve's pompous voice.

'Is everyone okay?' asks a female voice from the corridor. Too old for a Greenie.

The lights come back on. For a moment, I can't open my eyes. Through slits I can see Six moving towards the open door.

Twelve looks down at me. 'I've got him. He's here. I've got Seven. In here.'

Now I open my eyes a fraction more, I see he's almost bouncing with excitement.

'You're such a malak,' says Six, moving between Twelve and me again.

A tall lady walks in. Soaked grey hair clings to her face. 'Who is Seven?'

'I am.' Six moves forward, with her wrists held up.

The lady laughs. 'How very brave and noble of you, dear. Self-sacrificing acts are very heroic and it's clear you are a friend. But you are not who I'm looking for. Seven is a boy.' Her eyes focus upon me, then Three. 'Which of you is it, then?'

'It's him,' says Twelve, pointing at me, his eyes wide with intense glee.

The lady's eyes focus on me. 'Right, come on.' She holds her hand out.

I'm reluctant to take it, but she seems gentle and friendly. I couldn't see Serra doing this. She's acting so unRealm-like.

'Who are you?' asks Six. 'Are you exiles?'

'Time is against us. We must hurry. Seven, you must come with me if you want to live. Bring whoever with you, but it must be now.'

The other Greenies are crowding round, unsure what to do. Where are the Guardians?

'Is Smiler dead?' asks Six.

'The Guardian? No, I just knocked him out. Luckily the shot he fired missed everyone,' says the grey-haired lady. 'Come on.'

Greenies stare at us, unsure what to do.

Hell, I'm unsure what to do. But right now, there's nothing I want to do more than leave this place. I can work the rest out later.

'I'll come.' I turn to Six.

'And so will I,' she says, after a few seconds.

I start to follow.

Twelve tries to block our way, but I push past him. 'You're not supposed to leave. I'll tell the Guardians exactly what happened and where you're going. You can't defy the Realm, Seven.'

I punch Twelve on the face. As hard as I can. All the anger and anguish of the last few hours come out in one punch. He hits the floor hard. His nose erupts with blood. That's twice I've got him back and it still hasn't filled that hollow in my chest. Revenge isn't as satisfying as I thought it would be.

'Come, we don't have time for this.' The lady directs me through a series of doors. I'm glad she knows where we're going because I'm totally lost.

Once when I look back, I notice Three has come with us. Suppose that makes sense. He was going to be exiled anyway.

Finally, we reach a large door that I recognise. It takes us outside. We sprint through it.

A huge man blocks our escape. 'Mother, hurry. I think we've taken out most of them. Eagle has control of the tower, so if there's any left, they're inside.'

The mention of the word mother causes a sharp pain in my chest. The images carousel again.

'Where's our transport, Bulk?' the lady called Mother asks.

'Miller's getting it. We've to meet him at the gate,' the large man named Bulk replies.

'You three, follow me.' Mother marches towards the gate, her speed belying her age.

A door opens. BANG. The shot comes from the tower.

'Hit the deck,' shouts Bulk. He pulls Six and me down into the mud.

BANG. BANG.

'Clear,' says Bulk, hauling us to our feet.

I glance back and two Guardians lie dead, just outside the building. No time to think about it. Keep running. Close down the feelings. Don't think about Cherish.

When we reach the gate, I trip and fall onto the soft mud. I turn and let my head drop between my knees, my arms limp. Cherish is dead. She's gone. And I don't even know why she did it. Why didn't I ask?

Six lifts my chin and looks down at me, sadness pooled in those blue eyes.

And just then, in the worst possible moment, I begin to doubt what I'm doing. I can't give up everything I've ever wanted.

'I have to go back,' I say. 'At least, I don't think I can go. Not yet. I must find some answers.'

'No.' Mother stands in front of me. A frown hardens her expression. 'You will get in that truck, or you will be killed. She is gone, Seven. She would want you to leave.'

'Let me go!' I shout, my voice breaking slightly.

My mind is numbed, but for one thought. I need to know why she did it.

A truck's headlights illuminate the dark gate, and it speeds across the grounds before skidding to a halt beside us. Bulk lifts me into the back, pinning me to my seat.

Shots come from behind us, next to the building. Return fire from the tower keeps them distracted as our truck moves through the gate.

Just as we turn onto the road, two Guardians leap into the back of the truck. How did they get past the shooter in the tower?

Bulk reacts quickest. He thumps one of them so hard, his feet leave the ground, and he flies backwards out of the truck. The second gets in close, and launches a flurry of punches at Bulk's midriff, which buys the Guardian a little space.

He pulls a pistol from his belt.

Aims it at Bulk.

But the gun is slapped from his hand, and it slides out the back of the truck onto the road.

By Three. Three?

Bulk grabs the Guardian by the shirt and throws him out after his gun.

Mother pulls down the canvas cover to hide the defeated Guardian and the road from view. Bulk glances round at everyone. 'All okay?'

Six and I nod.

'Yes,' says Mother.

Three returns to his seat. He just saved Bulk's life. He reacted quicker than any of us to save the big man.

Bulk slides down next to Three and gives him a crushing hug. 'Cheers, kid.'

As soon as my body realises it's safe, the fight leaves me. I slide to the floor, exhausted. I can't believe she's gone. Cherish.

I'm pulled back into my seat and the tears come again. I cover my face.

Six sits next to me. She rubs my back gently, and I don't even mind the mild sting on my whip wounds. She wraps her arms around me, and I sink into her shoulder, grabbing her waist tight.

'I lost my mum, too,' Three says.

I nod my head slowly, not fully focussing.

'Who are you?' Six asks, one of her arms still around me.

'Friends,' says Mother simply. She pushes her sopping grey streaks back over her head. 'You need not worry, my child. No harm will come to you.'

'Why did you take us?'

'It was the boy we were wanting,' says Bulk, pointing to me.

'Why me?'

'We received a message that you were in danger. We couldn't allow anything to happen to you. Cherish was one of us. We take care of our *own*.' Bulk gives us a nod.

'One of who? Who are you?' Six asks.

'Very soon we will tell you everything, but it should be done by the person who sent us here.' Mother tilts her head slightly.

'And I assume you won't be telling us who that is?'

'Not yet, young ones. We may still be caught, and information is dangerous.' Mother nods as she finishes. Case closed. No point in asking any more.

Six and I lie back, her shoulder on mine, my head on hers, and my thoughts focus on Cherish. They were right. I couldn't have gone back.

If there are answers, they are ahead of me. Not behind. Even if I have to bang down the gates to Circle City myself, I will find them.

And then burn the place down.

CHAPTER 7
NAMELESS

Realm Rule 7:
Be mindful of current and future generations in every action.

The truck stops.

'Time to get out,' says Mother. 'We've got to leave the road.'

Six wakes and mumbles. She had only just fallen asleep. I watch her get out of the truck, uncomplaining. She has followed me, turned away from a life within the Realm, without question or hesitation. And Three, well he had failed his Test, so his prospects weren't great. A proverb that Cherish used to say pops into my head. *If you fly with the crows, expect to be shot down with them.* Hopefully it won't come to that.

'What's happening now, then?' Six asks. Rain thunders down. As I jump from the truck, my feet splash then sink into the puddles of mud.

'We need to get to the first checkpoint to meet Eagle and Malt. They have horses,' says Mother.

I should be asking questions about these people, but I don't have the energy and I don't think I care right now. If they can help me tear down the Realm and everything it stands for, then I'll follow them anywhere.

So instead of questions, I watch Bulk, his colossal frame dwarfing me, and wonder how he got so big. He's the biggest person I've ever seen.

The driver, Miller, remains in the truck and drives it off the road into some trees on the far side. He runs back to us, and we turn to walk in the opposite direction. We leave the road and march downhill into a series of fields with tall grasses. It provides great cover for everyone except Bulk. I don't need to ask how he got his name.

As we move silently through the fields, Six comes close and takes my hand. A surge of electricity flows through my fingers, up my arm and down to my toes. Our wet hands remain clasped for three fields of wordless walking. This feeling is worth a thousand conversations. After the last twenty-four hours, I need to feel something which isn't fear or hatred or anger.

Finally, she lets go. The fizz fades. I look ahead and see why. A small light. A fire.

'That should be Malt, waiting at the checkpoint,' says Mother. 'We can get dry and rest there.'

We stride it out to the checkpoint. I manage to whisper in Six's ear. 'Don't mention the whole thing with...' I swallow. '...Cherish. You know... I don't want them thinking...well, it's best not to say anything, if they don't know how it went down.'

Six nods and squeezes my hand.

An older man, round-bellied and bald, welcomes Mother, Miller, and Bulk. He smiles at us Greenies, sorry new Exiles, and nods.

'Which one is he?' he asks, almost bouncing.

'Not now,' says Mother. 'Get them inside the barn. Bulk, Miller, take cover in those trees and keep watch. Eagle shouldn't be too long.'

Miller and Bulk jog towards a small forest to our left. The tall trees overlook the grass fields. Three, Six and I follow our new friends. Or captors. I've not decided what this is yet. Sure, I'm alive, but what the hell do they want with me? I hope I've not led Six and Three into something bad.

The barn has a roof and a pile of mouldy straw. But it's dry and a small fire glows in the centre. Malt pulls the huge wooden doors closed behind us and I'm instantly warm.

'Sit by the fire, dears. Take your damp clothes off and put them on this wooden rail here.'

Six shakes her head and arches her eyebrow. Three also refuses.

'Well?' asks Mother. 'Do you want to die of hypothermia or what? Get those wet clothes off.'

'I'd rather risk it,' I say on behalf of the others. 'We're a little old to be...naked...you know?'

Nakedness was always discouraged amongst Greenies. No procreation before you earn your name.

'No one bothers out here, young ones, but please yourselves. Stay close to the fire. And Seven...hold this on your cut.'

'What cut?'

'Your eye's bleeding.'

I take the dirty material and press it hard on my swollen eye. I'm so wet, I'd not noticed the blood. Why hasn't it closed up yet?

We huddle close around the gorgeous gold-orange flames. My body purrs at the heat, even more than it did in the hot shower this morning. Or was that yesterday? I'm losing track.

Six is close again. Her soaked dark-blonde hair is drying into thin strands of yellow. Her little toes are close to the fire, curling back and forth. She trembles from the cold, and I have to resist putting my arm around her on the pretence of warming her. I might have done it, but Three is sitting across from us, staring without blinking into the fire, like a real sogberry.

Of all the Greenies, I would never have picked him to come along. Didn't think he had it in him to defy anything, let alone the Realm. Then again, the boxing match showed me different. To refuse to fight probably shows more defiance than fighting.

A small neigh behind Three makes him turn. Five horses' tails sway from side to side as they feed.

'Did you learn to ride?' Six asks me.

'Nope, I chose driving instead.'

'Me, too.'

At least I won't be the only one who can't do it.

'I can.' Three's mousy voice squeaks across the fire. 'Figured I would need it more out here.'

'How did you know you'd end up here?' I ask.

'I was never going to pass my Test,' he says, simply.

'Did you even try?'

But before he answers, Mother and Malt sit down beside us.

'Okay, we should move as soon as Eagle returns,' says Mother. 'We'll give her an hour and then we'll need to go, with or without her. The Realm Guardians will send out a hunting party before long.'

'Where are we going?' I ask. 'I want to know what's going on?'

'Patience, Seven. Patience. I know it can't be easy.' She gives me a crinkled smile.

'Why can't we know now? We followed you blindly, but you've yet to give me any reason why you came for me? Or how you know Cherish? Or who you are? I want some friggin' answers.'

I take a deep breath and push my head into my hands. I don't want to see anyone's face. My temper is sitting there, right on the edge, ready to erupt. The smoke from the fire is bringing it all back...smoke drifting from the end of the gun...STOP IT!

The mind-focus exercises come back to me and in a few seconds, my brain is clearer, less blurred with fury and frustration, but still just as consumed with sadness.

'Seven, I know this is frustrating, but trust us, as you did Cherish. You will find out all you want to know and more, if you can just wait a little longer.' Mother stands and pats my hair, then moves to the doors. Malt follows silently.

'Why aren't they telling us anything?' I ask Six once they've gone. 'They expect us to just trust them because they claim to be friends with Cherish. Do you think they might have put Cherish up to manipulating my DNA test? Maybe this was their plan that got her killed.'

'Listen, Seven.' Six holds my hand again. 'We all loved Cherish. She was the sweetest, kindest, and happiest soul in that camp. She helped us all at one point. And what happened...well, that was the worst. Unimaginable. But Cherish never did anything that she didn't want to – she was strong and loved you. She wouldn't do anything that might put you in danger because someone told her to do it. She wanted to do what she did. We may not know why, but we know that. You know this, so stop torturing yourself with these ideas. I think we can trust these people. If they wanted to harm us, they could have done it twenty times by now.'

'I agree,' Three squeaks.

I frown at him. 'Who asked you?'

'Just saying.'

'Hey, go easy on him, Seven. He's the only one who came with you. Those other Greenies all stayed. He came. He's with us. The smallest ever rebellion against the Realm.' She smiles, and it lifts the darkness clouding my vision and the crushing weight that's been on my chest.

'Sorry. I just can't get my head around...this.' I wave my arms all over the place. I've no idea what to say or do. Instead, I flop backwards and lie staring at the ceiling.

There's a hole in the roof.

And through it stares two wide, white eyes.

A long rifle points directly at me.

The barrel clicks into place.

CHAPTER 8
EAGLE

Realm Rule 8:
Control your emotions at all times.

An extremely thin woman drops from the hole in the roof and lands on the floor of the barn. She makes no noise, like the world is on mute. Six's gasp tells me it's not. It almost seems unbelievable. Without a flinch, her gun is realigned on me.

I put my open hand on my chest, my heart banging beneath. 'We are unarmed. Don't shoot.'

She continues to stare at me. Her long, dark hair and chiselled cheeks are beautiful. Three and Six are both stunned into silence.

'Eagle, stop playing with them. They are terrified and confused already,' Mother says, walking into the barn.

Eagle nods and slides, silently, to the horses.

'This is Eagle,' says Mother. 'The best sniper in Europa. Probably the best in all five Realms.'

'That's us ready. We should move now, Mother,' Malt says, walking in behind her. 'And cover our tracks. They will follow us, sooner rather than later.'

Miller and Eagle go outside and disappear into the grass.

Mother nods. 'Yes, pack up the horses, and saddle them for the young ones. We will walk.'

'No, we'll be fine,' I say.

She shakes her head. 'No, Seven. You'll need to ride. Once the adrenaline wears off, that head will really hurt, and you won't want to walk then. Plus, you've lost so much blood, the last thing you need is a long, tiring walk.'

It's not just blood I've lost today. My head is nothing compared to the gaping hole in my chest. When that trigger was pulled, it wasn't just Cherish's heart that broke.

Six and Three help them put out the fire and scatter the ashes. I sit staring at the ground. Even if I couldn't give Cherish an earth ceremony, I wish I could have done something...even a fire ceremony.

'All set?' Mother asks when Eagle and Miller return.

Eagle nods.

'Yeah, we made as many false trails in the grass and mud as we could,' adds Miller.

'Good. Time to leave.'

'Where exactly are we going?' asks Six. It's weird seeing her sitting on a horse, though she looks very comfortable with it. More than I feel right now. Three volunteered to walk first as there aren't enough horses for everyone.

'To our settlement. There you can meet Lasul, and you'll either be accepted, or asked to move on. Either way, we'll give you food and tend to those nasty wounds on Seven. You'll be better for it, trust me.' Mother smiles as she speaks. There's no threat in her voice, just an even, soothing tone that makes me think that maybe, if I could ever trust anyone new again, it could be her.

'I suppose we're walking, then?' asks Miller, shooting me an evil glance.

'Yes, Milly,' replies Malt. 'And as I said earlier, you could certainly do with the exercise.' He laughs, but Miller just stomps off ahead.

We move, in the opposite direction from the road, in single file. Miller walks at the front, then Six is second on her horse. Mother and Malt ride their horses just behind. Bulk and Three walk in front of me, then Eagle's at the tail, on the lookout.

I look at the people around me, all nameless – well, in the eyes of the Realm. They have shed their numbers, created identities of their own in this new world. Perhaps that's what I need to do. Say goodbye to E820907. But I can't. Despite it all, I still feel connected to the Realm. Despite all they've done, despite all that I have done, a tiny part of me wants to go back to my linear life, mapped out before me, full of the promise of a good life. It's a lie, but a comforting lie. What's in front of me now is so different, so unfamiliar and unknown. And I wonder if I can do it.

Despite the bumps and uneven movements, the saddle has me fastened in securely, my eyes droop, and I eventually submit. The last thing I see is Six's blonde hair blowing in the light wind, silhouetted by the waxing gibbous moon.

I wake at regular intervals, greeted by more dark countryside. Not that I've been paying much notice, but the whole area seems deserted. Coming from a training camp, which was constantly buzzing with all the Greenies, Gurus, and Guardians, it's so different to be away from that confined world. Everywhere I go from now on is completely new.

When I'm fully awake, I see Six's head's sagging towards her chest. I'm glad she's getting some rest.

Three plods along beside me, stumbling every so often. I'd never have thought he'd have it in him to walk for so long, without complaint or resting. He certainly never showed this kind of determination in his Tests. If he did, he might have passed and avoided exile.

Despite the occasional rain shower, the humidity makes me hot and sticky. The dark, discontented clouds are bearing down upon us, trapping us closer to the earth, almost like they are under Realm control as well.

I can't believe that when I woke up in my hammock this morning, my only thoughts were passing my Test and getting into the Military. And finding out my name. In some ways, that's what I was most looking forward to. I've always wanted to find my family. My real mum and dad, perhaps a brother or sister. Now, I might never know.

So, here I am, in the middle of nowhere, with a group of Exiles, no name, and a wanted fugitive of the Realm. It's frightening, thrilling and heart breaking, all at the same time.

My mind flashes back to the escape: the anonymous note, the unknown rescuers, and what Saull said to me. The Realm would have made me a Black Knight, he thought. Instead, they'll probably send one to kill me. Or a normal Guardian more like. They wouldn't send anyone important after a few escaped Greenies.

I look at Six again, her head still sagging and bobbing. She was the group Alpha. She had the pick of roles within the Realm. She's given up everything for me. Why? 'Cos I took a few lashes for her? Or because she's the second most selfless person I've ever met?

Mother ambles along just in front of me, so I dismount the horse, nearly falling onto my head, and catch up with her. 'Here, you can ride for a bit.'

'I'm okay, lad.'

'No, please. I'm rested and can walk for a while.' I look to Three who's been walking the whole time. 'Please?'

Mother glances to Three, then back. 'Oh, okay. As long as you're sure. I'm not long off that other horse, you know. Tried to get your friend to ride, but he refused. Bunch of gallant lads, so you are.'

I help her mount, and then I drift off to the side. The horse trots forward.

A sensation of motion still runs through me, even though I'm no longer riding. I stop for a moment to get my head straight.

Eagle stands directly behind me. Her silence is a little eerie.

'Hi, we've not really been introduced.' I hold out my hand, which she ignores. 'I'm Seven.'

She walks past me, barely acknowledging my presence.

'Sorry, if you want to be left alone, I'll just walk on then.'

My head spins now I'm walking. Must be all those blows back at the Testing centre.

A hand falls on my left shoulder. I turn and Eagle's staring at me. I notice her green eyes, with flecks of brown, despite the darkness. It's almost like they're luminous. She tears the lower sleeve off her top, and uses the material to wrap a rough, water-soaked bandage around my forehead, with a delicacy I'd never have expected. I don't wince, even once, as she covers my eye and creates a cooling head cloth.

'Thank you,' I say, feeling better instantly.

The corners of her mouth curl ever so slightly before her face goes blank again. She checks her rifle, and spends some time searching in her pockets, which I take as a sign to move on.

Malt and Miller walking side-by-side, holding hands. They don't seem a likely couple. Malt seems so nice and laid back, while Miller seems like an angry, grumpy man. But, who knows, I'm hardly an expert in relationships myself. Can't even tell Six how I feel about her. I guess I was so prepared for us being separated after the Naming Ceremony that I hadn't thought about us being together after.

To my left, the sky lightens. We must be close to dawn. The group's waiting for me and Eagle, just at the top of the next hill. Even Three's moving quicker than me. When we reach it, I take in a comforting scene.

Spread below us is a large village: a mixture of houses, mills, tents, and other buildings spread throughout the small valley. As the sun breaks over the horizon, it casts a golden glow to one side of each building. It's the kind of view that would be wonderful to paint, if the Realm allowed people to do that anymore. 'A waste of valuable time, which could go towards technological, genetic or warfare advancement.' That's their line on anything that's classed as recreational. In our history books, I always enjoyed learning about the famous artists of the past, like Kahlo, Johns, Hockney, Hirst, Emin, and Richter, who created masterpieces depicting our world as it once was. Before the Great Wars. Before the Realms.

'Welcome to our settlement. I call it home and a better home you'd struggle to find in all the Realm,' says Mother.

It's strange to hear someone speaking so fondly of somewhere else other than the Cities. Every Greenie in the training camp, and every Guardian, talked about nowhere else but New London, the closest and biggest City in the Realm. It's where all our families were from, so the other Greenies say, and why we were put into camp Echo. It's the only place I ever wanted to go, once I left the training camp. Once I passed my Test.

But now that dream is in pieces, and I must pick them up and make a new one.

'Let's go down. Lasul should be awake by now.'

CHAPTER 9
LASUL

Realm Rule 9:
Apply logic to every situation. Emotions cloud logic.

We file down the hillside, as the sun gradually rises. It's nearly breached the horizon by the time we reach the depths of the valley and walk through the streets of the village. People emerge from their homes, some smiling and welcoming the Exiles back. Others are wary when they see Six, Three and me. It's then I remember we're strangers and that we must be on our guard. After all, we barely know these Exiles, despite how kind they've been. And technically they kidnapped us, even if the alternative was staying to serve the hideous Realm.

Six, now dismounted, is just ahead of me.

I pull her close and whisper in her ear, 'Remember to be careful. Don't say anything unless you must.'

She nods and continues walking. Miller stands close, watching me intently, his eyes narrowed. I smile at him, but he doesn't soften an iota. Three is also watching me, but more with wariness than dislike. I wonder what the little sog is thinking.

We stop in front of the biggest house in the village, dead in the centre, with a wide circle of open ground round it, like a grass moat.

'Eagle, Bulk, will you take the horses?' Mother asks.

Eagle nods and directs them away behind some tents to our left. I watch her leaving; she has a softer side to her despite the harsh, silent exterior. I hope I'll see her again.

'Six. Seven. Three. Come with me. Miller and Malt, take everything we scavenged to the storehouse and check it in.'

'No worries, Mother,' answers Malt. Miller gives me a final scowl, and then moves off with his partner.

I wonder what his problem is. Probably didn't reckon we were worth the effort of saving.

'Seven, come on.' Six waves me towards the door she's holding open.

We enter a bright, circular room. The interior is one large room, divided unnaturally. The kitchen has some shelves separating it from the living area, and a large, thick curtain hides another section. I wonder what's behind it.

There's a desk, a couch, and some other small bits of furniture, but it has a haphazard feel to it. There's a fire blazing in the hearth, like it's been going all night and not died down. Sweat slides down my face. Three's soon drenched as well.

A man with a grey ponytail sits at the desk next to the window, writing. He doesn't appear to have noticed us come in, although we weren't quiet. I get the sense he knows we're standing here but is staying mute.

'Lasul?' Mother breaks the silence.

'Ah, Mother. You're back. I trust you had a fruitful trip?' He gets up and hugs her tightly, inspecting us over her shoulder. 'And I see you have picked up a few strays.'

He holds out his hand to Six. 'I'm Lasul.'

'Six,' she says.

He turns to me, and I grip his hand firmly. 'Seven, sir.'

He laughs. 'Less of the *sir*. You're not in one of those ghastly camps, now.' He turns to Mother, laughing again. She smiles.

'And you, young man?' he asks, turning to Three.

'Three,' he grunts, looking uncomfortable at being addressed.

'Have a seat, please.' He indicates the couch, so Six and I sit down. Perspiration pours from me. This room is scorching in comparison to the cool, dawn air outside. Three remains standing near the door.

'The boy's injured,' Mother says. 'I'll get Doc to come at once.'

'Yes, yes. But give me some time with them, first. You won't die on me, will you, Seven?'

I shake my head. He eyes me in an odd way. Like he's seen me before or knows me. But I don't recognise him. And as he's an Exile, there's no way we've come across each other before.

Mother leaves to get the doctor and Lasul goes to the kitchen. 'Water or tea? I'm afraid it's all we have. We live a humble existence out here, compared to the City people.'

'No, thanks.' I don't trust this guy, or anyone for that matter. I used to trust wholly in the Realm and in Cherish. As much as it pains me to say, Cherish kept something from me. She did something to my DNA samples. And these people are her secret friends, which she never told me about. From now on, my trust will have to be earned.

'Oh, yes please. Can I have tea? I had it once or twice as a reward,' Six replies.

'Absolutely, young lady. It's green leaf. Pretty much all we can get here. Unless we get lucky on a scavenge.'

He turns to Three, who shakes his head.

As he makes Six's tea, I scan the room. His desk's full of paper. He must write lots. But who to? And how would it get delivered out here? After the technology crash and the EMP exchanges, twenty years ago, we essentially had to start again, so I doubt there's anything electronic out here capable of transporting messages. They must physically deliver letters.

I scan the rest of the place; not one bit of tech. His bed doesn't look like it's been slept in for a while: it's perfectly made with a small layer of dust settled on top. Glowing coal and ashes spill out of an over-packed fireplace, which continues to burn merrily. What does he do all night that he doesn't sleep and keeps the fire burning so furiously?

'Here you go.' He hands Six a mug of tea. I look for anything suspicious. Sure, I've heard of tea, but never drank it. I watch warily as Six sips, concerned he might drug or poison her.

'That's lovely.' Her cheeks redden. 'Thank you very much, Lasul.'

Well, she seems fine with him. Maybe I'm being paranoid. Maybe this guy's okay. Maybe I need some sleep. Tiredness crashes on me and all I want to do is lie down. This heat's fuzzing my brain.

Several minutes pass in silence. I'm nearly falling asleep in the warmth and comfort of the room. Six gives me a nudge and I sit up.

Lasul finishes his tea and places the mug on the desk. He looks at us both but says nothing. Then he stares at Three, who's still shifting around near the door, trying to cool his pink face.

Lasul picks up a rectangular bit of plastic from under the papers on his desk. It's thin, like a book, but black, shiny and has a display, like a telescreen.

He presses something on the screen and then turns to us. 'I'm impressed.'

The room goes quiet again. He stares at us, but no one speaks for several seconds.

'By what?' asks Six, finally breaking the awkward silence.

'Your patience, of course. If I'd been you, I'd have asked a million questions by now. But you've sat there, impeccably mannered, and waited politely. Maybe there is some merit to the Realm's insistence on unquestioning obedience and discipline.'

'I do have questions,' I say, standing up. 'Like why have you brought us here? And what do you plan for us? And did you have anything to do with what Cherish did? And why she did it?'

CHAPTER 10
TRAPDOOR

Realm Rule 10:
Every child shall have the opportunity to become a Realm citizen.

'All fair questions. It will take some time, but I will answer them all for you. But let's go with one at a time,' Lasul finally responds.

'Are you with the Realm?' I ask.

I want to know who we're dealing with before I decide anything.

'No.' Lasul keeps his eyes fixed upon me.

'So, who are you? And how did you find out about us?' My heart's slowing, and I'm thinking clearer.

'I'm Lasul, head of this settlement. And as for the information, well let's just say I have someone on the inside. Someone sympathetic to our cause.'

A spy? The Nameless are supposed to be people who failed their Tests. The runt of the litter, my Maths Guru once said. How can they have infiltrated the Realm and be stealing information from them?

'I find that hard to believe.' Six's blue eyes are focused upon Lasul. 'As much as I hate them now, I can't believe they would allow a spy into their ranks. And that they wouldn't be able to track information leaving their databases.'

Lasul smiles at her. 'You are smart, as your scores suggest. Strange you didn't stay and become a Realm Academic. Isn't it? I wonder what, or who, convinced you to leave that much more appealing life behind.' He looks straight at me. 'Still, I'm glad that you came to us.'

Six's face has fallen. She looks a little fragile, which I've never seen before. Even back in camp, when times were tough, she was strong and determined...a leader.

'You haven't actually told us how you managed to get a spy into the Realm? Or who it is? Or, most importantly, why?'

Lasul laughs at me. 'Finally.' He stands up and places the plastic tablet onto the desk. 'At last you've asked the right question. The only one that really matters: Why spy on the Realm? Why spy on you?'

'Well, the spy is my son. You met him, I believe. Saull? He got the message to us about what happened. It's why we came and rescued you. He said you were an impressive young man and could be valuable to our cause.'

'Your cause?'

'Indeed. There's a lot more to say about this, but I am part of a leadership group of like-minded people who are not in favour of the current regime in the Realm. We'd like to see some changes.'

'You're part of the rebellion?' Six asks.

Lasul nods. 'But we are in need of a spark. Something or someone to help light the fire that's needed to torch the current system. To inspire the many thousands of oppressed Nameless to stand up and fight against the injustice of an inhumane system.'

'And what does that have to do with spying on us?' I ask.

But it's Six who answers. 'He means you, silly.' She punches my shoulder, gently.

I shake my head in confusion. It was only like five minutes ago that I was all set for graduation. To serve the Realm for life.

'How long have you been planning this?' I ask. 'And was anyone going to tell me?'

Cherish must have known this, too. I can't believe she would keep something like this from me.

But before I can ask any more, Mother returns. 'I must insist, Lasul, that they get looked at by Doc, and get some rest.' Her arms are crossed, and she frowns intensely. It reminds me of when Cherish was mad at me for stealing rations.

Six stands to leave, but I remain on the couch, unsatisfied. 'I'm not going anywhere until I get some more answers. Why tell us anything at all? And what makes you think we want to be part of your rebellion?'

But my words are betraying my emotions. I think I do want to help them. I just can't be sure, after all that's happened.

'And Cherish, my mother, was a friend of yours.'

'She was,' replies Lasul.

'Yes, and you did nothing to help her. Your people could have tried to save her, but they didn't.'

'Cherish knew the risks. We didn't have time to intervene. The plan was to let you stay within the Realm. To graduate and help us take it down from the inside. We'd gradually bring you over to our side. But that all went wrong.'

I ball my fists. Cherish died because of some stupid plan to make me betray the Realm. I hate the Realm, with an ever-burning fury, but I think the blaze of anger towards this man might be close to matching it.

'And as for joining us – where else would you go? You can't go to the cities; you'll be shot in a second. And everywhere else outside of the cities won't be like this. Settlements are very different, and in some you would be slung up, tortured, or even become a meal.' He shakes his head as Six's eyes widen. 'That's right, there's little food out here, and it makes people desperate. No, you'll be safest here, so I suggest you stick around.'

I shake my head.

'Thank you for rescuing us.' Six moves over to Lasul and shakes his hand.

'We appreciate you helping us. But Seven's right. He's been used and kept in the dark. He deserves better. We all deserve better.'

'I agree with Six,' adds Mother. 'We are usually better than this. And Lasul, they need to see Doc. Now!'

'Of course. Of course.' He turns away, back to his desk. 'The boy is overly emotional right now. Hopefully later he will see more clearly.'

'I am *not emotional*,' I say, but he ignores me. Fatigue suddenly smacks, and I slump in my seat.

'Six, Three, could you help Seven over to that large tent on the right, the green one, where Doc should be. I need a word with Lasul.' I can see from Mother's expression that Lasul is not going to get an easy time, and I don't have the energy to take in any more for now.

I get up, helped by Six, but turn at the door. 'Thanks for nothing.' It's all I manage. I stumble as I turn back to Six. My head spins. My muscles ache. She helps me over towards the green tent.

We leave Mother with Lasul. Three tried to help me, but I shrug him off. I guess he's really Nameless because he failed his Test, so he might want to settle down here.

I keep thinking about what he said, about being exactly where he wants to be. I also think about how poorly he performed in the Tests, and how easily he walked during the night, without stopping or complaining. And how he reacted so quickly to save Bulk. That's not the moves of a scared, lazy failure. He must have deliberately failed his Test – but I definitely don't have the headspace to work out that enigma right now.

'Nearly there, Seven.' It must be a comical site; tiny Six holding me. I'm grateful to her, once again, for the support. I want to tell her just how amazing she is, still to be with me after everything, but I don't have the words...or the nerve to say it out loud.

Mother walks out and sees us struggling, moving quickly to me. 'I can't believe that man. A ridiculous and thoughtless fellow, sometimes. But you'll grow to like and trust him, like the rest of us. Here, let me help you, son.'

Someone calling me 'son' makes me feel sick, rather than better. I'll never meet my parents now or be called 'son' in a factual way. All because of some rebel plan. I still can't figure out who I'm madder at, the Realm or the Rebels.

She puts her surprisingly strong arms around my waist and pulls me into the tent, taking me to the nearest bed. I fall onto it face first. The mattress is soft, and the sheets smell clean. Our sheets back at camp never got washed unless we did it. Safe to say, mine were never washed.

'Ouch.'

'Sorry, should've warned you. I'm Doc, the settlement doctor. Just thought I should get some alcohol on those wounds. Probably should have told you, huh?'

I open my eyes. She's very small, about the same height as Six, and not much older than us.

She wipes the wounds clean, with a large cotton ball, which she soaks in more alcohol. It stings worse this time, as she moves it across my back, but I bite down hard, making no noise. When she tosses it into the bin, I see it's covered in black-red blood.

'I'm going to put some cream on your back wounds and stitch your eye. Let me know if it's too painful and I'll stop.'

I nod and pull up my top, certain I'll be in agony, but trying to appear brave.

'Wait, you're not giving him anaesthetic?' Six asks.

'Sorry, don't have anything like that out here. Not for a while anyway. I'll be as gentle as I can be.'

'You can't do that.' Six moves between the Doc and me. 'Are you even qualified?'

'Yes, I am actually. I spent a few months training as a Medic at the University of New London, and I learnt from the previous

Medic when I first came here, three months ago, and I've been the main Medic here for the last two. So, if you'll move, I'll treat my patient.'

Fair enough, as long as she gets these damn wounds to stop bleeding. Plus, she must be really smart as only Greenies with the highest Mental scores get to do Medic training.

'A few months? So, you're not actually qualified,' Six continues. 'You've just learnt on the job? How do we know you'll...'?

'Six, just let her do it. This scutting hurts. We can discuss her qualifications later,' I say.

'Fine, but you better get him fixed. Don't mess it up.'

'Whatever, I know what I'm doing,' says Doc, continuing to work on me.

'Enough...both of you,' says Mother.

I can see Six hates this, but she does move. She stands behind the Medic, arms crossed, a look of hatred on her face.

Doc sews seven stitches above my eye and cleans the closed wound after she's done. The stitching doesn't hurt, but the anti-septic cream on my back does. Finally, she puts a bandage over the top of the stitches.

'There you are. I'll not ask how you got the wound. I'm sure I'll learn at your community inductions, so for now, just rest and I'll check on you in a few hours.'

'Thanks.' Now I can see properly, I notice Doc's got nice wavy, brown hair, green eyes, and lightly tanned skin.

'Thank you,' says Six, quietly.

I turn from Doc back to Six.

'You're both welcome. I have other patients, house calls, but for now, both of you get some rest. We have a spare bed here if you'd like it?' She points to the bed next to me, and Six nods her thanks.

Mother moves to the edge of my bed. 'Seven, Six, I'm glad you're both here and safe. I hope Lasul didn't overload you with information, as he has a habit of doing, as well as being very insensitive. Too much time alone, thinking and plotting, and not enough time in the fresh air, with people. Still, he's an outstanding leader of our community. Kept us safe and living in peace, for so long. Well, as much peace as you can get out here! Anyway, get some rest. We'll talk more later.'

She exits the tent, leaving Six and me alone. 'I'm glad you're mended, Seven.'

'Me, too. And thanks.'

'What for?'

'Caring.'

'No problem. I'm here if you want to talk. But first, I think we should sleep.'

'Six, who do you think we can trust? Mother seems nice, and so does Malt and Eagle. But I'm not sure about the others. Especially Lasul, with his lying and plotting.'

'I think we can trust them, Seven. And even if we can't, we don't have much choice. Nobody else is going to take us in. At least they seem better than anyone from the Realm.'

'Yeah, you're probably right. By the way, what's going on with Three? One minute he's clueless and struggling to run a hundred metres, the next he's walking most of the night and seems quite happy, if that's possible.'

'Yeah, I've been thinking about him a lot.'

I screw up my face, which she notices. 'You've been thinking about him?' I ask.

'Not like that, you sog. I just mean that I find him interesting.'

She doesn't seem to want to go into it, so I leave it and approach another subject.

'What about the whole rebellion plan? Can you believe that?'

'That they'd want you? Yes.'

'Haha, a compliment. You must be deliriously tired.'

'Maybe. Do you want to talk more tomorrow?' She stifles a large yawn.

'Yeah,' I reply, yawning, too. 'I'm shattered.'

'Good. Sleep time. Tomorrow we can take on the world.

Together.'

I smile, as she literally crawls to the next bed, slides under the covers, and passes out. Seconds later, I'm gone.

'Wake up, Seven. Get up.' Six thrashes at me in the dull, late evening glow of the tent.

'Get off,' I say. 'That hurts.'

She hits me a few more times. 'We need to go, now. They've found us. I saw them driving in on a truck.'

'The Realm?' I ask. Six nods.

Images flash through my mind rapid-fire: Test...Cherish arrested... beaten... murder... escaping the cell... riding across country with strangers... then the panic hits me.

Adrenaline floods my muscles and I leap to my feet, grab Six's hand, and run deeper into the tent. There's a small desk at the back and we find Doc, who's loading a small pistol.

'Is there somewhere safe that you can take Six and me?'

'Yes, beneath Lasul's house, there is a tunnel. It will take you far from here. Come with me.'

She disappears through the back of the tent, and we follow.

The settlement is burning. Flames erupt from the straw roofed houses, as well as those built from wood. The fires scorch the houses like funeral pyres. People run frantically, some screaming, others with makeshift weapons in their hands. Three Guardians move from house to house, igniting them, while the other Guardians fight off angry Exiles.

I stare at Six. I can't lose her. I've already lost too much.

I need to get her to safety.

She turns to me. 'Should we fight?'

'Let's just get away.' I shake my head and push her forward, fast on the heels of Doc. She pushes open the door to Lasul's house, which is one of the few not on fire. He appears at the entrance and ushers us in.

We sprint past him, and he locks the door behind us. 'Quick, under the bed. There's a trapdoor. Get in and keep going. Get away from here. You will come out in the land of the River people. They are good at heart if a little distrusting. I sent Miller and Malt there, so find them and they will help you.'

I nod and push Six towards the trapdoor, which Doc already has opened.

'Wait, what will happen here? They are burning the place down,' Six asks.

Lasul turns to her and shrugs. 'Our settlement has been dying for a while. Better to burn out for a good cause, than fade away for nothing. Make sure you keep each other safe. If we don't see each other again, I need you to go to Westmine. Join the Orphans.' He starts ushering us to the trapdoor.

'Hold on, I'm not leaving. I'm going to fight,' I say. 'Six is the one going.'

'Your stupidity is not needed right now, Seven. Get in that tunnel and go. I won't tell you again.'

'But, why?' I ask. 'Why are you helping us so much? We're not worth more than any of you?'

'We've watched over you for your whole life, Seven. Cherish has told us everything. And I know...I've known you for just as long if you can believe that...'

An enormous blast hits the front door. A large hole appears and what is left is ablaze. The house quickly catches.

'Go now, or you dishonour all our efforts by staying and being caught.' Lasul stares at me, unmoving, while his house burns. 'Fair journey.'

His sincerity sears into me. He means it. We need to go. I help Six down, and then follow her. I squat low, urging Six further along the tunnel.

Doc pushes the trapdoor closed.

I hear the bed squeak back into place and a loud explosion as the roof of the tunnel collapses behind us.

CHAPTER 11
RIVER

Realm Rule 11:
Every child is required to complete Greenhorn training.

Black, hot, and rancid. A boiling abyss of a stench hole. Our journey through the low, compact tunnel is relentless. My back scrapes against the roof so many times, I can feel fresh blood sliding round to my ribs and accumulating in a soaked patch on my top. Who the hell built these? Badgers?

'At last,' Six says. Her voice barely reaches my ears before it dies. 'I see some light.'

'Well don't stop. Keep crawling. I'm about to flip out.'

Claustrophobia doesn't cover it. I wipe my soaked face with my filthy hand for the fiftieth time. I'd just started enjoying clean clothes.

I drag my horizontal body inch by inch, crawling like a slow centipede. Back burns, shoulders ache, quads fail, head pounds. I focus on the dark soil beneath me, trying not to think about how far there is to go.

'Seven, it's here. Just a few more feet.'

Rushing water and squawking birds. Icy, clean air. The saturated sweat instantly cools.

I dare myself to look. Squinting, radiance swarms me. The exit, the best thing I've seen in my whole life. I follow the feet of Six, crawling up and out.

Sunshine attacks my eyes. The intense rays burn the area at the back of my eye – I think the Bio Guru taught us this – the retina? I should ask Six, she'll know for sure.

Six grabs my hand and pulls me. I grimace and let go. Scutting lashes.

'Oh, Seven. I forgot. Sorry.' She rubs my bare arm. Goosebumps. 'Come on, there's a huge river over there. We can wash the wounds.'

I follow her, cradling my arm to avoid tugging on the already gaping gash. Blood pulses to the cut, like a mini heartbeat in my shoulder.

I can almost fully open my eyes now. We're descending a large grassy hill towards a huge, roaring river. Makes the stream back at camp seem like a trickle. Six has run ahead.

'Six, wait up.'

'Ha, not often you ever say that to me! About time you did a little lagging behind. I'm fed up watching your backside.'

'Yeah, but not a bad view, huh?'

She catches my eye for a second, then turns away, skipping down towards the river. I amble after her. *Pathetic.* But the throb in my back brings me back to reality.

How can I be thinking about Six when I just left a village under attack? I should have stayed. In fact, when I get cleaned, I'm going back. We can't just keep running, we need help and answers. And we left Three behind, on his own, with people we've just met.

Six is cupping water from the river into her mouth in large gulps.

'Come on slug, or they'll be no water left for you.' She smiles and takes a few more mouthfuls.

I slide down beside her, but it hurts to stretch and get handfuls of water. I edge closer to the verge and lower my mouth to drink directly from the river. Cut my bleeding back out the equation.

SPLASH.

For a second, I'm in aqua land, face down on the sandy bed. I get to my feet, stand, and find I'm in the river, waist high. Six is killing herself laughing, rolling on the grass at the edge. I use my good arm and pull her into the water with me.

SPLASH.

I watch her thrash for a second, then resurface, the water up to her chest.

'That's what you get for laughing!' I say, grinning and nodding.

She spits a fast jet of water from her mouth straight into my face.

'Ha, I'll always get the last laugh, Seven. Gotta do better than that to get one up on me.' She pushes me and my foot catches on a large stone.

SPLASH.

I hold my breath. Ha, watch this, Six. I'll get you this time.

I drift slowly down the river, submerged. I open my eyes every couple of seconds to check she's still there. I can see a vague outline. But she hasn't moved yet. Just a little longer. Let the panic set in. Then I'll have her.

Thirty seconds pass and I must have gone several metres downriver. I can't see her anymore. Surely, she's not going to just leave me. Hurry up Six, or this won't work. I can hold my breath for a long time, longer than any other Greenie could at camp, but I can't do it forever.

I try to remain still even though I'm running low on oxygen. And my wounds are stinging. This is a stupid idea. I should just re-emerge. But I wait. And wait.

I exhale slowly, a bubble at a time. Why hasn't she dived down for me? This is *so* backfiring. I can't go back up or I'll look a sog. I wait.

My brain feels like it's swelling. My skull can't take it. My lungs are empty. I'm coming back up. I plant my feet on the riverbed and push up.

As I thrust my head above the water, I look back upriver.

Nothing.

I take several deep breaths, refilling my lungs and giving my cells oxygen for respiration – see I don't need Six for everything. I did listen sometimes in Bio. As I inhale, I turn 360, but the river and flanking grass verges are empty.

This doesn't make any sense. She was just here, like a minute ago at the most. It's not even possible for her to have gone anywhere in that time.

I panic. What if the Guardians took her while I was under? What if they're still here, watching? I jerk my head left, right, upriver, and downriver. Nothing.

I start to wade to the edge. I'll get out and run to the top of the hill.

SPLASH.

I'm under again, this time something is holding my legs, pulling me down. Then it lets go. I tense, ready to fight.

I resurface.

Six is laughing her head off. Her blonde hair soaked and stuck to her head.

'Why the hell did you do that? I was worried!'

'I couldn't resist. Ha, your face. I love it.' She arches her back and laughs to the sky. I've never seen her this happy.

Then I break and start giggling, too.

'Yeah, you did get me. I really panicked there you know?'

'Well of course you did. You couldn't live without me, could you?' She laughs again, this time a little quieter, her eyes never leaving mine.

'With friends like you, who needs enemies, huh?'

Seriously, Seven. She gave you an in and you gave her that crunk.

'*Whatever.* Come on, enough joking around. We're here to find Malt and Miller, remember?'

'Yeah, I remember.'

My stomach clenches again at the thought of us messing around with all that's going on. People are risking their lives for us and all I can do is flirt. Badly.

We spend a minute cleaning, not that we haven't been in the water long enough, but I get to properly rinse the dirt from my hair and clothes. Six gently cleans the cut on my back. It stings like hell, but I close my mind until it's over.

I pull off the bandage that covers my eye wound. It's soaked and falling off anyway. The stiches seem to still be intact. Seems like Doc is pretty competent after all. Best not say that to Six.

Six helps me out of the water and we walk back upstream towards the dense trees on this side of the river. Smoke spirals from somewhere deep within.

'Looks like someone's home. Hopefully we'll find them quick and can get back to the settlement,' I say. I smile at Six, but she doesn't return it. She has a glazed look, the kind she has when she's reading or thinking deeply.

We walk ahead in silence.

'Six, how the hell did we get here?'

'Through a tunnel and—'

'Yeah, good one. No, like what are we doing? It's all so crazy, isn't it? One minute we're both destined to pass our Tests and have long and rewarding lives serving the Realm, then the next day we're both fugitives, taking up with Exiles and now we're running again. What are we doing?'

'Honestly, Seven I don't have any idea either. But Lasul seems to. He values you and wants you. You never know, it might just have been a random attack back at the camp. Maybe they weren't looking for us. We might go back later, and they will all be fine. And we can help them rebuild their houses and maybe build our own houses and –'

'Get real, Six. You heard it, too. There were Realm Guardians there. Looking for us. They're not the good guys. I think those folks we left behind are in some serious trouble. They were friends with Cherish. Or so they say. Either way, I think we should help them. And we can't just leave Three.'

'But Malt and Miller?'

'Okay, we go check out if they're here, but then we head back. Agreed?'

Six nods. Her hair is still mostly wet, but strands of dry blonde threads are flying high above her head, like mini kites.

As we pass into the shadows of the wide oaks, I shiver.

'We should have dried off before coming in here. It's freezing without the sun.'

Six nods, also shaking. The noise of the river fades, as do the bird songs.

After several minutes of walking, it's just the noise of our feet crunching on leaves, twigs, and fungus. The temperature drops. I rub my arms; despite the pain it causes to my back. Six's lips are almost blue.

'Six, I really hope that fire is still going. You look like you need it.'

'I'm fine. It's you we should be worrying about with those wounds open to a zillion kinds of bacteria.'

'You look like you're gonna freeze to death. Come here.'

I pull her close to my chest. She places her arms loosely around my waist.

'Sharing body heat, huh? Survival technique? Or a way to get close to me?'

'Both.' I smile widely, knowing she can't see my face.

Her face moves on my chest. I hope she's smiling, too.

She rubs my back, slowly and precisely, avoiding my wounds and I rub hers in return. For thirty seconds I enjoy myself, not worrying about anything other than warming up Six.

'Okay, we'd better move.' She releases me and marches away. 'Not that I didn't enjoy it.'

I follow her, trying to work out what she means. I've never had to understand girls in that way. I've mostly just seen them as rivals for roles in the Realm. But Six is different. In fact, every girl is now different. I'm free from the rules and laws of the Realm. My emotions are unleashed. Nobody out here can tell me what is allowed and what is not and surely flirting with a girl is fine.

Though maybe my timing could be better. Maybe I should wait until we're somewhere warm and safe again. If that ever happens. The way things are going now, that could be never. Guilt squirms in me as I think of how happy Six makes me. Should I feel like this so soon after what I did to Cherish? What would she want?

'Be strong, Seven...live for a better tomorrow...'

We plough through the dense undergrowth of the forest floor. Inside, a shard of ice is piercing my heart.

'Six, can I stop? Maybe I can make a blanket with those branches and leaves? Sleep under that bush or in a tree?'

'Seven, shhhh. There's something ahead.'

Probably because I'm exhausted, I didn't smell it, but now it filters through the cold, forest air. Smoke. From the fire we saw earlier? I hope so. We move slower, more cautiously, careful not to make too much noise. Good or bad, we don't want anyone to see us coming.

The sky is darkening. Flickers of red and orange filter through the canopy. The fire is low but alive. We squat and crawl the last few feet. A wide opening, cleared of trees and plants, lies beyond the bush we crouch behind.

The remains of what must have been a huge fire is slowly dying. We watch, silent. Nothing moves except a few flames' last dance. Six raises an eyebrow.

I shrug.

We look again. A small movement. To our right, high in a tree. A person hangs, swinging slightly in the breeze. Dressed all in green, with long brown hair hanging over their head. Dead.

I point up. Six covers her mouth and makes the tiniest noise.

'Who's there?' says a gruff, male voice.

We freeze, looking for the source, but see nothing new.

'Who's there? Are you back to finish us? Well come ahead, you've killed the rest anyway. I've got nothing to live for. Come out and face me,' the man says.

Six shakes her head but something tells me this guy isn't evil. I could have said those exact same words.

I stand up and walk into the wide opening. Still, no other movement. I turn back to Six, who shrugs.

A sharp point of pain pierces my neck and makes me jerk round.

The vague outline of a man in green walks towards me.

But my eyes are heavy.

My knees give way.

I fall on my side and hear soft steps behind my head.

I watch the fire as he comes closer.

'Should'a killed you before, you little runt. But at least I got ya now.'

The laugh that follows is the last thing I hear.

CHAPTER 12
ASH

Realm Rule 12:
Respect your elders and remain silent, unless spoken to.

Six is shouting. 'Why did you do that? You knew it was him. There was no need.'

'Ah, girl. I'm afraid I mistook him for one of them Realm scumbags.'

I recognise that voice. Scumbag, huh?

'You've disliked us from the moment we met. You just saw an opportunity to be cruel and took it. Didn't you?'

'Listen, girl. I'm not going to stand here and argue with a know-it-all Greenie. I couldn't take any chances.'

I try to get up. I'm gonna smack him for talking to Six like that. But my body isn't complying. I can move one arm and my neck, but not a lot else.

'Miller! What did you do?'

Yeah, you tell him.

'Relax, Malt. It's only a sleeping dart. Look, there he's getting up already. They're not even that strong.'

I turn away from the grey glow of the dying fire and see three figures: Six, Malt and Miller. The dart must've affected my nervous system because I'm struggling to co-ordinate any kind of movement. Lucky for Miller.

'You okay, Seven?' Six kneels next to me, helping me into a seated position.

'Yeah, but my body feels like it's still asleep.'

'Yes, it will feel that for another few minutes at least. Just sit and relax. No point in forcing it.' Malt gives us a warm smile. It disappears when he addresses Miller.

'What were you playing at? The last thing we need is to waste time here, considering what's happening.'

'Well, better safe than sorry. If he'd been a Guardian, then you'd be thanking me.'

Six looks up. 'What *has* happened? Lasul sent us away to find you two because Guardians had entered the settlement. And where are the River People?'

Malt looks to Miller, who shrugs and walks off into the trees. Malt then sits alongside Six and gives us both a very paternal look.

'I suppose you should know. After all, you're one of us now.'

'Yes, tell us,' I say. I'm too eager sitting up and my back stings as the feeling returns.

'The River People are dead. Guardians from the Realm murdered them.'

Six and I both look up into the trees. The green body still swings.

'This is unbelievable. The Realm are responsible for this? But why? What did these people do?' asks Six.

I look up. Now that I know what I'm looking for, I see several more bodies like the first green one. All hanging from branches. Lifeless.

'Nothing. They were just in the wrong place at the wrong time. The Guardians spared no one. By the time Miller and I arrived they were hanging the last of them.'

'But why did they kill them?' Six pushes it. I'm not sure I want to hear the answer.

'Because of you. And you.' He nods to me, then Six. 'I heard them questioning the last one before they hung her. It was tragic, she didn't have any idea what they were talking about. They kept asking where they were hiding the fugitives. Of course, she couldn't tell them, so she was hung, too. It was horrible.'

'And where were you?' I ask. My fists are clenched, my jaw tightened.

'We were hiding, of course. We couldn't be seen, or we'd be hanging from those trees, too.'

'Oh, yeah and what about all these people? You could have saved some of them.'

'Seven, we couldn't. There was a whole troop of Guardians. Twenty at least. They'd have killed us, too. You don't understand, yet. Being rash will not help us.'

'What don't I understand? That you're both too scared to stand up for people when you see something unfair? That you're both too concerned about yourself to worry about anyone else?' I'm trying to stand, consumed with rage, but my body is struggling to obey.

'Hardly a hero yourself, kid, are you?' Miller smirks. 'You're doing exactly the same as us. Staying out of fights that are too big for us.'

Miller returns to the opening, looking equally as angry, and when I move towards Malt to question him more, Miller dives between us and pushes me to the ground.

'Don't dare, you little git. You've no idea the crunk we've gone through for you. Sit back down before I actually do something.'

I try to get up but Six places her hand on my chest to hold me down. 'Take it easy, Seven. This isn't helping.'

'Yeah, listen to your girlfriend, boy wonder.' Miller puts his arm on Malt's shoulder. Malt has remained calm and quiet.

'Seven. Listen to me and try to take it all in,' Malt says, his eyes gentle and sympathetic.

I see the fire in my own eyes reflected in his and take a deep breath. It's like a switch. I was well conditioned. Digital emotions, one or zero, on or off. I've never felt more like a machine, a vehicle of the Realm. They made me like this, and I hate it.

'We've been watching you for a while. Cherish has been in contact as often as possible these last few years.' Malt shifts from one foot to another.

'But why? I still don't get why it's me? Why not Six, or One? They're more capable than me in loads of ways.' I'm on my feet again. 'Why?'

Miller steps between us. 'Malt, we were told explicitly not to tell the kid anything.'

'I remember. But circumstances have changed. I don't think we can return to the settlement.'

'What?' Miller moves round to face Malt. 'We need to go back and see if Mother and Lasul are okay. They will need us. The kids just said it had been attacked.'

'No, it's too dangerous. If the Guardians are still there, we can't take the boy. You know how insistent Lasul was about his safety.'

'Would you both stop talking about me as if I'm not here! And I'm not a *boy*!' I can't believe they know something but aren't saying.

Miller moves towards me again, but Malt puts his hand onto his leg. 'No. There's no point in argument. We don't go back. I refuse to put the whole plan in jeopardy.'

'Fine,' says Miller, walking off. 'But I'm doing it for you, Malt. And Cherish. Not *him*.' He points at my chest, fury-fuelled and aggressive. Then he breathes out. 'I'm going to find us some food.'

'Good, and leave your temper out there.' Malt turns to us, smiling. 'We can't stay here long. Enough time for a quick rest and some food. Then we must move.'

'To where?' asks Six.

'Lasul was clear what to do if something like this happened. He wanted us to go to Westmine.'

'The mining colony?'

'The very one,' replies Malt. 'It has the biggest Exile population in the Realm. Surely the best place for a bunch of Exiles to fit in.'

I stare at Malt. What are they not telling me? I turn to Six who bites her bottom lip – her thinking expression. She probably has some ideas. I'll need to ask her as soon as we're alone.

'Wait here for a minute. I must speak with Miller.' Malt dashes into the trees, disappearing almost immediately in the fading light.

'Come on, we're going.' I start to walk back in the direction we came.

'What? No, we're to wait here, Seven. We're not doing anything stupid. Look what happened. Did you hear Malt? We're being looked for. You're being hunted and they don't care who gets hurt or killed in finding you. No, stay here.'

'I'm going, Six. Either come or wait, but I'm going.' I walk back into the dense forest, stumbling. I'm still a little lightheaded from that dart. I march for several minutes, and the forest closes around me, the trees tight. I stop to rest my sleepy muscles and look around. Crunk, how am I lost already?

'So much for your big exit? Don't even know the way, do you?' ask Six.

I shake my head. No point in lying to her.

'What would you do without me? Come on.' She marches past me and ploughs forward in the direction I was going anyway. Dammit.

'So, what changed your mind?' I ask to take my mind off how rubbish I feel.

'Pretty much the fact that you'll be way worse off and probably wouldn't live for more than a day without me.'

'Oh, is that right? Well, who saved who from those lashes?'

'Yes, once, Seven. Once. And I will never forget it, so no need to remind me every ten minutes.' She squints at me in the dark. I can just about see her pupils.

'Yeah, yeah. So, you coming back to the settlement with me, then?'

'Would I be here, if I wasn't?'

'I assume that's a yes?'

She continues to trek ahead at full speed. Obviously, she is, and I'm buzzing. Even though the frosty air is chilling my blood, I force myself forward through the forest. Finally, we reach the edge and walk back down river.

'I assume you think Lasul can tell you more about who you are? This is why you're so desperate to see him again?'

'Yes.' She knew the answer before she asked, but it's nice for me to say it aloud. To give myself new purpose post-Realm. 'I've wondered for so long. Who dumped me with Cherish when I was a baby? Why didn't they want me? And why Cherish did what she did – what was she hiding about me? And if I have to hang with some rebels for a while to get that information, that's fine, too. Stick it to the Realm at the same time.'

'Then I will help. If I can, if I'm not just a hindrance to you. I'm not really suited for this life of wildness and adventure. I thought I'd be spending my days at a microscope or reading books in a lab.'

'I think you're suited perfectly for it.'

She smiles back at me and in that second, that's all I ever want.

The familiar sounds from earlier are reassuring, but it's now so dark we can only see a few feet in front of us. Some moonlight shines through the sporadic clouds, but we've still got very little chance of finding the exit for the tunnel.

'Well, we know roughly what direction to go, don't we?' I offer.

Six scowls. 'Yes, but roughly could lead us anywhere. I want to find it, so keep alert.'

We walk on, my eyes hurting from the strain of examining the dark countryside.

'Found it,' comes Six's voice from just ahead.

'Great, I should go first though because I'll be slowest,' I suggest.

'Don't be brain-dead. We're not crawling back through there. We just need to follow the line of the tunnel and we can walk above ground. Seriously Seven, you need some sleep.'

I watch her ascend the hill, torn between annoyance and adoration.

'Come on, then.'

I trudge up the hill in her wake. The sounds of the river slowly retreat as I climb.

We walk for hours, my feet sore and head pounding.

'I think I can see it.' Six squats a little as we look from the top of the latest hill. She points down at the valley. It looks like the settlement...after a fire. Smoke billows from several sites, spiralling into the darkness from a flame foundation.

'No,' is all I say, at the site of the destruction.

I'm running. I've no idea how my legs are doing it. Sprinting down the hill into the valley, where the friends of Cherish rescued, accepted, and protected me, pretty much without question. All of this is my fault, but I don't fully know why.

'Seven!'

I know she's calling me, but I need to check. I need to see if Lasul and Mother and Doc and all those other folks are okay. And Three. Where the hell is that weirdo? I hope they haven't caught him. Malt is right, it's my fault. *If you fly with the crows, expect to be shot down with them.*

I slow as I pass the first cinder piles. Small fires still glow, but the main party is well over. I hear no one. I see no one.

'Hello?' I shout. 'Anyone still here?'

Only a few hours ago, the whole settlement was full of houses, huts, and tents. Now, nothing. The fields look scorched, the trees scalded. The people gone. Or dead.

'Seven, wait up.'

Six skids to a stop at my heels, breathing heavily. 'Why...did... you...run...like...that?' She's bent over with her hands on her knees.

'Sorry, I had to see. What have we done? We brought them here. This is all because of us. Because of me.'

'Seven, we can't think like that. They welcomed us in. We didn't know this would happen.'

'We should have at least stayed and fought.'

'We would be dead or imprisoned if we'd done that.' She shakes me and I look her properly in the eyes. 'Seven, they want to kill us. This isn't camp anymore, where you can pick a fight with any old Greenie and probably win. We are traitors. These are Guardians. With guns. This is serious. People are dying.'

'I KNOW IT'S SERIOUS.' I'm shaking. Fury, frustration, desolation. 'I know, Six.' I take a huge breath. 'I know. But I still can't help it. All my life I always wanted to help people, protect people. That's why I wanted to be in Military. And even now that we're no longer part of the Realm, I wanted to help the people here, for Cherish, but I didn't. I ran when I should have stayed, hid when I should have fought.'

I flop down onto the blackened grass. The sky begins to glow orange at the edges. I can see Six's blonde hair gently blowing in the early morning breeze. She stands for several minutes looking around, her eyes narrowed. I watch her, and then I watch the horizon above the hill. The light slowly peels into sight. As it does, it frames the figure of Six. The golden glow washes over her slight body, highlighting her small but strong outline.

When the Sun glimpses over the skyline, she sits next to me.

She puts her head on my shoulder and leans in, placing her hands between her knees. I enjoy the moment, knowing that at any minute, we'll need to move. Even if the Guardians are gone, we can't stay.

There is nothing left.

The Nameless settlement has died.

Burnt to the ground.

And so have all my hopes of finding out more.

CHAPTER 13
PARTING

Realm Rule 13:
We are stronger united than apart

'I'm gonna beat you, ya little turd.'

Miller has finally caught up with us. Malt follows some distance behind him. For all his faults, Miller is fit and strong.

'Miller, leave it. Look around you. There's bigger things to worry about.' Six is standing up for me, bringing reason to a crazy situation. I think Miller and I would have killed each other by now if it were not for her. And Malt. Here he comes.

'You big buffoon. I told you they looked safe. Why did you run off like that?' Malt speaks to Miller like a Guru telling off a Greenhorn. I love it.

'I just wanted to check they were both okay. You know, just in case.'

'You liar. You knew they were fine. You just wanted to open that big gob of yours, didn't you? And what a lot of good that has done. Honestly.'

Malt finally arrives at the spot where we've been resting for the last hour, watching the remnants of the settlement burn away. He flops down beside Six and me.

'I'm off to check there's nobody still here.' Miller marches off towards the large hill we descended the first time we arrived at the settlement. Was that only yesterday?

Malt lies flat on his back, his arm over his forehead, blocking the early morning sun from his face. 'Well, young ones. What was all that about? Didn't want to listen to old Malt, did you? Wanted to come and see for yourself?' He sits up and looks at me particularly.

How does he know it was my decision?

'Well, now you've seen it with your own eyes, what do you think? Still love your Realm and your glorious Autokratōr? Still want to serve and be a hero?' Again, he looks at me. How did he know that? Surely Cherish wouldn't have shared that.

'It's horrible. So horrible I can't even describe it.' Six looks all around as she speaks. I see a small tear slide down her sooty face. 'First Cherish, now this.'

'I tried to avoid this. I didn't want you to be exposed to it. Not yet. But it may well be a good thing,' says Malt.

'A good thing?' I say, turning on Malt. 'How exactly?'

'Now you know what they're capable of. What we are up against, day in day out. The fact that they could wipe us all out in an instant if it suited them. Just like they did here.'

'I know what they are capable of.'

Forcing a Greenie to shoot their own mother to prove their loyalty to the Realm.

I stare into his eyes, and he returns it, not full of anger, but sympathy. Some of the tension leaves my shoulders.

'How can you be so calm about all this? These were your people, your friends,' I say.

'Do not think for one second boy, that I don't care. That I'm not hurting inside more than you could possibly imagine. That every inch of me is not on fire with fury and wants nothing else than to get revenge for this.' He takes a second to breathe and compose himself before continuing. 'I believe in looking for ways to move forward, not back. This has happened. What matters now, is what we do next.'

'I think we rescue them. Lasul, Doc, and Mother, and Three. Anyone who needs us.'

We share the last of Malt's expedition rations. It's not much, just a few nuts, seeds and habbit. It's better than that crunk we had back at camp and it's good to eat some meat. It drastically improves our mood.

'You know, even though it's totally GM, this habbit isn't so bad,' says Six when we finish.

'Ah, they teach you such stuff in the camps?' asks Malt.

'Yes,' replies Six, her smarty-pants face is back for the first time in days. 'We learnt all about cross species modifications. Habbits from rabbits and hares of course, but also dots and cheep. Though apparently the dots didn't work all that well. Six hundred and fifty-seven attempts until the first one worked, and it cost millions.'

'A dot, eh? What's that then?' Malt asks to be polite.

'Well, it's a cross between a cat and a dog. Really tricky because they have different chromosome compliments and huge differences in their genome. It's actually fascinating. I wanted to study genomics when I got into Academics...' She picks up a stone and throws it at a charred tree stump.

'You really are a brilliant girl,' says Malt. 'A bright star amongst the dullards about here.' He turns and winks at me.

I look down before my face reveals anything.

Six giggles.

It grows silent. Not even the usual twitter of bird song to entertain us. I pull my knees up to my chin as we wait for Miller to return. I can see his shape outlined at the tip of the hill. Hurry up, it's getting cold. I rub my arms. I'm used to the cold, but this is worse, as if the amount of death in the air chills my blood.

Six begins to whistle a familiar tune – the Realm's anthem, *Glory, Glorious Realm*. I used to love that tune, humming the words when things got difficult, or I was doing extra laps after compulsory training. Now I only think of murder.

'Six, stop it, please.'

She squints at me for a moment, then presses her knuckles onto her forehead. 'Sorry, I wasn't thinking. Just an old habit.' She shakes her hand and stands, looking out beyond the area of the settlement, away from the Sun.

I watch her for a while, wondering how I might spend time with her if things were different. If we had this whole part of the country to ourselves, we could spend all day splashing in the river. All evening lying under the stars, cooking habbit and chatting about clever stuff to please Six – well, she'd be the one saying clever stuff, but I'd listen. We could enjoy the scarlet red sunrise without the reminder of the bloodshed.

'Right, so far as I can see, they've gone east.' Miller's back. 'Towards New London. Probably went last night once they'd sacked the place. Maybe got eight hours head start. Don't see no bodies, so I reckon they've taken them prisoner. Maybe some of them got away as well. Gotta hope, huh?'

Malt nods. 'Let's hope many of them got away. If they're thinking straight, they'll make for Westmine. No, we can't do anything for those scattered. They must fend for themselves. At least, they're still free.'

'Mmmm,' says Miller, looking east.

'Well, let's get going then,' I say, standing up and moving east. No one follows. 'Come on, they've already got a huge head start.'

'Kid, if they're going to New London, we've got no chance. They'll make straight for the nearest road where trucks will be waiting. Our only opportunity would be to catch them before they reach the main road. It's a ten-hour walk, give or take, so they're probably already there. Give it up.'

'What is it with you two? Mother would help you. Eagle and Bulk would help you. I know they would. If you're willing to rescue a nobody Greenie like me, then why not them?'

'Seven, please sit down.' Malt with his easy, relaxed tone thinks he'll smooth me over. He'll speak with reason and logic and try to calm me down. No chance.

'I'm fine standing, thanks.' I know I'm being as big a sog as Twelve, but I can't help it. I hate sitting around doing nothing.

'Okay, stand if you wish. We will not be rescuing anyone. We need to go to Westmine and inform Hess. She needs to know what's happening, so they can prepare.'

'Prepare for what?' asks Six.

'Let's just say it's a safe place to be. At least, safer than out here, on our own. And it's what Lasul wanted.'

'But why? Why does he want us to be so safe? And why Seven specifically? It's clear that this is all about him.' Six leans close to Malt.

'I'm afraid I don't know those answers, or not fully. What's more important, right now, is that you both agree to come with us. It's imperative you come.'

'So, you expect us to follow you and the biggest sog in the world...that's you Miller...into the countryside to some mine, crawling with Realm Guardians, no doubt, and you won't tell us anything we ask?' I move close to Miller when I call him a sog. I enjoy watching him tense. But when Malt holds up his hand, Miller relaxes.

'This bickering is useless. Whatever we decide we need to go, now. Either way time is precious.'

Miller nods and moves behind Malt, placing his hand on his shoulder.

Six stands. 'I'll come to Westmine. If you tell me one thing... are you a faction of the Orphans?'

Malt looks up to Miller, who shrugs. He then nods to Six.

'And going to Westmine will help their cause? Will help against the Realm?'

'Yes, my dear.'

'Then, I'm in. I need a new goal now – that life that I always hoped for in Academics is gone.'

'Six, I am totally with you, but what about those people who got captured?' I say. 'They're taking our places on those trucks. They took us in and now they're taking our fates. Three could be with them. We need to help.'

'If I went with you, then I'd just slow you down. I'll be much more useful in Westmine. They might need someone to work out how to mine more efficiently or something.' She smiles at me, and I understand. She's right. She always is.

'You'll be a real asset in Westmine, my dear. I'm glad you'll be coming. But so will Seven.'

'I don't want to leave you, Six. But I think I need to go after those prisoners. If Lasul is the spring of all knowledge, then I need to save him. I need to know why Cherish did it. I need to know why I'm so important. And it seems like only Lasul can tell me that.'

'But we don't even know what happened to Lasul. Or anyone. You'd be taking a big risk for possibly no reward,' Malt says, reasonably.

'I know how much this means to you, Seven, so go if you must.' Six touches my shoulder as she says it, and my body loses all its tension. 'I'll be fine, and if I can help the Orphans, I will. And in some ways, it's so much better than being imprisoned by a monitored and restricted life in the Realm. If I go with them, at least I'll be free.'

I smile at her, always so calm and wise and reasonable. My antithesis (see, that's a word Six taught me!), but you know what they say about opposites.

'Thank you,' I say. For a second or two I begin to doubt myself, but then the memory of Cherish and that room and that gun come flashing back and I'm resolved again. 'I need to go.'

'I cannot stop you. I'd hate to try, as you seem a pretty capable lad. Fit, too, by the way you outran us last night. It's the Orphans rule – if another is caught, we do not then identify ourselves by trying to rescue them – but, if you must go, so will Miller.'

'WHAT?' Both Miller and I shout it at the same time.

'I am not going off alone with that little squirt.'

'Miller, he's not that little. But I'd rather you went with him. You're not going to catch up with those Guardians, unless you're very lucky. And when you don't catch them, you'll need to make your way to Westmine. Seven doesn't know the way, so it makes sense that you accompany him.'

'No way, Malt. If he wants to play the hero, leave him to it.'

'Miller, please.' Malt holds his hand. 'Do it for me. Please. I ask so little, usually. He needs to be protected. And he's more likely to survive with you.'

They are locked in a gaze for several seconds. In that time, Miller's face softens, his furrowed brow becoming flat. They're close. Close enough that Miller would even travel with me, for Malt. I spy a tinge of sensitivity in Miller. A small crack in his icy exterior.

'Six and I will stop at a small village, Lasul knows it well, called Stonewood and we will wait there for you, for a day or so. I will leave you a sign if you do not arrive while we are there. And if you arrive first, do not wait for us. On to Westmine,' Malt adds.

'Right, let's go, squirt.' Miller breaks his handhold with Malt and walks quickly east.

I was so absorbed in their moment that I am frozen for a second.

Six brings me back to the present with a warm hug. She breathes a few times on my chest, before looking up and into my face. 'Be careful. Do what you can but stay alive. I'll see you in Westmine in a few days. And don't you dare stand me up. If you're late, I'll kick you in the balls.'

I laugh. She doesn't.

'I mean it.' Then she finally laughs, lets me go and stands beside Malt. *'Be strong. Live for a better tomorrow.'* Cherish's last words. Six must have heard them, too. Maybe she understands the meaning better than me. Maybe that's why she's letting us separate.

'Bye,' I say.

'Bye,' says Malt.

Six is quiet, looking at me like she does when studying a book before an exam.

I turn and sprint after Miller. He's already a hundred metres ahead and something tells me he isn't going to be slowing down for my benefit.

When we've run to the top of the hill, I turn briefly and watch Malt and Six walking across the charred settlement. Will it be the last time I see her? *I promise it won't be, Six.*

Then I fly down the hill behind Miller.

I enjoy the feeling of running fast, again. I'm no good at staying still. My back is pulsing again, but it's not as bad as before. My legs are getting to an enjoyable level of sore. I control my breathing to maximise my efficiency. Six would love that.

I see a sliver of metal, way off to my right. The sun hits it and I see it again. It's a gun.

BANG.

PART II
IDENTITY

From the audio diary of E820906. Entry 1.
Recovered from her sensory recording implant.

The first time I met Seven, he looked like this lost Greenie, but who appeared, on the surface, to follow all the Realm Rules. I could tell he would never be a follower. It was so strange back then to see a Greenie with such deep emotions. Sure, we were all a little sad from time to time, or quite pleased when we did well in class, or got promoted in the class ladder. But Seven, he hit the deepest funks or the highest euphoria.

It's what interested me about him, initially. I'd never met a Greenie like him. It was he who told me about the emotion-suppressing drugs that they mixed into our food. It was him who convinced me to climb the great Beech tree, nearly a hundred metres high, to show me the view, to see the world outside of our camp, to appreciate that we are only a small piece of a much larger puzzle. He opened my eyes to so much, he made me feel deeper than ever before, and he made an emotional connection between us that will never be broken. I'd never met anyone so impulsive and I'm sure I never will again.

CHAPTER 14
PURSUIT

I lie flat on the ground, hiding behind a bush. Like that's gonna stop a bullet if the sniper wants to hit me. I wonder why I'm not dead. A minute has passed since the shot.

I glance over at Miller, squatting behind a small beech tree. He presses his open hand in a downward motion. Stay low. He picks up a stray, thin branch, holds it out and starts waving it.

BANG. CRACK.

Miller quickly retracts his arm, dropping the bullet-broken branch.

'That was some shot,' I say to him.

'It's okay. Only one person in the Realm could make that shot.' He starts to whistle. Low pitched and almost sore on the ears. But there's definitely a pattern to the notes. Like a horrible song sung by ghosts.

'What the hell is that?' I say aloud.

Miller smiles as he finishes. 'Listen.'

We wait several seconds before a response comes. The same tune. The same pitch, tone and rhythm. Miller must know this person.

'Who is it?' I ask.

'Never you mind, nosey. Just stay behind that bush.'

Miller strolls out from the cover of the tree. I nearly shout a warning at him, but then I remember I despise him and don't really care if he gets shot. He stands waving his hands. Is he crazy? Okay, I take it back – don't get shot Miller, I do need someone to help me right now!

But he smiles at someone, steeped in warmth. The kind of smile I'll never see from him. Or want to. It's a little creepy. He must know the shooter, so I figure it's safe and trek out after him.

BANG.

I freeze. Soil erupts from beneath the wounded grass. That was close. Miller is nearly rolling on the ground in laughter. I stare into the distance and see two figures marching towards us, both with long rifles over their shoulders.

'It's Eagle, boy.' He laughs again. 'Honestly, that was priceless. The look on your face as you completely scut yourself. Whatever happens after this, that one moment will make it all worth it.' He chuckles.

Laugh it up, crunk-for-personality. Your time will come.

'Who's she with?' I squint again.

'Your fat pal.'

'Three?'

'Aye, that one. Weirdo.'

'He's not my pal. But keep your mouth shut if you're not going to be nice to him.'

'What do you care, sog? You even said he's not your pal.'

'I don't like how you talk to people.' I move closer, maintaining eye contact.

'Well, I don't like one little thing about you, boy wonder. Prodigy? Pah, you're down in the pig crunk with the rest of us now. There's not one thing about you that's special, or different.'

'Whatever, just quit the insults.' But I have to agree with him. I'm no better than many of the Greenies. This is why I need Lasul.

'No bother, arse-wipe.'

I shake my head. No point. He's just a scutting sog and I'll never change that.

Three and Eagle cross the field and hurry towards us.

Miller moves forward and embraces Eagle in a tight hug. I stand back, a little awkward, watching the hug, not sure what to say to Three. I've never spoken to the guy. He's not exactly easy to talk to.

'Still alive, huh?' he asks me.

'Yup. You too, I see.'

He nods and holds out his hand. I raise my eyebrows but extend my own and give a brief shake. Kinda formal and awkward, but it's better than usual. Between him and Eagle, we won't get much chat.

'Eagle, so glad you've not croaked it.' Miller steps back from the hug.

She places one arm on his back, the other gripping her rifle.

'This is great news. I thought I was going to go chasing those Realm Guardians with just the turd, but now I'll have some good company.' Miller shoots a dirty look at me as he speaks.

'So, what happened? How come you're here and not captured with the rest?'

Eagle nods and turns to Three.

'We saw it all.' It's Three who speaks. I've never asked why but Eagle never speaks. 'Eagle was training me to shoot, just over those hills behind us, when we saw the smoke. We ran as quickly as we could, but by the time we reached the lip of the hill over-looking the community, it was all over. They were all on their knees. They were being questioned by the looks of it. We couldn't hear what was being asked. Then, they were marched away.'

'Were they on horses?' asks Miller. 'Or on foot?'

'Some of them had horses, maybe about ten, but there were more on foot. Probably thirty Guardians in total. And one Knight.'

'A Black Knight?'

Eagle nods, her eyes wider than usual. Even I know a Black Knight is not good news.

'Why didn't you go after them?' I ask.

'We were going to, but one of them spotted me. So, we had to get away and hide out for a bit. Two of them came to look for us.'

'Did they find you?'

'Yeah, unfortunately. They are both dead now. Bodies are way over there. Eagle got them both.' He nods to his trainer.

'Well, that's game over then, boy. We're not going after them.' Miller sits down and pulls out a small bag of nuts.

'Yes, we are. Or I am...if you're too scared.' I narrow my eyes at Miller.

'You have no idea what you'd be facing, scut. A Black Knight would destroy you in their sleep. They are the best of the best. And ten horse-mounted Guardians, with more on foot. No way.'

Part of me knows he's right. But part of me thinks I could take on a Knight. If they let someone like Twelve become a Knight, they can't be all that tough. He seemed to think it was about connections rather than ability, but I don't know if I believe him.

'I'm going.'

'Fine. Good luck, kid. You're gonna need it.' He turns his back on me and starts crunching his nuts.

'Three?' I ask out of politeness. There's no way he'd be up for running several hours and taking on a full-blown rescue attempt against thirty Realm Guardians.

He tilts his head and squints one eye. Is he thinking about this? No way!

Eagle shakes her head and points to her own chest.

'You'll come?' I'm surprised but I probably shouldn't be. I've suspected all along that's she one of the bravest out of all the Exiles.

'I want to come, too,' says Three.

His lower lip is sliding out. What's come over him?

Eagle shakes her head. She points to Miller and nods.

'I've not got much left around here to stay for. If you're going Eagle, then so am I. Plus someone will need to carry the fat kid when he eventually can't run anymore.' Miller stands and shoulders his rifle, stashing his nuts in his pocket.

Three moves real close to Miller. He's shorter by a head, but he holds his gaze and doesn't blink. I see his body tense. Miller doesn't back down either. He just smiles.

'Three, he's just a scut-hole. Ignore him.' I put my arm between them and push Three back, away from the confrontation.

Miller laughs and turns to Eagle.

'So, we should get moving if we're gonna be heroes and rescue the rest of our sorry lot. Chubster, if you're quick you can head over that hill there and catch Malt and the girl. They will be heading for an abandoned barn that you'll come to if you keep walking straight. Don't get lost.'

Three is shaking. Eagle moves over to Miller and in one swift movement has him on his back. She kneels over him and repeatedly shakes her head. I thought they were friends. And to stick up for Three like that. I mean he went way over the line, but he always does that.

'Fine, the kid can come if it means that much to you,' Miller says.

But Eagle shakes her head again and releases Miller. She hugs Three, rubbing his back. I see his shoulders relax and sag.

'So, what's happening?' I ask. Between Eagle's silence, Miller's insults, and Three's rage, I'm lost.

'Beats me, kid, seems like Eagle's got her own ideas.' Miller skulks off in the direction I'm about to run.

Eagle looks Three in the eye. She points south.

I keep wondering why I haven't heard Eagle speak yet. Maybe she's the strong and silent type, or maybe she can't.

'Malt and Six have started to travel that way,' I say. 'They are going to Westmine. It's a big Exile settlement. I think an extra gun might come in handy.' I nod towards his rifle.

'Fine, I'll go. Clearly, I'm not wanted. I should have shot him, not the stick.' Three shouts it, so that Miller hears.

'*That*, was you?' Miller moves nearer. 'You shot the stick from that distance?'

'Yes.' Three says it with no hint of arrogance.

'But how? I thought Eagle...'

'Well, you thought wrong. Three here is a crack shot, obviously.' I smile at him, keen to make some kind of connection. But I am also genuinely impressed. 'And even more reason to go with Malt and Six. They may need someone with your skills.' I add the last bit to ham it up and make his dismissal seem easier.

He gives the smallest of smiles. *Breakthrough.*

Eagle nods again and Three nods back. He holds up his hand. 'Fair journey.' He turns and runs south.

'Fair journey,' I mutter. Eagle holds her hand up.

I watch him run away with a pace I've never seen in him before. Three, a sharp-eyed shooter and running. I'd never have believed that a couple of days ago. I wonder why he never showed anything like this in camp. Or in his Test. Not for the first time, I think he wanted to perform badly.

'Right, can we get this scutting idiocy going. The kid will be fine. If Eagle trained him that well, he'll be okay.' Miller looks at Eagle with a smile that doesn't suit his face.

I snigger at his crunky attempts to get back in her good books.

Eagle ignores him and starts running. I follow.

'Crunk it.' Miller hot on my heels. 'Let's get this suicide mission started.'

FROM THE AUDIO DIARY OF
E820906. ENTRY 2.

The first time I broke a Realm Rule I was with Seven. It was his fault, really. We had snuck out our tents, like we often used to, and he had a small packet of dried fruit. He told me that Cherish had stolen it from the rations store and given him it because he felt down. But he wanted to share it with me, so didn't eat it until we met up. We sat on a rock, in a small clearing between the trees, staring up at a full moon, in silence. The fruit was delicious.

CHAPTER 15
PLAN MAN

Years of training did not prepare me for this. We run at a pace set by Eagle for several hours. By Realm standards, for a sixteen-year-old, I'm fit. Compared to these pair, I feel like Three. Or Greenie-Three.

I lie on my back, chest heaving, legs less than jelly. My feet, normally impervious to the tough ground, are bloody and blistered.

'Our wee run too much for you, boy?' Miller sneers at me. Surely, he's equally as tired as I am. He just doesn't want to show it, trying to get one up on me.

'The Realm's Greenies ain't all that tough, huh Eagle? Prodigy, my arse. Look at him.' He looks to our silent companion. She doesn't acknowledge him, her eyes intent only upon the Realm holding house down the hill.

'Why do you keep calling me prodigy? I've never said that.'

'Och, just something Lasul told us when he sent us to rescue you. It's not important.'

I want to press him, but I don't want to give him the satisfaction of refusing me when I ask. I manage to haul myself up, and edge over next to Eagle's shoulder, to take in the scene.

'You feeling up to taking out some of your Realm buddies?' Miller asks.

'That's not who I am, anymore. I'm done with the Realm. I'm an Exile now. Nameless, like the rest of you.'

'I have a name, boy. We're Exiles all right, but don't call us Nameless.' Miller screws his eyes up.

'But Mother said a name doesn't define you. It's okay to not have one.'

'Aye, and she's right. But neither does not having a name define you.' Miller, for once, looks less angry and more fatherly than I've seen him. Perhaps he's not as much of an idiot as I thought.

Eagle hisses and points down the hill.

The main door to the holding house opens and several Guardians emerge. I count six. They position themselves at the four corners of the building, plus two climb onto the roof.

Eagle smiles and loads her rifle.

'Wait.' I place my hand on her arm. 'I have an idea.'

Miller gives her a sceptical look, but nods. 'Let's hear it, kid.'

'If we attack from this place, they will immediately throw their full force on us. Thirty, or about that, against three. So, if we hit them from three sides, we'll be more difficult to deal with. This is probably the best point to shoot from, so it's probably best for Eagle to stay here. Miller, you should walk round to the south and find a covered spot there.'

'And what about you?' he asks.

'I'll walk round with you and continue until I reach the east slopes, opposite from here. That will leave them only one way to run – onto the open, flat field to their north. And Eagle can then pick them off easily if they do run.'

Eagle nods. Miller gives me a funny look. 'Not bad, kid. Just one problem. How do we save the people inside? You think the Guardians will just run out of there and leave their prisoners?'

'No, but don't worry, I'll deal with that. Just keep shooting,

Eagle. And be careful about who you shoot. They might send out some of our people when they realise what's happening.'

'Should I keep shooting, too?'

'No, when you see me moving towards the house, you need to creep down the hillside at the back and follow me in. Leave Eagle to deal with anyone outside.'

'Doesn't sound the most solid plan. What if one of us gets hit? Those Guardians will shoot back, you know.'

'I know, Miller. We just have to chance it. Come on. Eagle, look out for my signal.'

She nods.

I move away from the lip with Miller, leaving Eagle solitary upon the top edge of the hill, the rifle sight to her eye. I'm glad she's on my side. I've seen what she can do. It helped me get rescued back at the testing centre. I hope it will help us save the Exiles today.

The day's exertions are showing on Miller. His lip is dry, his forehead soaked. He walks with a slight limp in his left leg, and he takes two breaks as we loop round the hill to arrive at the south side vantage point. He seems relieved to finally fall on his front and line up the sight on his rifle.

'Remember to follow me in once you see me.'

'Yes, hero.' That's polite for Miller. He's clearly too tired to bait me more.

I walk around to my position on the eastern rise of the three-sided slope, knowing I'm about to put my body through its greatest test. Hours and hours of combat training have made me handy at most disciplines. But this isn't a duel in a ring. This isn't other Greenies I'm up against. These guys have guns, and they'll kill me in an instant. I'm a fugitive of the Realm. Miller is right, this is close to suicide. But Cherish's words ring in my mind. *Be strong.*

I close off all the fears racing through my mind. I close down my emotions. The Realm wanted us focused. Now, they're about to see just how thorough their training was.

I crawl the last ten feet, peaking through the waving grasses, down to the fort we're about to storm. Six Guardians are in position as before. Classic Realmism. Disciplined to the core. Full focus. But I'm relying on that. The whole plan relies on that.

Time for the signal. I raise an arm and wave. Wait. Nothing. I raise it again and wave again. Wait. Nothing. I stand and wave both arms.

BANG.

I leap backwards down the slope. That shot was at me. I pat down my body, searching for red, trying to detect pain.

I'm fine. It missed. And that tells me one thing for sure. That wasn't Eagle who shot. It must have been one of the Guardians. I'm trapped. If I stood up now, they'd shoot me before they saw who it was. That I am unarmed, pretending to surrender.

Great plan, Seven. Stuck until Eagle or Miller starts shooting. What are they waiting for?

Voices, getting closer. 'I saw someone up here. No, this way. Get the others out here as well, there may be more of them.'

I skulk backwards towards a row of bushes growing further down the slope. I fall behind them, peeking beneath the bulky foliage. I should be able to see their legs at least.

'Just up here. This is where he was. I shot something. I'm sure of it.'

'Can't see anything, Bear. You sure you it wasn't a cheep or a gow?'

'No, it wasn't an animal, Sarge. It was definitely a person, waving. Keep alert. I think there might be more of them.'

'Spread out. Sega and Hermit, you take the left flank. Slim, Puke, you're on the right. Bear, I'm with you, straight ahead.'

I'm done for now. I wish I had a gun, or something. Anything. Doesn't matter how good my boxing is, they'll mow me down with bullets before I get a chance to hit anyone.

I crawl further under the bush, but it's no use. I'm too lanky. No matter what I do, some parts of my long limbs hang out. They'll see me for sure.

I slow my breathing, position myself into a crouched stance, ready to pounce. Maybe, just maybe, I'll surprise them and perhaps I'll knock one of them down and give myself half a chance.

The feet come closer, and closer.

'What's that in the bush?'

BANG.

A shot rings through the air. It's not close. Eagle has started firing. Or Miller.

'Guardians, take position at the edge of hill.'

The feet run back up the hill. I watch the six Guardians take position on their stomachs, like I was a few minutes ago. They'll look for the source of the shots and shoot back. Eagle's good but it's two against six. I need to help.

I creep slowly up the hill. It's hard for me to get low, but I try to step lightly. All six of them are too focused on spotting the shooter.

BANG. BANG.

I jump, but it's not the Guardians. Hopefully Eagle has taken out two more of them.

I move forward again. Slow. Cautious. Breath held.

I decide to go for the Sarge. The decision maker. We always learnt that hierarchical systems work less efficiently when the person at the top is removed. Pawns are dispensable. Losing a Queen is like game over. Six loved her chess.

Delicate. Stepping on tiptoes. Be a ghost upon the wind. I crouch, just behind the toes of the one I think is the Sarge. His boots are shiniest.

Be strong.

I lift his legs and drive forward pushing his torso headfirst down the slope. I release, but don't watch him fall. I kick two faces, one with my left foot, one with my right. The right crunched a nose. I roll left, landing beside the Guardian on the end. I slide my arm around his waist and pull him to his feet, putting him between me and the other Guardians.

They leap to their feet; their rifles aimed at me, or more accurately, their comrade. I use him as a shield to back away from the edge. Don't want to get shot from down below.

'Weapons down.' I try to make my voice sound less boyish. I squeak at the end and fail miserably.

'Kid, you're outnumbered. Put your weapon down. Now. Or we'll shoot, human shield or not. He's dispensable.'

Incredibly, the man I hold doesn't argue. He doesn't fight, his muscles relaxed in my hold. I'd be fighting for my life. Scut, I am fighting for my life.

This is it. Surrender or fight? Surrender or fight?

I grab his right hand, loosely holding his rifle and raise it, my hand over his, covering the trigger. Painfully, it reminds me of my last moments with Cherish. The anger makes me continue.

'Down the hill. Or I'll start shooting,' I say, as loud as I can.

One of the female Guardians nods to the other who's still standing. One moves left, the other right. They're trying to flank me. Crunk. I need to stop them.

BANG.

The bullet smashes into the ground. I won't kill them. They look young, probably not long in the Military. They're just like me, only their eyes are still closed. No, I won't kill them. But they need to know I might.

It does the trick. They stop. Movement in the corner of my eye tells me one of the Guardians I kicked is moving. I glance at her and see her nose is in bad shape. She picks up her rifle and aims it at me.

'Sega, hold your fire,' instructs the other female. She must be in charge now.

'He broke my scutting nose.'

'Control yourself. You've had worse.'

'No, I've had enough. Searching all over the stinking fields for some little rebels. I've had enough. I'm getting rid of this problem.'

BANG.

I fall to the ground, landing on my back. I can't breathe. The sharp pain in my ribs makes me moan. I'm weak and my head spins.

'Get him up.'

The limp body of the Guardian is rolled off me. Two arms grab me, and I'm hauled to my feet.

BANG. The background shots are very frequent now. At least Eagle and Miller are still putting up a fight.

'How many of you are there?' the Guardian-in-charge asks.

'Just me,' I mumble.

'Liar.'

Another BANG in the background.

'Wait, Sega. I know his face. He's one of us.'

'You sure, Atari? He just held a gun to us. And he's dressed like an exile.'

'No, I'm pretty sure I've seen his face once before.'

The Guardian with the broken nose moves close to me. She's back on her feet. Four of them against me. I'm not getting out of this now.

'Yeah, well I don't care who he is. I'm finishing him now. This is for my nose.' She lifts her rifle. I thrash but the Guardians hold me tight. No escape.

'No, he isn't to be harmed. I think he's the one we're looking for. Atari, you'll be in deep water if you damage this one.'

'Fine, but if he tries to escape, I'm taking him out.' She turns and moves back to the edge of the hill. Another BANG echoes up the hillside.

'Slim, Bear. Don't let him go. You know how important it is.'

'Yes, Corporal.'

They grip me even tighter. I watch the Corporal and Sega, with her broken nose, peak into the valley. I want to see. I want to know what's going on. I hope all those shots are ours. But I'm not hopeful. The Guardians are better drilled than I thought. And they're disciplined. If someone had bust my nose, there would be no stopping me whacking them back.

If only I was strong enough to shoot them when I had the chance. I had the upper hand, but I hesitated, like a scutting coward. I wonder what Cherish would think if she'd seen me wimp out like that. I can shoot my own mother, but not my enemy.

BANG.

One arm releases me. I swing my free arm into the groin of the other Guardian. He lets go and I follow up with a kick to his ribs.

BANG.

The Corporal becomes still. But broken-nose Sega is quick to reach her rifle and aims at the shooter. A single bullet is released.

BANG.

The shooter falls to the ground.

I leap onto Sega and grab her round the neck. My long limbs are helping me in this close wrestle, as I pull one of her arms behind her back. I pin her to the ground, face down. I don't want to kill her, but she just shot someone. Hell, she wanted to shoot me.

I have her head in position.

Be strong.

One twist and I could break her neck.

I look over at the still body of my helper.

I recognise the baldhead.

It's Miller.

And he's completely still.

FROM THE AUDIO DIARY OF
E820906. ENTRY 3.

The first time I realised Seven was not just different, but special, was during some combat training. I had worked out that he was strong and quick but fought with a passion and a determination that I saw in none of the other Greenies. His eyes glinted with an ambition and a distinctiveness that made him stand out. The other Greenhorns were jealous and that's why none of them ever became close to him. I always think that it was a shame he never had any male friends in camp, but maybe if he did, then we would never have become so close.

CHAPTER 16
SMILER RETURNS

I drop the Guardian's body to the ground. Unconscious. Not dead. Though they probably deserve it.

I sprint towards Miller, but the colossal scut has yet to move. I kneel and place my hand on his cold neck.

No pulse.

I hold my hand over his mouth.

Shallow breaths.

My head to his chest.

Weak heartbeat.

BANG. BANG.

I jerk my head around. Another Guardian lies dead at the lip of the hill. Eagle is still shooting. I need to get back to it.

'Sorry, Miller.' A whisper. 'I'll be back.'

I flash across the grass, and stride down the slope. My body's at an unnatural angle, but my speed keeps me from falling on my face.

Another shot.

Here they come. Seven of them. Circular formation. Classic. A non-lethal capture arrangement. Militia studies come in handy once more.

They won't shoot, but close in, synced.

One of them falls. Good shot, Eagle.

Closer to the building, I hear return fire. If she gets hit, I'm done.

Six of them left. There's a small gap. I sprint for it, but it closes, and I collide with two Guardians. We're all scrambling on the ground. I'm punching something. Someone. A blow to my back ends that.

I take a second. Breathe; they're not going to kill me.

Hands grab me rough-like, as Bulk would say, and stand me up.

Another shot.

I'm scrambling again, my elbows finding flesh. I kick one in the balls. Always effective.

Four of them still stand, circling. Two more lie on the ground. An invisible barrier separates us. They don't want to properly attack me. Like their Sarge said, *'he's not to be hurt'*. I'm confused, but I can work that out later. Now, the captured Exiles need me to help them.

Even if the Guardians don't harm me, they'll make damn sure I don't get into the holding house, so I start to move left, further from the building. The Guardians seem confused and let me get further from my target, probably thinking I'm about to run for it.

A few more feet...

I shuffle left, my arms in the air. They think I'm surrendering. Smiles creep onto their faces. They think they have me.

More shots.

Two fall. The other two run straight into the holding house, realising Eagle has the high ground and will kill them all, if they stay exposed. I turn and give the signal. All the Guardians are now inside. The hard part now begins.

I quickly count fifteen bodies on the ground. Two have fallen from the roof. Six up the top of the hill, where Miller also lies.

That leaves only seven, if Three's estimate was right. I can't imagine, they'll all line up, one by one, to fight. Even if they did, there's no way I'd beat them all. I'll have to rely on their reluctance to attack me.

I bend low and approach the building. I sneak round the stone structure towards the main door. It's closed. But I bet it's still guarded.

I hammer on the door. It remains silent and shut.

Why would they stay inside and not try to take me? Two minutes ago, they sent more than twenty Guardians out to get me. Now, they won't come out even though I'm here, on my own.

They're waiting. For help. Idiot, Seven. Of course, they'd need a truck to transport all these prisoners, so the Guardians could get back to scouring the countryside. For me. I wish Six was here. She'd have worked all of this out already.

I pick up a Guardian's rifle. I raise it over my shoulder and tense to smash it into the lock.

A sharp, shrill whistle. I stop, then turn.

'Eagle, was that you?'

She nods. Points to my rifle and shakes her head.

'How will we get in, then?'

She goes down on one knee and clasps her hands. A perfect foothold. We're going on the roof. But why?

I place my right foot into her clutched hands. With surprising strength, she hauls me up and I grab the ledge. My back muscles scream as I pull. I scramble up and over, carefully. My wounds give me a big reminder that they're still not healed.

I lean back over the edge and lower my outstretched arms. Eagle grips my wrists and pulls herself up, using my arms as leverage. I hardly help her. She's light as a feather, strong as a bull.

We move on our toes across the broken, wooden roof. Twelve cells. Six on each side. One central room in the middle where the remaining Guardians stand tense. Rifles are raised.

Eagle points to a large *me* sized hole. I creep across and wait. Eagle moves her rifle across the room below. Is she deciding who to shoot first? Or whether to shoot at all? If Miller weren't dying,

I'd be convincing her not to kill them. But now, I don't care. Kill or be killed. They don't hesitate, so we shouldn't either. I breathe deeply, turning off my digital emotion switch.

Eagle nods. I drop through the hole.

I slam onto the shoulders of a Guardian, using her body as a cushion.

Staying low, I slide across the floor, sweeping the next Guardian. His rifle falls. I smash his jaw. Out cold.

Eagle fires three more shots.

They return fire.

Bodies fall as I fight the next Guardian. She's good and lands a solid jab to my cheek. I stumble backwards, tripping on a prone body. She leaps on top of me, followed by another Guardian, pinning me. I can't push off their combined weight. They slide to opposite ends, to stop my scrambling. One squashes my chest and holds my arms, the other my legs. My back is ablaze with agony.

More shots.

Come on, Eagle, take them out. I squirm but nothing is getting these two off. They're too heavy.

All around me, voices float through the air, some familiar. I hear Bulk's deep tone and Doc's accent. They tell me to get up, to fight.

I'm trying! I really am!

More shots.

'They're all down,' says one of the Guardians restraining me.

'Well, pick up a rifle and fire. I'll hold him.'

The load lifts from my legs and I immediately start to fight. She hits my face again, but that only makes me angrier, and I thrash, finally lifting her off and rolling on top.

BANG.

I turn around to see the last Guardian crumple. A shadow moves across the roof slats.

My jaw explodes in pain. Another jab. I'm on my back. Stupid distraction. And the Guardian has given up restraining me.

It's Smiler. How did I not recognise him before with those teeth? He dives for a gun. He's going to kill me, the change in his eyes makes that clear.

I look around me, desperate. But I'm helpless. I turn to sprint out the door.

CRACK. The bullet smashes into the wall above my head. Inches away. How did he miss from that range? I turn around.

One of the prisoners has the shooter pulled back against the bars of her cell. Her thin arms stick out between the metal and strangle Smiler.

'Stop.' I don't know why I told her to stop.

Smiler falls to the ground, gasping. I creep closer, eager to see my saviour.

'Doc?' I ask. 'Is that you? Are you okay?'

'Yes.' Her hair is tangled so bad, carbon black from fire smoke. But her eyes glow like burning coals in a dying fire.

'Thank you.' It's weak. I want to say more. She just saved my life. She looks beautiful. I can't take my eyes off her. Is it the soot? I don't know. But she's just different from before. Weird.

A gun loads. Smiler aims his rifle at Doc.

'All this death for a talentless Greenie like you, Seven.'

I launch towards him.

BANG.

I hit the ground. Hard. My shoulder, ribs, and jaw all hurt. But it's sore. Not agony.

My hands feel my body, searching for the bullet entry. Nothing.

Smiler is down. Dead.

The evening sun streams in the door, partly blocked by a lone figure. Eagle.

Her rifle is lowered. She moves forward and starts searching the dead Guardians.

I check my body again, but I definitely wasn't hit. My neck

swivels round to Doc, who is now sitting, her mouth wide open, shaking.

'Are you okay?' I ask.

She nods but is staring at me funny. What's going on?

Eagle taps me on the shoulder and hands me keys.

She unlocks the cells opposite. I do the same on my side. When I open the cell with Doc in it, she leaps out and floors me with a huge hug.

Despite the pain, I lie back enjoying the closeness. The warmth. Then I choke on a piece of charred hair.

'Sorry,' she says, getting up and pulling me to my feet. 'I forgot you were hurt. But I am so...thank you. I cannot believe you did that.'

'What?' I say. I'm confused. Eagle did all the hard work.

'Protecting me, silly. You were willing to take that shot to shield me. That's pretty awesome, hero stuff.'

'Err, sure. But I really didn't do anything. Seriously. Plus, you saved me just before. I'd have a bullet in the back of my head if you hadn't grabbed that Guardian.'

'Whatever, Seven. Modesty suits you. Let's call it evens, then.' She smiles and starts to help the weak and injured Exiles.

I turn away, beaming. Eagle shakes her head and walks outside. The sun glows in, on all of us. My insides are mush. I help an elderly Exile outside onto the grass.

Once everyone is outside, we sit in a circle.

I nod to Lasul, who looks very bloody and bruised. He sits like he's in a lot of pain but says nothing. Doc kneels beside him, cleaning a nasty looking wound on his arm. Looks like a gunshot. I hope it's not infected.

Eagle sits next to me and squeezes my thigh, smiling. I think that's high praise from her. Or maybe she's trying to make me feel better for not killing a single Guardian, while she killed most of the thirty or so. She's something else.

I can't believe I once thought I could make it in the Realm military. A Black Knight? What a joke. The Guardians' bodies still lie scattered around the house. As I wait for Lasul to speak to us, I stare at them. They were just like me, not so long ago. Some of them look not much older than I am. And now they're dead. Why are so many lives worth mine? They could have shot me a hundred times over. Or is this bigger than me? Surely it can't only be about retrieving a fugitive kid. I want answers and I know Lasul has them.

I turn to the Exile leader. He's watching me. For how long? His glare is not kind, his eyebrows knitted together. Puzzled? Angry? I can't tell.

Six would know. She was brilliant in psychology. I remember us looking at animal expressions and determining their emotions. I once wrote down that the growling bulion was either angry or constipated. Six and I laughed so hard, until the bulion leapt into the wire mesh of the cage, and I quickly scored out that answer before our Guru saw it.

Bulk brings me out of my daydream by smothering me. I think it's a hug, but he knocks the wind out of my lungs.

'Cheers, kid. Thought we were prisoners for good, then.'

'You rescued me from the Realm. Now, we're even.' I seem to be settling all kinds of scores, today.

Bulk gives me a nod and flops onto his back beside me. His size is truly terrifying. I wonder how they managed to overcome him and take him prisoner.

'Friends, we are free.' Lasul stands as he says it. The group applauds. 'I think we all want to thank Eagle and Seven for coming to our rescue. I was sure we were on our way to the Circle City prison cells. But luck has intervened. Thank you, friends.' He bows and holds his hand over his heart. The group copy the gesture. Then, everyone claps again.

'You must all forgive me, but we cannot loiter or tarry. We must move quickly. News of this will travel back if it has not already. They had a couple of radios. Unless, anyone has any objections, we will head south. Our compatriots at Westmine will be able to aid us by the time we arrive, I believe.'

'Wait, we need to help Miller. He was shot.' I say it without thinking. I'd forgotten about him in the commotion. Everyone gasps and whispers fill the group.

'Check on him.' Lasul says. He looks at Eagle. She sprints up the hill, followed by Doc. 'Come, people. We must move.'

We reach the summit and crowd around Miller. He's so still. The usual glare or smirk is gone. Doc works on bandaging Miller, while Eagle applies pressure to the bleeding wound.

'He'll be okay,' says Doc. 'An inch lower and he'd be dead, but it hit just above the heart. He'll be weak and need treatment, but in a few days, he'll be back to his usual, grumpy self.'

'Heard that,' Miller whispers.

Everyone is so relieved they laugh a little and relax, finding nearby spots to rest before we take off.

'Seven, a word?' asks Lasul, walking away from everyone else.

'I want to say thank you, personally. I would expect Eagle and Miller to help us. We are like family after all. But for you to help shows your commitment to us, and for that I shall reward you.'

'Honestly, I didn't think, I just came because I knew it would be what Cherish would want me to do. And because I need to know what you know...about me and where I came from? Why did you rescue me from the camp, and why did Cherish mess around with my DNA test? I need to know.'

'It is time I told you, but not here, with all these people around. This is information I don't want to share with anyone else.' He smiles and starts to walk away. 'I must check on Miller.'

'No, tell me now. I left Six to find you. I WANT TO KNOW NOW!'

I watch him limp away, half-hating, but fully needing, him.

FROM THE AUDIO DIARY OF
E820906. ENTRY 4.

Seven was always obsessed with Sharan. At least in the early days. We had all seen her on the Telescreen, when we had our compulsory viewing times, and she was impressive. I always suspected she was too impressive. Something about the lighting and the way her enemies always attacked her one at a time, made me suspicious. I'd never say this to Seven, but I reckon the whole Sharan thing was made up, filmed to make us believe we had an invincible Guardian fighting for us. A phony idol for every young Greenhorn to aspire to. Perfect propaganda for a Military recruitment campaign. I was glad that over time he talked about her less and less. I'd hate for him to have spent years worshipping a false hero.

CHAPTER 17
LASUL'S PAST

Doc's head rests on my left thigh, her gentle breaths punctuating the silent night.

A light fog has fallen across the field in which we camp. Almost everyone is asleep, except the night watch - Bulk and me. Eagle sits in a tree above the stream that runs alongside our camp, hidden by the white cover of mist. I doubt she ever sleeps. She's superhuman.

The last few days have been quiet. No Guardians. No running or lying or killing. A little time to recover for whatever is bound to come our way next.

My right hand brushes some stray hair from Doc's clean face. When we washed in the stream earlier, the memory of Six and me messing around in the river flooded back. I really like Doc, but Six and I have been through so much. We nearly kissed that one time, I'm sure of it. If Six saw me right now, what would she do?

The image makes me carefully move Doc's sleeping head off my leg and walk out of the camp. I take my new rifle, stolen from a dead Guardian. A spoil of war. But I'm no warrior. Still, it might come in handy.

I walk alongside the water, watching it flow downstream, the moonlight reflecting off the rippling surface. It's like my life. Only my life is moving much faster. More like a waterfall, or tidal wave, or tsunami.

'Seven?'

I swing round, ready to shout at someone. The mass in front of me blocks out the moon. Bulk.

'What?'

'Lasul wishes to speak with you.'

'Here? Now?' I scan the darkness around us. No-one.

Bulk moves aside and Lasul limps forward. He takes a minute to reach us. He looks tired and badly hurt.

'Thank you, Bulk. That will be all.'

The big man nods and wanders back towards the camp. Lasul waits a while before speaking. He stares at me, a small smile on his face.

'So, Seven. I think I've seen enough to believe you're on our side, now. And more importantly, I think you have convinced the others of your worth.'

I decide silence is the best way to get him to keep talking.

He remains mute for a long time, before continuing. 'You have been brave and reckless. Often a poor combination for a leader during times of peace, but the perfect combination for a leader in times of war. Of uprising and rebellion.'

He lets those last words take effect, waiting for a reaction. I simply nod.

'Seven, I must tell you something because there are dangerous times ahead. When I was captured, I thought I might die with the information you need to know, but luck or fate is on our side. Are you willing to hear what I say?'

'Yes.'

'It will change everything. You will be placed on a path that you will not be able to turn from. Your life is already at risk, but you don't understand why. If I tell you this, you will be in even greater danger. I need to have your absolute assurance that you are happy with this. It is not what Cherish would have wanted; it is what she protected you from for many years, but I think you need to hear it.'

I shiver at the mention of her name. What did she not want me to know? If she didn't want me to know, it was to protect me. I'm sure of it. She would want me to avoid danger, to avoid this. But I've no choice, now. I'm committed to this path, even if I did want to turn aside. I committed the moment we pulled that trigger...together.

'Okay, let's hear it.'

'Let us walk and talk. These words are for your ears only.' He places his hand on my shoulder, and we walk further from the camp, continuing downstream.

'You know Cherish was not your real mother, yes?'

I nod, hoping he's going to tell me more than that.

'And you have no idea who your own parents were? Where they came from? You have no memory of your infancy?'

'None.' I close my eyes. It's true, even after I found out she wasn't my real mum, years and years ago, Cherish never told me anything. She said she didn't know.

We walk in silence again. Why's he torturing me? Just say it already.

The trees across the stream rustle, but I can't see anything with this damn mist. 'You hear that, Lasul?'

Silence.

'Lasul?'

'Get down,' he hisses from beneath me.

I lie low next to him, and he silently points across the water. 'Guardians.'

'We should get back to camp,' I whisper. 'We need to warn everyone.'

'No.'

'Yes,' I say.

He clamps his hand over my mouth and shakes his head. He places two fingers in his mouth and whistles something that sounds like a bird. He produces three long, high-pitched noises, and then pulls me further downstream.

The noises across the river disappear upstream, towards our camp.

I remember Doc, lying asleep. 'We must go back.'

'No. You can't, you just can't. If you were caught...well, I can't let it happen. Eagle is there. And Bulk. You've seen what they can do.'

'We can help.'

'No. You're what they want. Think about it? If we go back, we make everyone's situation worse. You'll put everyone's life in even more danger by showing your face.'

'But they'll be taken prisoner.'

'Seven, look at me.' He fixes me with his concrete grey eyes.

My shoulders sag and I slow my breathing.

'Trust me, please. Stay here. Remember that we still have all those weapons we took from those Guardians back at the holding house.'

He pulls me into a small line of dense bushes that surround the field. This, combined with the mist, hides us pretty well. We wait.

Several shots ring through the air from a short distance away.

This doesn't seem right. 'I'm going.' I begin to crawl out.

'Wait...look,' Lasul whispers.

He points ahead into the mist. Two shapes appear, one large, one smaller. I tense.

'I left them down this way, somewhere,' says Bulk.

'If they've been caught, then it's all over,' says Doc.

They're five feet from the bush. I look to Lasul, who nods.

'Hey, in here,' I say.

'Seven?' asks Doc. 'Where are you?' She glances all around.

Lasul emerges from the bush, and I follow.

'I am glad to see you both,' he says. 'How are we faring back at camp?'

'Good, nobody injured. Eagle got most of them. They had no

idea where she was shooting from. That was genius, sir. Just how did you know they were coming?' Bulk nods to Lasul.

Lasul simply taps his nose.

'Yeah, but you took out two of them as well, Bulk. You're always so modest,' says Doc. She gives me a warm smile.

'You are all invaluable to me. I am but an old man, who has too many years of experience and caution. But it doesn't take a genius to know that you should hide your best shooter in a tree. Anyway, we must be quick. Those would have been scouts. Guardians will follow and as good as Eagle is, she will not be able to deal with a troop.'

'What are the orders, sir?'

'Bulk, you will come with us.'

The big man nods.

'Doc, return to camp and send Eagle with us, also. Bring Miller if he is willing, too. We will have to separate from the rest of our group for a time – tell them to head south. Malt, Three and Six are travelling to Stonewood and we should try to meet with them before turning south, too.'

'Off you go, as quickly as you can. Tell Mother to get those people moving.'

She nods and runs off into the grey vapour. I watch her outline gradually disappear.

'Let's go,' says Lasul. 'They will catch us.'

We follow the river downstream once more, walking parallel to it for several miles. The night is silent, except for some far off howls. I'm glad we're not near the wox.

As we walk, quiet with our own thoughts, the others catch up. Eagle nods to Lasul and walks next to him. Doc and Miller walk alongside Lasul and me.

I follow them without complaint and as the afternoon progresses and the sweating and chaffing gets worse, I try to increase my pace and ignore the pain and the brief dizzy spells. I was so fit before; I don't get how this is happening. Maybe it's the lack of sleep, the rescue exertions, or getting hit on the head when I tried to save Cherish. Whatever it is, I despise being thought of as a complainer or slow and weak. This must be how Three feels. I feel bad about being so harsh to him now.

We stop briefly for food and water, and when we start again my legs feel a little better, my head clearer. Bulk is reading his small book again. I try to read the title, but it's faded. It looks really old.

I decide to probe Lasul for that information he started to share last night. It's been nagging at me all afternoon, but I didn't want to ask.

'Lasul, about what we were talking about, you know, about my parents or something? Well, you said it was important. You could tell me now if you want?'

'No. Wait until we next stop. It is not for everyone to know.' He nods to Bulk up ahead, and Eagle bringing up the tail.

I nod and continue the walk across the never-ending fields. I reckon when I go to sleep tonight, all I'll see is green. Then it strikes me how weird it is that we've not seen any people or animals, or anything really, since we saved the prisoners. Well, except that scouting group. Maybe no one lives around here, but the lack of animals is bizarre. Even I know that rich habitats like this should be teeming with life.

I stop for a moment and scan the horizon, rotating on the spot to see if I can spot a bird, a cheep, or a wox anywhere? Nothing living, but I do see something else in the distance.

'Lasul, look. Is that some houses?' I point straight ahead.

'Aye, it is. Eagle with Doc, Bulk with Miller. Keep an eye open. The boy and I will approach from straight ahead. You four flank and work inwards.'

As Lasul and I reach the nearest of the stone buildings, it's clear that this is an abandoned settlement of some kind. Probably many people lived here; there's enough space for more than twice the

Exile settlement we've come from. And there's evidence that the fields around here were once farmed, judging by the fences and the odd bits of rusted equipment.

It's so silent. The absence of natural noises, such as birdsong or swaying tree branches and leaves or even wind. Some wind would be good right now to break this awful silence. Where is everyone?

The first building is abandoned, nothing but a shell, as is the second. We move further towards the centre and as we pass between two taller buildings, we emerge into a large, square cobblestone yard.

'Wow,' is all I manage.

'Yes, it is impressive. Or it was. I doubt anyone has lived here for a number of years, but this was once the marketplace. You can see the remains of stalls scattered around the edges. Let's find somewhere to have a rest. One of those large buildings over in the corner would be ideal. The ones with the upper floor windows, so we can see anyone coming.'

'Have you been here before?'

'Yes. Not for a long time.' He scans the square. 'I was born here. Before I was taken to my camp.'

'You went to a Realm camp?'

'Yes.'

'And did you graduate?'

'Certainly, I was the Alpha. Had a nice life in the city, too. Professor of Genomics.'

'You were an Academic for the Realm? And you had a name?' I subconsciously take a step back from him.

'Many years ago, Seven. I have not served the Realm for sixteen years. And yes, I had a name. One I no longer care for. Lasul is the one I took for myself.'

We move across the yard, and I stumble on the stones.

'Watch your step, lad.'

As Lasul speaks, I hear something from the building behind

us. The heavy silence makes the noise even more noticeable. I turn but there's nothing moving.

'What's wrong?' Lasul stares at the building as well.

'Nothing. Just thought I heard something.'

'Probably just a stray animal, or Eagle sneaking up on us. A favourite game of hers.' Lasul smiles and walks on.

I watch the building for a moment more, then turn and walk across the rest of the square.

'Lasul.' Doc jogs up behind us. 'Guardian scouts in one of the farmhouses. We need to get under cover. Eagle, Miller, and Bulk are taking position in the watchtower and will try to ambush them if they follow us here.'

'Did they see us?' Lasul asks.

'We're not sure. Best take cover, just in case.'

'Quite right,' Lasul says. 'You two, wait in the building, on the upper floor so we have a good vantage point. I will return presently.'

'Where are you going?' asks Doc.

'I need to hide something. I won't be a moment. Go ahead.'

I nod and move through the door on the right, as Lasul goes left.

Inside it's stuffy and smelly, like mouldy fish and I need to cover my mouth. As I climb the stairs, I have to dodge bits of broken furniture, and stone that has crumbled from the walls. Doc follows, her top over her mouth to muffle the stench.

We move onto the highest floor and it's even worse. The source of the smell is up here for sure, but I'd never find it, as there is so much crunk up here. It's strange because it's almost like there is too much furniture. Like it's been piled up for some reason. I dodge between the rubble towards the window and stare out onto the cobbled stone yard. Doc stands beside me.

Lasul was right. This would be a great place to look out for anyone approaching. I move to the second window that looks over the square and it's got an even wider view.

Guardians.

There must be twenty of them, spreading out from the narrow road like ants emerging from an anthill.

They enter each of the buildings in pairs.

'We're trapped. And so is Lasul. I need to get to him,' I whisper to Doc.

'No. Wait. He's clever enough to stay hidden. We'd only give ourselves away.'

I nod and glance out again. Two of them have remained in the yard, looking around. We'd never get to Lasul without being spotted. Better to sit tight, perhaps he'll be able to hide too, and they'll miss us all.

I wait for several nervous minutes, silent. Doc clutches my hand. I know there's nothing more in it, but it settles me.

When I look out again, many of them have re-emerged and are working down the buildings towards us. I reckon I have five minutes, tops.

I move quietly around the room, trying to find the best hiding place. There's so much stuff in here, I'm almost spoilt for choice, but I decide to hide beneath a large, collapsed desk that has a small gap below it. I'll be able to see approaching feet from here and it faces the top of the stairs. Doc moves silently to my side.

I hear the general rabble of the Guardians as they search building after building, but nothing that sounds like they've found anyone. I hope Lasul is well hidden.

Then I hear them. Two pairs of steps, climbing the stairs, kicking those bits of rubble and wood out of their way. They have no need to be quiet when they have guns and numbers. I wonder if they know we are here, or if they are a random scouting group? Suppose it doesn't matter right now. Either way, we're in trouble.

I finger my stolen rifle. I better be ready to kill now. *Be strong.*

The first head appears at the top of the stairs. Then his body, and finally I can only see his feet. The other follows. My heart bangs, so I try to slow it. Keep my breathing steady.

They push furniture aside and I hear a couple of retches. Clearly, they hate the fish smell, too. One set of feet moves towards the desk. Five metres. Four, three, two. I can hear him breathing.

'Over here. Help me move this desk.'

Crunk, they'll find us. I tense, ready to shoot.

A rifle fires.

The two Guardians sprint away from the desk, and back downstairs.

It sounded close. It must be next door.

I emerge from my hiding spot and move to the window, edging round to see the neighbouring building. Ten Guardians stand outside. The others must be inside.

The ones outside begin to back off. They retreat from the building as the ones inside emerge. Two of them are holding someone covered in blood.

Lasul.

I nearly shout, but luckily nothing comes out.

He very subtly shakes his head without looking our way. I'm frozen by his look of calm. The bullet went into his shoulder judging by the stream of red on his shirt, but he smiles as they ask him questions repeatedly.

'Where is the boy?'

'Where were you going?'

'Who else is with you?'

He continues to grin at the woman asking the questions.

I'm torn between wanting to stay safe and doing something to stop them harming my one chance for the knowledge I am so desperate for. Doc has shaking hands over her mouth.

'Lasul, you are a traitor of the Realm. You are also an Orchestrator with the Orphans of Thasos. If you will not tell us the location of the boy you are hiding, then I will kill you and find him anyway.'

'No Lasul. Just tell her,' I whisper.

Doc looks at me wide-eyed. She shakes her head at me, pleading with me not to shout or reveal our position.

Lasul looks up at the lady's face. 'You will die today.'

'And so will you,' she replies.

'But my legacy will not.'

She pulls a small pistol from her waist and pulls the trigger.

Lasul falls limp to the ground.

'Some legacy.' She spits on Lasul's lifeless body. 'Burn every building. We'll smoke him out, like the rat that he is.'

My fingernails are buried in the wooden sill of the window. They've already taken everything from me. And now they've taken away my last chance at understanding why.

'The Realm will burn,' I say.

I aim my rifle at the killer, but Doc touches my hand, softly.

'Please don't. He died for nothing if you also die. We will avenge his death. We can take on the Realm and bring it down. We all believe this. We believed in Lasul. But not by giving up our lives.'

Maybe she's right. Maybe the rebellion will be better off if I don't shoot now. But will I be?

I brush her hand off and take aim once more.

Time to decide who I really am.

FROM THE AUDIO DIARY OF
E820906. ENTRY 5.

Seven always looked out for me. When I was much younger, Rex and I had been sort of together. There was no real spark between us. There was no interaction or conversation. I was just a trophy to him. Another thing that made him stand above the others. I think I was just glad of the attention after my parents had disappeared. It was nice to be more important, for a while. When I finally grew up a little, I stopped the façade. I kept my distance, where possible. It only made him more interested. Just after Seven arrived into our training group, Rex tried to kiss me. Several of his friends were with him, too, and I was terrified. He was being physical and aggressive. I screamed and old Smiler sent them away. Well, Seven found out about this. Actually, everyone did, but they all ignored it, even the Guardians. Rex was untouchable. His dad was close to the Autokratōr. But Seven didn't care who he was, or who his dad was.

CHAPTER 18
HERITAGE

Smoke coats my skin, fumes poison the air, heat roars like an aggressive lion, whipping its fiery tail all over the room.

I've been holding my breath for over a minute. My top is off, used as a rag to cover my mouth from the lethal carbon monoxide. I stay low to the ground, where the air is slightly less toxic, and crawl towards the window. Doc stays beside me the whole time.

I'll be seen, but I can't help that now. Better to get captured and live, than die in this room.

I haul myself onto the window ledge and peer into the courtyard.

A huge man fights several Guardians just beneath my building. Others are shooting at a building across the courtyard. Return fire always hits its mark. They fall like dominos.

I look around us, but there's no other way out except the window. We can't go down the flaming stairs and licks of fire begin to engulf us. I spot some old rags and begin quickly tying them together.

Doc spots what I'm doing and helps. But the final rope isn't long enough to reach the ground, even with my top added to the chain of rags. 'We'll need to climb down as far as it goes, then jump,' I suggest.

Doc just coughs in reply. She's not looking good.

'You go first,' I say. 'I'll be able to hold your weight as you go down, then I can tie it up to hold me.'

She nods and climbs out the window, holding tightly to the makeshift rope.

As she reaches the end, I can see she's exhausted and struggling. She let's go, her body flailing through air, heading towards the cobbled stone below. I shout out and Bulk sees her and runs with almost super speed to the spot.

And he catches her, her skull about two inches away from crashing onto the hard rock.

I breathe again, though I wish I hadn't. The acrid, choking smoke claws at my trachea, assaulting my lungs, and making my head spin.

I need to get out now, so I quickly tie the end I was holding to something that looks like an old bed. One side of it is on fire, so I need to be quick before it burns through my escape mechanism.

We used to do rope climbing drills during physical training, so I'm quick to descend, but when I'm about halfway down the rag-rope, I feel it's tension disappearing. The fire must have reached it and the knot is about to give.

I'm still a long way from the ground, and I glance over to see Bulk fighting off Guardians while protecting Doc's prone body.

He won't be able to catch me.

I search around for something softer to fall on, but it's solid cobble all the way.

But then I spot a small window just a few feet below where I hang, but about two metres to the right. It's too far to reach. Surely.

I'm going to fall any second, so I act. I swing to the right, and just as I do, the rag-rope gives way.

My world spins and somersaults.

I throw out my arms, trying to catch the ledge of the window.

The feeling of cold, hard, smooth stone in my hands is an unexpected relief. I made it. My fingers clinging to the ledge.

I hang there for a moment, but when a gunshot smashes into the wall beside my left ear, I find the strength to haul myself up and into the lower window.

I turn my head and see Bulk storming towards the last few Guardians, still shooting at Eagle and Miller. I don't even watch. They are superhuman. They will kill the Guardians. Instead, I cover my mouth and head to the stairs.

They've now crumbled in the heat and flames, but there's a small patch of Earth on the bottom floor that's free of smoulder and I drop myself down and fall onto that. The impact is hard on the knees but I'm okay. Finally, I force my way out of the front door and fall onto my front, coughing and spluttering, and trying to see through my stinging eyes.

I crawl towards our leader, just a few feet from me.

The warmth of Lasul's blood covers my cold hands as I try to stop it.

Doc slides beside me and tries to plug the wound. She measures his pulse and shakes her head.

He can't die. I need him. We need him. He just can't. Not after Cherish.

'Up you get, Seven. We need to go.' Bulk lifts me away from Lasul's body, despite my resistance. I kick and I punch, but he doesn't even notice. Doesn't he realise that Lasul had something important to tell me about my parents? It might not matter to them, but it matters to me.

I run round the giant to get back to the body. 'Try to help him. There must be something we can do?' As I shake him, something falls from his hand and clinks on the ground. A small key.

I pick it up and look at it closely. It's worn and tarnished, and it looks useless, but I pocket it anyway.

I look up at Bulk, his soft blue eyes staring back at me.

'No, he's dead. And he was clear that we should leave him and follow the plan if that happened. It's the Orphan way.'

'And what's the plan?' I ask.

'Get to Westmine. There are big things happening.'

'Yeah, well I'm not interested in your big plans.'

'You're just upset, Seven, like us.'

'Really? Upset like me? Was he just about to tell you why Cherish died? Or who your biological parents are? Was he just about to tell you the one thing that you've spent your whole life wondering about? You have no idea what I feel, or what it's like to be me.'

'I do.'

'Really? I doubt it.'

'Kid, I didn't know who my parents were either,' Bulk calmly replies.

'Well, maybe you understand, but I doubt Eagle does. She can't have an emotion in her body with the way she kills for fun. How many has it been in the last couple of days and not one sign of feeling or remorse? Look at all those bodies lying round us right now. Hell, she probably isn't even worried about Lasul dying. Just another body to her.'

My back smashes down into the cobbled street and the full strength of Bulk's right arm pins me. I don't fight it, allowing him to crush me. My chest is searing with pain, as is my back, but I remain still. Maybe he'll crush all the hurt out of me. I'd take physical pain every time over this emotional torture.

Bulk releases his grip and I open my eyes. Eagle has a hand on his shoulder.

'Hold your tongue, boy, or I'll cut it out. Important or not.' Bulk picks up Lasul's body and walks away between two buildings and out of the square.

Eagle holds her hand out for me. She pulls me back up, the deep pain in my back amplifying.

'Sorry, did you hear any of that?' I say.

She nods.

'I didn't mean it. Lasul was important to me. He knows so much that I wanted to know. And now that has died with him.'

Eagle opens her mouth, and a small noise comes out. She's trying to speak. I notice she has no tongue. Not cut out. Just not present, like maybe she never had one.

'Leave?' I ask.

She nods and strides off.

What happened to Eagle's tongue? Was she born without one? Then the questions smash my chest as hard as Bulk's fist; what if Eagle is the one who knows? Would she be able to tell me? She can make noises, almost form words, but could she tell me lots of important information accurately? I doubt it. The thought bursts my balloon of hope and swells the bubble of hurt.

I breathe deeply several times, playing with the key.

Doc is the only one still with me.

'Why would he be holding this key?' I ask her.

'It's just an old key, old and useless like this place.'

I run into the building which Lasul was removed from.

'Where are you going?' shouts Doc.

'To find the lock that this key opens.' I avoid the still burning furniture and wooden beams, searching for a lock. 'Lasul said he was hiding something in here. Maybe this key will open whatever it was.'

We search for a while in the wreckage, but we find nothing.

'It's getting too hot, Seven.' Doc looks faint. She's been through a lot.

'We should leave.' But as we head to the door, I trip on something on the floor.

A handle. 'It's a trapdoor,' I say to Doc.

'Have a look, if you must. I need to get out.'

I want to follow but the urge to look in the trapdoor is too high. The handle is too hot to pull, so I run out and grab some of the leftover rag-rope from earlier and return, tying it around the handle and hauling it up.

Beneath is a small crawlspace. Containing only a small box,

made of stone, sitting unaffected in the midst of the carnage above it.

And it has a small lock on the front. I grab it and race out of the smoky building.

'What's that?' asks Doc.

'This is a lock...and we have a key.'

We bury Lasul in a small section of woods, not far from the town. There is a small cottage hidden in the trees to my left, where we found spades that allowed us to dig a deep hole.

At least he is getting a proper earth ceremony. Cherish could still be lying, decomposing on that floor. Or cremated, more likely. I'd give almost anything to never have to do *this* again. I'm sick of death.

'I'd better say a few words. I'm not good at this stuff, but I'll try.' Bulk throws a handful of dirt into the hole as he speaks. 'Lasul, you were a great man. Sometimes I didn't agree...actually, a lot of us didn't agree with you. But you rarely steered us wrong and we're alive today because of you. Eagle and I owe you everything for rescuing us that day. We've both had much better lives ever since because of it, and so I need to say thanks. Rest in peace, Lasul.'

He moves away from the grave, leaving us.

'Well said, big man. Well said.' Miller walks after Bulk.

Eagle picks up dirt and tosses it in. For a long time, she simply stares down at the dead body beneath. She's probably saying goodbye in her own way. I stand silent, waiting.

Eagle nods to me and steps aside, joining Bulk and Miller at the edge of the woods.

Doc comes to my side, taking my hand. 'You want to say something, Seven. I'm not sure I can.'

I nod. 'Lasul, you seemed like a good man. And you died for me, too. You should have told them where I was, I think. I wouldn't have thought it betrayal if you had. And you would be alive now.

Able to tell me all those things you had locked up in your head. All those things that are precious to me. But I'll keep searching and I'll find out who I am. For Cherish and now for you. I'll try not to let you down. And I'll try to make a difference. To *live for a better tomorrow*.'

I walk over to the piled dirt, pick up a spade and begin to load the dirt back into the grave. Eagle and Bulk join me and together we fill the grave quickly. Eagle fashions a crude grave marker from wood and spikes it into the ground.

For a long time, as the owls and woxs howl, we stand looking at the grave and the sky. Bulk reckons we should stay in the cover of the trees until the deepest part of the night.

It's eating at me. The guilt continually crawling up my throat. I vomit, but it stays in there. I try drinking water, but it won't wash down. I sat and hid in the building as they shot Lasul and I continued to hide as Eagle and Miller started taking them out with their rifles, and Bulk with his pistol and blade.

They're warriors, not like me. I'm just a traitor of the Realm, responsible for the death of many, many people who tried to help me, but not willing to risk my own life when it counts. Sure, I rescued some of them, but I did that because I was angry. My rage made the decision, but now that's gone, consumed by remorse, what next?

Eagle sharpens a short knife on a stone. And Bulk stares out to the lands beyond. Where did they come from? Surely the Realm wouldn't discard two people with their skills. I walk over to the big man. It's time for me to understand more.

'Where did Lasul rescue you from? Where were you before?' I ask him. I need to be direct. I didn't ask Lasul the right questions when I had the chance. I won't make that mistake again.

'It's not the time, lad.' He continues to stare out into the distance.

'Please,' I say. 'Lasul told me so little. I need to understand this world better. I'm so lost at the moment, and it might help if I knew where you and Eagle came from.'

'We were experiments.'

'Experiments?'

'Yup, genetic, and biological experiments. Part of the Autokratōr's early attempts to create better Guardians. He's always been obsessed with genetics.'

'What did they do to you?'

'Horrible things, Seven. I would spare you the details. It was not nice.'

'But you escaped? How?'

'Lasul used to be a scientist within the Realm. An Academic, they're called now. He was part of the group doing the experiments. Only he didn't like what they were doing, and after a while he decided he would let some of us go. Of course, he had to come with us. They'd have killed him if he'd stayed in Circle City. They don't like traitors much. As you know.' He nods to me, respectfully.

'Is that why Lasul hated the Realm so much?'

'I think so. It's why he knew so much as well. We'll not get a leader like him again, I wouldn't think.'

It all makes sense. Lasul's spies: they must have been old friends from his days working for the Realm. And Bulk is far too big and strong to be natural, Eagle too good with a rifle, and silent like an assassin. They are the perfect warriors. I think about Sharan, our most famous Guardian, and wonder if she is like Bulk and Eagle.

'We should open the stone box, Seven.' Doc gently reminds me.

'What box?' asks Miller.

'I found it in the building where Lasul was found by the Guardians. He had a key in his hand. I think he wanted us to find the key and the box.'

'Well, open it then, boy.' Miller edges closer.

Everyone crowds round.

I slide the old key into the lock and turn it. Stone scrapes as it rotates. I lift the lid and inside are five scrolls, each bound by a red ribbon.

'They're sealed with the Orphan brand,' says Miller.

I lift the first one out. 'It's got your name on it, Eagle.'

Her eyes widen as I hand her the paper.

'There's one for each of us.' I hand them out.

Each of them takes their letter and moves a little away, to read in private.

I take the one which has *E820907* on the outside.

I loosen the ribbon carefully, my hands shaking.

Dear Seven,

As a cautious man, caution learned from many, many dark experiences, I have written this letter to tell you all you wish to know, in the result of my death.

First, about the cause. We are only a very small faction of the Order of Thasos. However, as you already know, we have many extraordinary people in our group, with skills that will serve the cause with great effect. They must all arrive at Westmine and soon. If my information is correct, something big will be happening soon. A rebellion, a strike against the Realm and our best chance of success lies with these individuals making it.

I have named you my heir. Having no natural children of my own, I want you to lead this faction to Westmine. I have explained this to the others, especially Miller, who may not like the decision, so you will not need to discuss it with them, nor provide proof. However, keep this letter in case of any such issues.

You may ask why I have named you heir and promoted you to lead our faction. Well, that answer is ravelled within the answer to the biggest question – who are you? Why are you important? Why did we take you from the Realm?

The first thing you should know is that I once served the Realm and the Autokratōr, with great loyalty. I did all I was asked, regardless of the ethical implications. For years I experimented on animals and latterly on humans. The Autokratōr sought genetic perfection, both in his soldiers and then in his offspring.

I am ashamed to say I helped him with both. First, I created a legion of soldiers, using the DNA from the best in the Military. You've seen Bulk and Eagle in action. They were part of this group. Suffice to say, it worked.

Buoyed by this, and greedy for success on the battlefield at the border fronts, he ordered this to be done on a larger scale. He wanted thousands. At this point I began to doubt his intentions. When he had come to me initially, I thought I was working on eliminating inherited conditions, now I was designing people to kill people.

So, I began to waiver in my loyalty.

Then I was asked by the Autokratōr to speak with his wife. They had been struggling to conceive an heir. His wife desperately wanted children. I said I would help. Her intentions were purely based on love. She just wanted a child to love. The Autokratōr wanted to make her happy, but he also saw it as a chance to make his heir stronger. He asked me to modify the genes of the embryo that would become their child. And I did. I modified all eight of them.

Of those eight, only four began to develop when implanted into his wife. She grew big, but I hid the fact that she was having quadruplets from her. Fortunately, when she went into labour, the Autokratōr was away from the City. A day's travel. This gave me time to deliver the four babies, from behind a small curtain via c-section, and to present his wife with one.

The other three were taken to far corners of the Realm by various servants and I kept watch upon you all. Initially they all kept me updated. But after a while, only Cherish continued to do so. She took you to your Greenhorn camp and I decided it was time.

I pause reading for a moment, unable to process all this information properly. I'm the son of the Autokratōr? And I have siblings? Possibly three of them. No, this can't be right. There's no way...I look at the others – do they know? Surely not. They'd have hung me on sight, especially Miller. I pull the letter even closer to me and read on.

I left the service of the Realm, renounced my name, and became Lasul, an exile. I formed our community, not too far from your camp, welcoming all those of good heart and with a common point of view.

Cherish kept a close watch on you, making sure your genes could never betray who you truly were. We had originally planned to use you, perhaps as a bargaining chip, perhaps for protection, but Cherish grew to love you so much, she would not allow it.

So, we waited. We wanted to see what kind of man you would become. And you became a fine, brave, and honourable young man. Cherish was proud of you. You did what you had to do.

If I had lived, I would have taken you to Westmine, to meet the leaders of the Orphans. I would have convinced them to let you lead. Your face, with your heritage revealed, leading a rebellion against your father's Realm would have been very powerful. It still could be. Nobody ever defies the Realm and the impact of his own son doing it, could unlock all those years of fear and resentment in others.

So, now you know your origins. I have told you everything.

It is now up to you, how you use that knowledge. But I hope you do so wisely and with much thought. Lead the faction to Westmine. See them join the Orphan rebellion. That is the only price of the knowledge I've just given you. After that, you are free to become who you wish.

And remember, a person is not defined by a name, or their heritage, or where they come from, rather they are defined by their actions, intentions and where they end up going. When I gave up my name, only then did I discover who I truly was.

Please forgive me, Seven.

Lasul

. . .

As everyone finishes their letters, they slide them away. Nobody discusses the contents or says anything else. I wonder what was in their letters, but right now I can't even take in what mine said.

No reaction, no snide comments from Miller about me being leader or about being the Autokratōr's son. No-one knows what my letter said, and I intend to keep it that way. I'm wanted by the Realm already, but if I tell them who I really am...surely they'd never accept me.

But Cherish knew. This explains everything. Why she took such good care of a random Greenie (or not so random, now), why she manipulated my DNA tests – she was trying to protect me. Even at the very end, always protecting me. At the cost of her life.

How do I ever repay something like that?

'We should go.' Miller breaks the silence. 'Malt left his mark back at the town. He's already passed through with Six and Three. If we go quickly, we might catch them.'

Eagle leads the way, leaving the grave of Lasul behind. Bulk helps Miller start walking.

Doc waits back for me and holds out her hand. 'Come, Seven. Let's go.'

I take her hand, grasping it tightly in mine, close my eyes and let her guide me forward. Then she kisses me. I'm surprised at first and do nothing. But after a second or two, I kiss back.

After what I've just read, I need something human, something tangible, something I can understand. Anything so I don't need to process the contents of the letter.

FROM THE AUDIO DIARY OF
E820906. ENTRY 6.

Seven beat Rex. Badly. He got a fair amount of time in the Cage for it. But Rex left me alone after that. Cherish used to give me food and I'd sneak it to him while he was in there. Water and vitamin pills were all the Guardians gave him. He got dreadfully skinny that time. It was his longest stretch, I think. I was worried that he'd continue to fight with Rex when he got out. And he did, but rarely physically. He became wiser and realised that fighting wasn't the only way to solve things. Well, mostly. He had to battle his impulses, which I knew was difficult for him. After that stretch in the Cage, Seven rarely ate camp food if he could avoid it. Cherish kept him alive. She was breaking so many rules for him, to keep him alive and safe, but she did it. Then one day, the scientist from New London came.

CHAPTER 19
DOC

The kiss lasts for approximately seven seconds. I quite like it, for a first attempt. Her lips are warm, thick, and squashy, and taste like mint. She must have been chewing some mint leaves as she walked. I make a mental note to pick a bunch the next time we come across them.

I keep my eyes closed, I'm sure that's the right thing to do. That's what I've seen other Greenies do. Nine and Fourteen were always at it when old Smiler had fallen asleep. I couldn't help but peek out my tent when they were snogging behind the water well.

It's a little awkward when we stop. She just gives me a huge smile, squeezes my hand, and we walk on in silence. What's the protocol for a post-kiss conversation? I could tell you the quickest way to skin a lango fruit, but I haven't a clue about what to say to a girl I've just kissed.

I settle for a quick smile, then stare straight ahead.

After a few moments, the tension becomes unbearable, and I have to speak.

'This fog is crazy, huh?'

'Erm, yeah I guess. Last night was worse.'

Silence, again. Come on, Seven, think of something funny or witty to say. You're better than this.

'So, you kiss real good.'

Doc looks at me, eyes wide and shakes her head.

Crunk, that was wrong.

Then she starts to giggle.

Maybe not so bad?

'You had a girlfriend before, Seven?'

'Sure. Loads.'

She laughs louder this time. Gee, thanks!

'Well, maybe not loads.'

'One?' she asks.

I seriously don't want to tell her I've never kissed a girl before, so deliberately catch my foot on the ground, release her hand and tumble.

'Are you okay?' Doc springs down beside me.

'Yes, just my stupid lumbering feet, again.'

She puts out her hand and helps me back up.

We start walking, again in silence. Good, hopefully she's forgotten her last question.

But the quiet makes me think of Six, and the guilt starts to rise up my throat. I release Doc's hand. I always thought Six might be someone who, you know...well, maybe she'd be the first person I'd kiss. I dunno, the last couple of years I've thought about it a lot.

A sense of betrayal worms its way through my brain. Not only about Six, but also Lasul and Cherish – two people dead because of me, and all I can think about are girls.

And I'm not even trying to process that I'm the secret heir to the Realm just yet – apparently, I need to lead a rebellion against my Dad first.

I step away from Doc and slowly let the space between us get bigger, hoping that distance will make all my problems go away.

'DOWN.' Bulk falls flat to the ground, in sync with Eagle. Doc and I are slower and clumsier, but get down more quickly than Miller, who is last to fall. He basically saved my life and I'm spending all my time worrying about kisses with Doc. Maybe I should say thanks at some point. Maybe.

About twenty metres away on our right, two bright, beaming headlights approach us. The vehicle appears to be driving along a rough, muddy track, but it's moving at speed and skidding all over the place.

My chest swells into the cold, wet ground with every rapid breath. Please don't be Guardians. Then I spot it. The emblem of the Realm, emblazoned on the side of the truck as it passes directly in front of us. Loud shouts come from the back of the truck, where multiple Guardians are seated.

The noise echoes through the silent night louder than a howling wox. Fortunately, none of them seem to be looking our way as they pass. The tiny red taillights start to get smaller and smaller. Finally, the truck disappears from sight, and only a slight rumble of the engine can be heard.

'What the hell is a truck full of Guardians doing out here?' Bulk asks. 'There must have been about twenty of them in there. That's no random patrol.'

'How did they know we went this direction?' I ask.

I can see Eagle's eyes moving to Doc.

'Not sure they were looking for anyone. You see how fast it was going? And those Guardians didn't seem very alert. I reckon they were taking something or someone important away. If you weren't standing right here, I'd have guessed they'd have caught you.' Bulk nods to me.

'We should get away from this road while the fog still gives us some cover,' I say.

'I agree,' adds Doc, looking around nervously.

Several hours of walking, combined with little sleep or rest, as well as everything else that's happened, has fatigued every scutting cell in my body. I can't go on. I look at Miller, who's now being carried by Bulk. At least I don't have a bullet hole in my shoulder.

The weight of my learned heritage and new responsibilities aren't helping either.

There's part of me that just can't believe the Autokratōr is actually my father. Like, there's no way they'd just not notice Lasul stealing three babies, is there? And I don't look much like him. Although maybe when they spliced my genes, that made me look a little different to them.

But there's only one place I can find out for sure. And it's in Circle City, about a hundred yards from the Autokratōr himself. But there's no point wasting energy on that. I have a new job to do.

I am now the leader of this group, so I best do something about that. Taking some action might help me escape all these confusing thoughts – I feel like I'm being pulled in so many directions.

'We should rest,' I suggest to Bulk.

He looks at each of us, our moods steeped in sadness. He nods, Eagles shrugs.

'No fire. We can camp here. Looks like there's some strawberries in that field there, so I'm gonna go pick some. Eagle?' Bulk places a sleepy Miller down into a comfortable position on the ground. 'Doc, you can keep an eye on him, yes?'

She nods and moves over to him.

He marches off with Eagle to the field on our right.

Why didn't Lasul make Bulk leader? I know I'm "important" but he's way better suited than me.

I have no idea how he can see there are strawberries in that field. It's the middle of the night and the fog's as thick as old Wheezy, our group Omega. But then again, they are GM. It's weird to think about. A person who's been modified. Plants, yes. Animals, well I'm not a fan, but I can kinda see why it happens. But humans, I can't get my head around it. How must those guys feel? Like experiments? Less human?

Like me. Lasul said I was modified, too. Me, and my brothers. Feels weird to say that.

'Hey, what you thinking?' Doc's soft voice.

I turn and stare into her green eyes, still bright in the darkness. Jeez, this is tough. I really, really like her.

'Nothing,' I say, hoping Miller is either asleep or far enough away that he can't hear.

'Really?'

'Yes. Why?'

'Well, I thought you might be thinking about what we were discussing earlier. Or maybe about your letter?'

No, stop it. Don't say it. If Miller hears, he'll mock me forever.

I ignore the part about the letter. 'What did we discuss again?'

She smiles and shakes her head. 'About having a girlfriend, silly.'

'Oh, yeah.'

'Well, have you? It's not important, but I just wondered.'

My face burns. I want to disappear real bad. Miller hasn't moved. Please be asleep.

'I don't know what to say, Doc.' I look down at my hands and fiddle. Anything to not look at her.

'Does that mean you haven't?'

I nod, still looking away.

'That's so sweet. I kinda reckoned that maybe, you know... well...you and Six were pretty tight when you arrived. So, I thought maybe...'

'We are tight. Were. Well, hopefully we will be again. I mean, not that we were together. Just close. Close friends. Good friends. Yes, good friends.'

'Okay, well you aren't together, so that's great. I don't want to step on anyone's toes.'

The guilt is back, no longer squirming but now thrashing.

She puts her hand onto my cheek and slowly turns my head.

But I turn away. 'Sorry. I can't. Not that you're not amazing. Way too good for a Greenie like me. It's all too much just now.'

As we sit for the next few seconds, the silence is uncomfortable. Then Doc just smiles and slides her head onto my shoulder, and we stare out into the dark, foggy night, my mind full of thoughts not in any way related to the Realm, parents, Six, or unsaid words.

'We're not going to talk about our letters, are we?' she asks.

'No.'

A loud, feral howl erupts from the noiseless black night. The silver sheen has lifted and the shimmer of stars and reflected light of the moon illuminates the bare and uninhabited countryside around us.

It's the cry that wakes me. Wox, most likely. Doc also comes around, looking a little groggy. We must have slept for an hour, at least. Eagle and Bulk have not returned. Miller lies in the same position.

My arms shiver, my clothes and hair are damp from the wet ground, and Doc has frostlets in her hair. Our breath comes out in ragged puffs.

'They've been away for a while,' Doc says. 'I'll check on Miller.'

I nod and stand up, rubbing the skin on my arms. The landscape is deserted. Nothing moves. I suddenly feel very exposed. The fog had covered us nicely, but now anyone within a 2000-metre radius could see us easily.

'You reckon we should move?' she asks, while kneeling over Miller.

I don't know what to do. I want to think that they are just delayed or are picking enough strawberries to last us several days, but the field on our right is definitely empty. They must have gone further afield.

'Yes. Something doesn't feel right.'

We move in the same direction as earlier, before we slept...and all the awkwardness with Doc. She and I flank Miller on either side to help him along. His shivering worries me, but not as much as his lack of chat. He must be in a lot of pain if he's not taking the opportunity to slag the crunk out of me.

I also wonder what his letter said. Knowing Lasul, the little I did, he probably asked him to support me. We'll see.

We reach the top of a gradual ascent. The view is wider all around.

'Can you see anything?' Doc asks. We place Miller down for a rest.

I scan the countryside, turning 360 degrees. When I get back to where I started, I spot movement. Someway off, probably more than 1500 metres. I pull Doc to the deck with me. We watch, lying on our stomachs.

'How many can you count?' I ask her.

She shakes her head. 'Three, maybe?'

'Too few for Guardians?'

'Probably, and they wouldn't be on foot this far out from a town or city, would they?'

I nod. 'You're right. They don't walk like Guardians, neither. I'm sure that's Bulk at the back, carrying someone.'

They get closer and I see five figures moving towards us. They must have seen us already. I pull Doc back to her feet and we wave. Bulk lifts his arm.

'Who have they found?' I say, watching the quintet approach.

The others shrug.

I walk down the slope towards the party, leaving Miller with Doc.

'What's going on?' I ask Bulk.

And then I spot Three. 'We've had a hell of a night, Seven,' he says.

Once Three speaks, I recognise that the bundle in Bulk's arms is Malt, who looks unconscious. But someone is missing.

'Where is Six?' I ask Three, dread engulfing me.

'*They* have her.'

I shake my head. Why did I separate from her? And I just kissed Doc, while she was being taken. I hit myself on the head several times.

'And how is Malt?' I ask, regaining my composure for a second.

Bulk lowers him to the ground.

'Dead.'

FROM THE AUDIO DIARY OF
E820906. ENTRY 7.

Seven was worried, but that was nothing compared to how Cherish felt. She was terrified they were going to take him away. The scientist took a sample of Seven's blood and packed it away, to be taken back to the City. He asked Seven lots of questions about his childhood: what he remembered, who his parents were, how long Cherish had been his foster mother, as well as the standard Realm loyalty questions. He answered them all, not honestly. He told me the scientist was the biggest liar he'd ever met and said that he had lied in return. The next day, I saw the scientist leaving. He was leaving Cherish's tent, which was strange as he had his own. She kissed him on the lips, and I saw her slip something into the scientist's bag. I never told Seven.

CHAPTER 20
IMPOSSIBLE CHOICE

'Where did they take Six?' I ask.

'We don't know. They came and took her away in a truck. About twenty Guardians.' Three can't look at us.

I look at Doc, and then Eagle.

'Will they have taken her to Circle City?' I ask, fury scalding me.

'Yes, I am certain of it. Three said they took off at full speed once they had her,' says Bulk.

'Then we have to go.' I turn to Bulk and Eagle. 'We have to go now.'

They both stay silent. Bulk shakes his head.

'Sorry, Seven. Lasul's last wish was...'

'I don't give a scut about Lasul and what he wanted. I want to help Six. We need to help Six.'

'No, you can't help her that way. The only way to help is to hit the Realm where it hurts and that's why we go to Westmine.' Bulk looks at me, awaiting my refusal.

I wonder if they are thinking about their letters. They were all probably given instructions, too. But how can I lead these people to Westmine when I know Six is going in the opposite direction? And because of me.

I walk away from the group.

Miller lies on Malt's still body, weeping and holding his hands.

Doc is checking Three, making sure he is okay.

'I'm fine. Just tired. And hungry,' Three mumbles.

He must have carried Malt's dead body after they took Six. Eagle hands him a blanket and some food.

'Lasul made me leader of this group,' I announce.

Everyone turns to me.

'Aye, so the letter said. What of it?' Bulk takes a step forward.

'Then you will all come with me to New London. We will work out a plan and rescue Six.' I watch them all, one-by-one, turn their heads away.

I wait for a reaction, but none of them speak.

'You will come with me.'

'If you command us, Seven, we will come with you,' says Doc. 'But it's the wrong decision and we all know it. You included. You're letting your emotions cloud the logic. Lasul made you leader to help with the rebellion, not to rescue one person.'

'It is not the Orphans way,' says Miller, his voice thick with anger. 'Malt is dead. Lasul is dead. Many of our people are dead, ya little shit. So, we're not fucking off to save your girlfriend. We're going to Westmine.'

'You will do as I say.'

'You're pathetic.' Miller leaps for me and has to be restrained by Bulk. 'Leave him, Miller. Save your strength, you are hurt. He will see sense.'

'Off you go and rescue your girlfriend,' Miller hisses. 'Get your-self killed. Like I care, kid. Bulk can lead us. He'd be much better at it, anyway. At least he's actually killed someone who's not his unarmed foster-mother.'

I ball my fists, but Doc lays a gentle hand on my forearm, and I take a deep breath.

'Be a leader,' she says. 'I know you can do this.'

But I turn and walk away from the group, a long way down the hill and into the strawberry fields. I need some time to think where that scut isn't annoying me.

Doc joins me.

'Don't bother lecturing me,' I say. 'I need some space and time to think.'

'Okay, I won't lecture you. And I will leave. But when you think, ask yourself, what would Six do? What would she want? But if you do decide to go, we'll still be going to Westmine, we'll just be in a much weaker position and Lasul and Cherish will have died for nothing.' She rises and leaves me.

I sit for an hour, reading and re-reading the letter, then thinking.

I must find out if the Autokratōr is my father. I must. I really don't want it to be true...I just hope they took all the evil out of my genes when they modified them. I don't want to be like him.

And I also need to save Six. They are in the same place. It's a no-brainer.

But I know that's what is best for me.

Lasul thought I could lead. And a good leader puts the needs of others before themselves. And the last thing Doc said sits heavy on me. Six would want me to lead the rebellion. It *is* what she would die for. And Cherish *would* have died for nothing if I abandoned the rebellion.

I walk back up to the group. They're dozing or resting.

'I've changed my mind.' They sit up as I speak. 'We shall go to Westmine. We will help the Orphans rebel at Westmine. We will honour the memory of Cherish, Lasul, and Malt by helping to wound the Realm. To show them that the people they've discarded are a force to be reckoned with. We will be strong. We will live for a better tomorrow. For all the Nameless.'

PART III

THE UPRISING AND THE TWIN

From the audio diary of E820906. Entry 8.

I wasn't always the best in class. Once, Three was the best in class. He got the Alpha prize for General Excellence in Academics several times. But around about the time when I turned twelve, he seemed to stop trying. Sure, he was still smart, and that doesn't just disappear, but he stopped answering in class, he stopped studying for exams, he stopped speaking to the rest of us. He just stopped. I don't remember anything specific happening. He got worse as the years passed so that by the time we got to our Tests, he had dropped down the ladder. When Serra announced he was the group Omega, though...well, that's when I knew something was up. I knew he deliberately failed.

CHAPTER 21
DOUBT

'I'm sorry, Seven. I know you were close.' Bulk puts his left arm onto my shoulder and squeezes.

I remain silent; thinking of Six only makes me want to change my mind.

'We need to get to Westmine. Soon. I've been thinking and I reckon they might send more Guardians down there if they suspect that's our destination. What do you think?' I ask.

'Possibly, although I doubt the Realm believes Westmine to be a threat. Why should they? There has been very little trouble ever since they introduced the slaves. It's ruled with an iron fist, apparently. Or so Lasul's reports suggest.'

'So, do we have a chance?' asks Doc.

'Certainly.' Bulk stands a little taller.

'How?'

'Numbers. We have far greater numbers, and, in the end, I think that will be enough. As the Realm has grown and more of us have been discarded, deemed weak by the Autokratōr, the stronger the Exiles have become. They may call us Nameless now, but soon they will know who we are. It's Lasul's big vision.'

The group eats some more strawberries and gets prepared to

move on after our rest. Bulk's reading his book again. I watch him for a while, scanning the words, chuckling every so often.

I stare out into the endless hills and grasslands. What am I doing? I'm not sure I've been able to really answer that question since the Destination ceremony was cut short. Certain I would go into the Military, my silly dreams of being a war hero and fighting alongside Sharan on the front are long dead. The Realm is a sham and now I'm supposed to lead an uprising against it. To lead all those people, many of whom are much more capable than I am, and definitely have much more experience. How can I get them to trust me, to listen to me, to show them that I'm even part of their cause.

'Hey, we are going.' Doc places her hand on my shoulder and turns me gently. 'I know this is tough for you but remember we all feel the same. We need to stick together, okay?' She lifts my chin. 'Okay?'

'Yeah, I just can't get Cherish out of my head.' I decide not to share my insecurities.

'She would want you to keep going, to fight for her, no?'

'Yeah, you're right. You're always right.' At least I know I have someone on my side.

'I'm glad you've finally realised that.' She punches me on the arm and strides off.

I watch her move. I want to like her. I want things to be simple. A world with just one girl, not two. Six has always been there. But Doc is here now. They are both great. And if Six liked me that way, would she have done something by now. Maybe she thought it didn't matter - we were supposed to be separated after the Test. If I ever see her again, what would she say. What would I say.

Still, it could be worse.

It is worse: I am the son of the Autokratōr and I'm marching to war against his Realm.

. . .

I walk with Miller, who has been staring into the distance, almost without blinking, for the whole day's journey. Out of respect, I've avoided asking him the question that still gnaws my soul. Why does he hate me so much. Does he know who my parents are? If he does, I need to show him, and the others, that I'm nothing like the Autokratōr. That we can burn this world down and create a better one from the ashes.

'I can't believe he's gone,' says Miller, still staring ahead. I don't know if he's speaking to me or wants me to respond.

Silence follows, but it becomes awkward, so I place my hand onto his good shoulder and squeeze.

'Thanks, Seven.'

'Miller, did Lasul tell you anything about me?'

'Other than you being a little turd-licker? No.' There's the real Miller.

Miller stops and turns to face me. 'You will come with us to Westmine, won't you?'

I shrug. 'For now. But I can't stand not trying to help Six.'

'But don't you see that this is exactly what they want? By taking her, they have the best possible bait to make you go to them. It means they don't have to scour the countryside for you. They can just wait. There's a reason they make you pass that Test and it's to make sure they have the best minds and bodies on their side, working for them. Don't let them win. Alright, kid?' He gives me one last look, then walks ahead.

I let my pace slow, falling back behind Eagle. Miller is right. That feels weird to say. It is a trap. I'm not stupid, but Six gave up a happy life in the Realm to follow me out here, and her reward is to be captured and imprisoned. And that's the best-case scenario. I don't want to think about what else could happen to her.

The people who have died saturate my thoughts. I can't let someone else die because of me. I have to switch off, focus my mind elsewhere or I'll just go mad with guilt.

I stride ahead to walk alongside Eagle, knowing that I'll be able to walk in silence and force out all the crunk that is circulating in my head.

A fierce, bright fire at the bottom of the hill illuminates the mud-stained side of a goods vehicle. The emblem of the Realm is just visible. Three Guardians laugh, eat and drink.

'Okay, we need at least one of them alive, so we can get information on how many of our people they've taken, and what other patrols are in the area. I'm sure Eagle could just take them all out with her rifle, but best to keep this quiet if possible.' As I speak people move in closer. 'Bulk, Eagle, and I will charge them. Doc, you bring Miller and Three down once we've given the all-clear. There may be more than three of them.'

Bulk and Eagle nod.

I creep forward with the two GM's, hoping to get close before they hear us.

But a wox howls to our right and the Guardians look our way. Bulk is hard to miss.

'Who goes there?' shouts one of them.

Eagle replies with a bullet and he falls dead.

One of the other Guardians runs away in the opposite direction, while the other runs for the truck.

'Bulk, Eagle get the runner. I'll get to the truck.'

I sprint hard and thump into the Guardian just as he reaches the door. The momentum takes us both careening into the side of the truck, headfirst.

FROM THE AUDIO DIARY OF
E820906. ENTRY 9.

No one ever came back to see Seven after that scientist left. I suspected Cherish had something to do with it, but as time went on, I forgot about it. For about a year after it, we spent almost every night speculating about why they had taken his blood. Seven had the wild notion that he was being primed to become the new Sharan. I never told him what I thought of that. He had his heart set on it, so I didn't want to let him down. It was around about this time, that I started to eat less of the drug-containing gruel and began to rely upon Seven's emergency food packages from Cherish as well. It had an enormous effect upon me.

CHAPTER 22
INSIDE INFORMATION

Doc. Flames. Miller. Three.

My eyes take in images that my brain struggles to process.

'Take it easy. You have a concussion,' says Doc. She presses some damp material to the top of my skull. As it touches the swollen lump on my head, I bite down to avoid making a noise. My brain is processing pain. Lots of pain.

I close my eyes. 'What happened?'

'Good question. We don't know. The only things I know are that two of the Guardians are dead, and the others must be chasing the last Guardian. I saw him run away after the fight.'

'Why didn't they just shoot him?'

'He dropped his gun, so they didn't want to shoot anyone who's unarmed. Plus, we needed one alive, remember? We found you lying face down in the woods. You feeling any better, yet?'

I rub my eyes and massage my forehead. 'A little.' The top of my head still throbs. I try to sit up, feeling blood drain from my brain. Doc helps me into a seated position. I lean against the tyre of the truck. That's what all this pain is about.

'At least I don't have to walk for a bit,' I say, forcing a smile.

'Here, hold this on your bump.' She passes me the wet material and holds it on my head, despite the agony.

Three climbs up on top of the truck, squatting with a rifle cradled naturally in his arms. He seems better. He peers out into the night, obviously watching for the return of our friends. I struggle to comprehend the transition in this guy since he was a Greenie. From fumbling, terrified mute, to confident, scary, and well, still pretty quiet. But it's just so different. I really think he must have been deliberately underperforming to be exiled. But why? I mean, I understand how decent the Nameless are now, but back then none of us could know that.

Doc offers me a small drink of water from her canteen. Well, probably one of the Guardians' canteens, but I don't think about its origin as I gulp down the liquid. I watch Miller standing a little away, his right-hand shaking. I've noticed it hasn't stopped doing that since he found out about Malt.

'Thanks.' I hand Doc the canteen.

'No problem. We have so much in the back of this truck. It will keep us going all the way to the coast. There are weapons in here, too, which we may need at some point, unfortunately.'

Miller wanders away from the firelight and stands watching the moon. Poor guy. He's suffered as much as anyone with losing people they love. It's probably not something I'd have noticed a few weeks ago. The emotions of others mattered very little to me. And now, more and more, they are meaning so much.

I turn my head to Doc, who is busy tidying up the camp, like she's ready to leave already.

'Are we going soon? The others aren't even back yet.'

'Yes, Miller wants us to leave as soon as they return. With all the noise and the increased patrols, we'll be lucky if no one heard the scuffle. And I'll need to put this fire out, too. Sorry, Seven.' She uses a large blanket to smother the flames, which go out after the second covering.

.   .   .

We take a quick itinerary of the truck's contents and dump a whole load of mining equipment that won't be any use to us. Enough food in there to feed us for months, enough weapons to arm a legion of Guardians and lots of other hi-tech stuff that I don't fully understand.

'What is all that stuff?' I ask Doc.

'I think some of it is tracking equipment, other communications and I think this last one is a list of the latest Military orders. And guess whose name appears more than once.' She points to the list of numbered commands on the screen. I scan the list, focusing on the ones with my number on them.

Sunday 18th March 2091
20.24 PM
Priority One – recapture and transfer E820907 and return him, unharmed, directly to the Autokratōr.
Priority Two – capture known associates: E820906, E820903.

Monday 19th March 2091
18.04 PM
New Priority Two – capture known associates: E820906, E820903 and the rebellion leader known as Lasul.

Thursday 22nd March 2091
02.43 AM
Update – known associate Lasul terminated due to resistant behaviour. Capture impossible. E820907 still unaccounted for. Continue scour.

05.34 AM
Update – known associate E820906 captured. Currently in transit to New London. Cease scouring of Nameless territories and remain in station.

'They have her in New London. They've taken her to get me to come to them. The friggin' sogs.' I sit down on the metal swivel chair behind us.

'Maybe they took her because she's valuable, Seven. Seriously, it's not *always* about you.' Doc tuts loudly as she leaves the truck. I sit alone, pondering my next move. I have a truck, so maybe I could drive it to the city and sneak in?

I smack myself on the forehead, pain erupting from my skull. Stupid, stupid, stupid. I put my head back, close my eyes and take several deep breaths. I've already promised to help the other Exiles. Plus, how the frig am I supposed to just drive into the capital city without anyone noticing I'm like their most wanted crim.

I relax, determined to put complex thoughts and questions away for a moment or two. The subtle heaters in the truck make me real comfy and I listen to the hum of the engine, thinking of Cherish. Why didn't she tell me more? If she didn't tell me anything, I know it was out of love. She thought I'd be safer without the knowledge. But right now, it's consuming me, eating away at my insides, and messing with my old composure.

I slowly drift to sleep, memories of Cherish and Six merging into a blissful, peaceful dream.

'Wake up, they are back.' Doc helps me off the floor.

I must have slid down when I fell asleep. My head spins and I take a few seconds to get my bearings before I exit the truck.

Bulk holds both arms of the runaway Guardian directly behind his back. The poor guy looks like his arms are about to be pulled from the sockets.

'Good, that's everyone,' says Miller, nodding to Seven. 'Time to vote. Do we leave him out here, with the risk of him finding another patrol and telling them all about us, or do we keep him as a prisoner, which is a real pain, but will give us a better chance of remaining unfound?'

'Shouldn't we question him?' I ask. 'He might know stuff which could help us.'

'Like what, kid?' Miller asks.

'Well, how about why you lot are after me?' I ask the Guardian.

He stares at me, trying to make out my features in the dark. Then he recognises me. I see the change in his face, his eyes widen, and his mouth falls open.

'It's him. I mean you. E820907.' The Guardian starts to wriggle, but a quick yank by Bulk stops him instantly.

'He prefers Seven,' says Doc, winking at me.

I ignore her. 'Why are you hunting me? I'm a nobody. And why did Cherish do it? Who am I?' I move to within inches of his face, spitting as I speak. The frustration grows inside my chest.

'It was just an order. I don't know anything. I'm just a Guardian.'

'I don't believe you. Tell me what you know?'

'Seriously, all I know is your number. The orders have been flashing on the screen for days. We are just Transporters. The lowest of the Guardians.'

'You're lying,' I say.

The Guardian remains silent, shaking his head.

'TELL ME!' My voice rips the soundless night air.

I'm now so close, I smell the man's stinking breath. He's sweating, clearly terrified, but it hasn't loosened his tongue. My body tenses, my fist curls and my arm slowly rises.

As I attempt to punch him in the face, Miller grabs my wrist.

'No. Leave this to us.'

'Let go of me. I need to know.'

I force my wrist out of his grip and pull my arm back. Again, he grabs it. Every angry piston in my body is now pumping. I turn to Miller and push him with all my force onto the ground before launching a punch at the Guardians nose.

'SPEAK!'

Bulk catches my closed fist inside his own. His other arm grasps the Guardian tightly. Eagle moves over and pulls me away. She's stronger than I am, but I resist. I struggle and swing my arms and legs. Three grabs me as well, then Doc. As I thrash, I see Miller struggling to get off the ground. He looks even more hurt.

The anger goes. My muscles relax. I let it all out. I start crying. Tears flow and flow and finally flood. I'm lifted onto the floor of the truck. The doors close and I'm left on my own. I continue to cry the tears of frustration, unable to stop. Why? Why? Why?

The questions circulate in my head, and each time they pass, I cry even harder.

Finally, the tears stop, but my face remains scrunched, and I sob.

Then I breathe.

I'd forgotten to. And with each intake of oxygen, I become calmer and calmer.

The truck doors open, and I hear people getting in, taking their seats. Several people join me in the back, but I keep looking at the side of the truck, too embarrassed to speak to any of them.

I feel an arm wrap around my waist. A body slides in behind me and holds me tight. It's Doc. I can tell by her hand, her scent, her presence. For a long time, I forget my confusion about us. I forget about Six and Cherish and all those questions I have. I forget about everyone else in this truck and whole Realm.

I enjoy the simple comfort of lying, with my eyes closed, being held close in the arms of someone warm and caring and who seems to like me.

FROM THE AUDIO DIARY OF
E820906. ENTRY 10.

It's incredible how our bodies adapt. Long term use of any drug, followed by abstinence, always results in withdrawal symptoms. Famously, our world was once addicted to nicotine from cancer-causing cigarettes, and it was claimed that this was one of the hardest to give up because the withdrawal symptoms were so severe. Well, let's just say my withdrawal was quite the opposite. Yes, there were the headaches, and the mood swings, even the aggression and the odd relapse where I'd return to eating my gruel just for a tiny hit, but the emotional expansion was the greatest compensation I could have imagined. It's like I had lived my whole life with an emotion spectrum of about 10% of what it is now. I was able to think more freely, to make my own clear opinions, to question what we were learning and to look at our Realm, our society, as a whole. I didn't like what I found.

CHAPTER 23
LEECHES

I pretend to sleep for several hours.

Doc left me once I stopped shaking. Unfortunately, the truck has not stopped friggin' shaking. The 'road' we've taken clearly isn't the smoothest. Still, it beats hiking the whole way.

I've been listening to the odd bit of chatter from the others. They decided to bring the Guardian with us, despite Bulk's loud objections.

More sweat drips from my forehead. I need a break, to cool down and to move from this position. I spin round to face the others, cramped together in the back of the truck, clearly designed for half this number of people.

I count them: Miller, Doc, Three, Bulk. Eagle must be up front, driving. Plus me. That's six of us. And one Guardian, tied up with the boxes at the back.

Five faces look at me, some scowling, others wide eyed and worried, but the worst is Miller, who simply looks away.

'Hey.' It's all I manage. A grand apology was supposed to spring from me, but it just didn't come out.

Miller gets up and joins Eagle in the front of the truck, pulling the curtain that separates the cabin from the back, closed with a snap.

'I probably deserved that.' I look at Doc, who nods.

'We just heard, there's something big happening down at Westmine. All sorts of orders coming through on the screen. We think it means the Exiles have finally cracked and are fighting back.'

'So, we don't have to go then, do we? We can go back and help Six?' I keep my eyes away from Doc as I say it.

'No,' says Bulk. 'We are going directly there now. Quick-like.'

'Great. Just great.' I'm almost done caring. Perhaps some fighting would be good. Get some of this frustration out of my system.

'But we won't take anyone who doesn't want to,' the big man adds. 'We can drop you at the settlement in Westpool?'

I don't answer. I'm not interested in his baiting.

'How far away are we?'

'A couple of hours maybe. It may take longer as we'll be taking a diversion. We'll get there and we'll make a difference.' Bulk looks far from excited though. For a big unit, genetically engineered to be a fighter, he doesn't seem to love it.

Three, however, is polishing a new rifle, stolen from the stash in the truck. The weak kid from camp, who didn't believe in fighting.

THUMP.

'What was that?' Doc shouts.

'We hit something,' Miller says, popping his head back from the front seat. 'Maybe an animal. Better check it out to be sure.'

'I'll do it,' says Doc. She leaves and Three goes with her.

The cool air flows in and I shiver. I enjoy it for a moment, the clean oxygen waking me up. But after a while I start to shiver.

'Close that door,' says Bulk. 'Cold-like.'

I get up and start pulling it. Then I see people. Running. Fast.

'Hey, check this out. There's more Exiles out here.'

'They ain't no Exiles, they're leeches. Scutting cannibals! DOC,

THREE, get back in here, now.' Bulk loads his rifle. 'Eagle, check your mirrors, we need to move. Quick-like.'

I hear the engine starting, but Doc is still outside. So is Three.

I jump out and see him standing over a body in the bushes.

He looks up at me. 'We killed her. Look.' A young girl lies dead at his feet. That's what we hit.

'Doc, get in the truck. We need to go. Look over there,' I shout across to her. She's wandered off to pick some quenchberries.

She gazes in the direction of the newcomers and her eyes widen. 'Leeches.' She sprints towards the truck.

Three jumps back inside and tries to pull the door closed.

'What you doing?' I say. 'Doc's still out there.'

I open the door fully and run out. She's still too far away. I won't get to her and back before this mob arrives.

'We need to drive to her,' I say, turning to face my friends inside the truck.

'Seven, they are Leeches. They'll cook you, eat you and kill you. In that order. We are leaving.' Miller says it with enough authority I almost obey.

The Leeches are now screaming. They carry an assortment of weapons. Many blades, thick sticks, and ropes. They are less than 100 metres, now. Some of them have broken off from the main group and run directly to Doc. It's going to be close.

'Seven, we need to go. She'd do the same in our position.'

'Wait,' I say. 'Give her a chance.'

I stand with one foot in the truck and the other out. Hopefully they won't leave until I'm inside. Come on, Doc. Quicker.

Fifty metres.

Forty.

Thirty. She won't make it.

Twenty.

'Get in, Seven. Eagle, get us away from here.'

BANG.

Bulk is firing.

BANG. BANG.

So is Three.

I remain half in, half out.

Ten metres. Bulk grabs me and hauls me inside. Gun shots go past my head, felling the closest Leeches, but more come, like ants flooding towards their prey.

Then Doc is just there. Two metres from the door. I reach out and grab her hand. I clutch Doc's hand, while Bulk holds me. Several Leeches grab Doc and pull. I grip as hard as I can, but her hand's wet and she's slipping.

Her fingers slide out of my hand, and she screams. The Leeches continue to try to get into the truck. It starts moving forward.

'No wait,' I say, but I can't move. Bulk has me. Shots fly past us.

One or two leap into the still open door of the truck, but Bulk quickly boots them out and Three loosens several rounds of bullets into them. They slam onto the ground. Finally, Bulk slams the door shut.

'We can't leave her,' I say. Thumps continue on the roof. They must have climbed on top. Three and Bulk shoot upwards, holes appearing where the bullets penetrate the ceiling.

I can't stand it. I can't let Doc be taken by the Leeches.

I open the truck door and throw myself out, landing on my feet but falling sideways onto my shoulder.

'Seven, no!' It's Bulk's voice. But it's cut off by the slam of the door. The truck continues to speed off. I glance up and see several Leeches still attached. Gunshots continue to smash upwards.

I pick myself up, my shoulder throbbing, back burning with agony again. A large group of Leeches, maybe about thirty, are standing in a circle. Obviously, that's where Doc is.

I sprint towards the group. A few stray Leeches come for me. The adrenaline and fury swimming inside my muscles amplifies every blow, and I hit several of them so hard, I might have killed them. I don't feel any guilt. *Be strong.*

As I approach the larger group, there are shouts and many of them break off and charge me. At least ten of them. Some of my fury is morphing into panic now. What good can I do here? Bulk was right, but I've gotta try. How could I live with myself, knowing I left Doc with a mob of Leeches?

The struggle is brief. They are strong, despite their slim, malnourished bodies. Knuckled fist after knuckled fist comes raining down upon my body. I try to close off the agony, but it's impossible.

I want it to end, but they keep going.

Finally, when I think I'm nearly dead, my eyes close and the pain vanishes.

FROM THE AUDIO DIARY OF
E820906. ENTRY 11.

When I was younger, I had an unflinching belief that I would become a top Academic with the Realm, and my work would help advance the fields of genomics and medicine. The more I studied, the greater my interest became. First, it was Biology and Chemistry, next it was Cellular Biology, and finally I got to genomics. I think the main thing that drew me in that direction was meeting Seven. His fascination with finding his parents was so compelling that I wanted to help. I wanted to pay him back for what he did with Rex. But, on top of all of that, I was still wrapped in the Autokratōr's romantic vision of a genetic disorder-free world. If I could contribute anything that would help save the lives of people, I would do it. It was only towards the end of my time as a Greenhorn that I began to question the real purpose of the Autokratōr's interest in genetic modification.

CHAPTER 24
LEECHES LUNCH

Upside down, the world is.

Every part of my body aches. I try closing my eyes, try becoming unconscious again, but it won't happen. My head is so swollen with blood, I can hardly think. My naked body is sweating from the heat of the fire and probably from the mass swellings, like everywhere where they beat me. Man, I hate being naked. But sweating naked and hanging upside down is up there with the worst thing I could imagine.

Two huge fires are visible, and many people, singing and dancing. The music lovely and soothing, the lyrics sweet and poetic. There's also the steady sound of fast-running water, like a river or more like a waterfall. If I wasn't terrified for my life, I'd find it nice.

A punch to my stomach makes me vomit. Puke slides up my nose and into my eyes as it squirts from my mouth. I spit and spit until I get most of it out, but some sticks at the top of my throat and in my nose, gravity defying my efforts to dispel it.

'That's it; get all the horrible stuff outta yae. Keen for a slice of you, we is. Slug, we gots one awake, nows.'

'Fressssssshhhhh blood. Mmmmmm. I'll lick and suck the blood from this one, yes I will.'

I feel the tongue of the Leech on my back, licking my open

wounds. I hope they're infected. I hope they're overloaded with disease, and it's kills every last one of these scuts.

'Get off me,' I shout, squirming in the ropes that bind me. I can't move my legs, which are tied tightly above my head, but my arms are looser. But not loose enough to even contemplate escape.

'Stay still, little meat. I is a-licking you good.' I continue to struggle, so a fist smacks my head.

I spin, literally, and I'm so dizzy I spew again. This time very little comes out. Acid. Bile. I spit and spit. I keep my eyes firmly closed, hoping I'll wake up, but I don't.

At least the licking has stopped, and they appear to have gone.

How are you getting out of this one, Seven?

Looking up, I see we're tied to a long branch. Maybe I can break it, but it's too thick where I'm tied. It's a bit thinner further along. So, as I spin, I also swing, moving inch by inch along the branch, closer to Doc. If we can put our combined weight through the same, thinner point on the branch, maybe it will break.

It's silent for several minutes before I stop spinning. I'm not sure if it's just in my head or whether I spun that whole time, but now I'm still I can see Doc properly. Next to me. Unmoving. Naked. I avoid looking at her body.

'Hey, Doc? Doc?' I say. Nothing. 'Doc?'

Her body jerks. 'Seven?'

'Yeah, it's me. Try and get out of your ropes. They're going to eat us. Hurry.'

I watch her struggle, but they clearly know their knots. She's as securely tied as I am.

'No good. I can't.'

'Try shaking the branch. Maybe we can snap it.'

She nods and we both do our best to struggle and put as much force through the wood as a possible. Nothing. It's too strong, even for our shared weight. We need more force.

One of the Leeches approaches.

'Ah, awake we are, yes?' She turns. 'Pan, they're awake. Dinner time.'

Pan limps over. He has a large chunk bitten of out his right arm. But I can see why they don't eat each other. They've no fat on their bodies at all, and very little muscle. His hair falls in long strands in some parts, but in others it's completely bald, like he's ripped it out.

Pan stops in front of Doc, staring at her naked body with his gaunt, black eyes. Drool falls from his mouth.

'Stop it. Oi, stop it.' I shout at the Leeches. 'You're sick, you know that? Sick! Stop looking at her like that.'

The first Leech, Slug I think she's called, turns to me. 'Let's us have a wee tasties of this one, yes? Snackies before dinner.' She pulls out a small sharp piece of metal.

'Pan, come hold while I gets the juice out.'

The other Leech stops staring at Doc and moves behind me, before bear hugging me round the middle. The only part of my body not tied up.

'Now, we's play, yes we does. We plays and gets fressssshhhhh juice.'

While Pan holds me, Slug moves her knife to my thighs and slices. Blood squirts from the wound and Slug's mouth clamps over the cut, her throat moving like she's drinking. She makes noises of enjoyment, while Pan continues to grip me hard.

I jerk and thrash but I'm locked in place, forced to suffer. I try to ignore the sharp pain on the wounds, the wretched touch of Slug's mouth.

She starts cutting my other leg and sucks at that wound for a while, before swapping roles with Pan. He kneels and cuts just above my hip, once more latching onto the slash and sucking. It's disgusting me, but as long as they don't go near Doc. They better not do that.

As Pan drains the 'juice' from me, I alternate between struggling hard and falling limp. It's hopeless; they're too good at this to have given us a chance at escape. Behind me, Slug is laughing and whispering horrible things as the nightmare continues.

I want to shout out, to taunt the Leeches and make them stay on me, but I can't stomach it. I have to force myself to take it.

They've swapped again and Pan holds me, but his eyes are now fixed on Doc. I can't hold my tongue anymore.

'Stop looking at her like that, you sick scut!'

The Leech releases me. He moves closer to my face. Slug is too busy drinking to take notice.

'Little meat talks bad to me. He thinks I am a bad man. Girl meat will taste good as you watch, yes it will.'

'Come here,' I whisper.

'Whats?'

'Come here.' I say it so quietly he needs to move his head closer to mine. I deliberately hiss a few words as quiet as I can manage. His head is next to mine and turns his ear to my mouth to hear.

'Whats?'

With all my energy and momentum, I swing my head and smash our skulls together. It's such a loud collision, that I hear the clash of bone. The pain that follows blinds me. My eyes are firmly closed as blood from my forehead streams through my scalp. It soaks my hair and I start losing consciousness. I open my eyes; I try to remain present, focusing on what will happen if I pass out. I need to distract them for as long as I can.

'Bad meat. Bad meat.' Pan lies on the ground, clutching his skull, swearing, and pounding the ground with his fist.

Slug, who fell to the ground in the commotion too, gets to her feet and moves close to me.

'Stupid Pan. Stupids. Never get too close to the head. That's what the Master says. Yes, she does. Never close to the head.'

She walks round me several times. I don't close my eyes, despite my head feeling like it's been cleaved open. The ferrous smell makes me nauseous, but I focus on staying alert.

'Let's getting slicing, Pan. I ain't thirsty no more, but the flessssshhhhh. Yes, the flesh is firm in this one. Let's get a-cutting.'

I watch Pan get to his feet. He also has a stream of blood down the side of his head. He looks dizzy, unstable. Slug hands him the sharp metal.

'Chunks,' she says. Pan nods, then smiles.

'STTTTTOOOOOOOPPPPPPPP!' I scream it so loud I nearly faint from the effort. I can't let them do this without some kind of resistance and my voice is all I have left.

The music stops. The singing dies. The Leeches approach. Thirty or more, old and young people, male and female. How have they got this way? They were probably all Greenies like me at one point. Most of them are skeletal, but one towers over them all. She's as big as Bulk. She must be GM, too. She seems very well fed, muscular and has a full head of hair. Less crazed looking than the rest of the Leeches, most of whom are covered in scars, have large patches of hair missing, as well as chunks of flesh absent.

She steps forward, looks at the two of us, then at Slug and Pan. Every Leech is looking downward. They respect her. She must be Master.

'I see two of our number have decided to get started early, without the rest of us. How selfish of them, how greedy. You know the rules. Bring me a bucket.'

A Leech runs beyond the fire and returns with a large, clear container, which is placed just at the feet of the Master.

Pan and Slug slouch back towards it. They both kneel over the container and place their fingers into their throats. Making themselves vomit.

A large volume of the blood, leeched from me, is spewed into the container. They both continue to bring up the liquid until they've got it all out of them. The sight makes me feel sick. I'm glad my stomach was already empty.

'Good, that blood is to be shared.' She nods to Slug and Pan who move away from the Master and the container.

'My children, tonight we have a feast. It's a long time since we had fresh, well-nourished people to eat. As always, the right to first bite is open. Step forth, worthy candidates.'

She moves back into the shadows beyond the fire and seems to disappear.

Once she's gone, they lift their heads and focus on us.

One of the Leeches comes close to me, his cracked, thin lips licked by his slim, black tongue. 'I first with him.' He turns around. The other Leeches seem afraid and remain silent. 'Good. Firsties.'

Then one of the other Leeches attacks Black Tongue. It's Slug. I watch them viciously punch, kick and bite each other for several minutes. Both Leeches are covered in thick, running dark blood. The other Leeches look on, drooling.

Black Tongue attacks and knocks Slug to the ground, then sinks his teeth into her neck. The scream would rent the air for a million metres, all around.

When the screaming stops, Slug becomes still. Black Tongue stands, his mouth overflowing with blood. 'My brothers and sisters, we has three now. I has this one. Slug is your appetiser. Dig in.'

The Leeches leap towards their newly killed compatriot, fighting each other to tear a chunk of flesh.

I'm ready to die. If I could, I'd kill myself rather than let this happen to me. And Doc, how could this happen to her.

Black Tongue looks at us, weighing it up. He moves towards Doc. 'Young flessssssshhhhhh. Yes, young and tenders.'

'No, me first. You wanted me first.'

I watch his head flick to me, then back to Doc. Then he moves towards me.

'Yes, I have delicious blood. Me first. The girl last.'

'You's all get eats. Orders doesn't matter to me's. No. It don't matters.'

He circles, and when he is behind me, I feel him stroking my back. I jerk and writhe, which earns me another punch.

'Hold him.'

Two of the Leeches grab either side of me. With the ropes binding me, they don't have to hold me too tight, but they do anyway, their filthy nails breaking the skin.

The nauseating feeling of his tongue on my back makes me thrash again, but I'm held so tight, it's pointless. He moves up my back and when he reaches my bum, I feel teeth. Biting. Hard. Tearing the flesh. I try everything, but I'm not getting out of this.

This is my end. How I die. At the hands of cannibals, trying to save Doc. Is this being *strong*? Is this *living for a better tomorrow*?

And as I thrash for my life, there's a loud snap, and I fall to the ground.

The branch finally snapped. I glance over at Doc, also on the ground now, but barely moving. The Leeches have all jumped backwards, shocked, and I don't waste a second, sliding my hands and feet out of the now-loose rope, and standing upright.

The world spins, and my legs are unsteady. I can't fall over. I must stand. I must fight our way out of here.

But the tiny delay as I orient myself again is enough for the Leeches to close in again. They don't look very strong, but they have way more numbers. Beside me, Doc moves close, also trying to get to her feet.

'Don't worry,' I say, lying. 'I'll get us out of this.'

I pick up the broken branch that we'd been tied to and hold it like a quarterstaff.

'I'll make a gap, and you run through it, and don't stop, okay?'

Doc nods. 'And you'll follow.'

'If I can, I'll be right on your tail.' I know I'm not strong enough to fight and outrun them right now. But I can maybe do enough to let Doc get away.

A quick glance and I notice that there's fewer of them behind us, so that's where I charge, swinging the branch wildly, and knocking two of them over, creating a small gap. And Doc sprints through it. But the Leeches are quick to respond and being sprinting back and forth, knocking over anyone who goes in the same direction as Doc.

After a few seconds, they must realise they're not faster or stronger than me, individually, even like this. They begin to group together and move quickly towards me, leaving Doc for now.

Good. I side-step away from them, edging away from the direction that Doc ran. And then I notice something on the ground, glinting in the firelight. Slug's knife.

I jerk down and grab it, as one Leech leaps for me. But I stab the blade through their arm, and they dive back, howling in pain.

It's only a matter of time before they all come for me at once.

I glance around, trying to decide the best way to go, when I'm aware of the running water again. The noise is coming from behind, so I continue to back away, using the branch and knife to deter anyone who gets too close.

The water sounds close now, but it's very dark and I'm struggling to see the Leeches as we get further from the fire.

I glance around, hoping I'll see the river, but instead I see a massive precipice and a huge drop. There is water, which I can just about see in the reflection of the moonlight, but it's a long way down.

The Leeches must realise what I'm about to do.

So they charge.

And I jump.

Thin hands grab my arms and legs and pull me under the water.

The rapids are carrying us downstream fast, but several of them followed me off the cliff, clearly so desperately hungry, they'd risk their life to follow me.

I kick and thrash and do all I can, but their sharp nails and teeth are digging in all over my body.

But I have one advantage over them. I've trained for years to swim and hold my breath under water. So I go limp, and let myself fall further below the surface of the fast-moving river.

They'll need to breathe before me, or at least that's what I'm banking my whole life on!

They try to pull me up to surface but I push back down, and one by one I feel their grip loosen on me, then eventually disappear.

I'm heading towards my own limit on air, the lungs starting to screech, so I come up and take a breath, scanning the river and the banks for any sign of pursuit.

Several are running alongside the river, but the current is hurling me away from them faster than they can surely run.

There's also a couple in the water behind me, I know I have the advantage if they come at me again.

When I've lost the Leeches on land, I decide to lose the ones in the water with me. As we turn a corner, the high banks make this spot really dark, so I push myself under, reaching out to grab absolutely anything that will stop me.

I claw my hand around a large rock and bring the other hand around to hold tight. If I stay here for a minute or so, they'll simply float past me.

Then I just need to get away from those on foot.

I try to shut down my mind, the old calming technique I was once taught, simply counting the seconds in my head until I reach sixty.

Then I push myself back up and manage to scramble to the side of the river, and slowly haul myself out.

I lie for a moment, gasping and staring up at the moon. It's a blood moon tonight. Six used to teach me all about the night sky when we'd sneak out. The phases of the moon, the transit of the planets, the constellations of stars.

Maybe one day she'll be able to talk me through it again.

But first I need to find Doc and the others. I've no idea how far downstream I've come, so I head up the bank, away from the edge, and start walking back up stream.

At one point, I see the pursuing Leeches run alongside the river, but they've slowed and decide to turn around eventually, meaning I have to stray further from the river.

I limp through the darkness, taking cover in the trees wherever possible, heading in the general direction of where I think Doc ran.

I'm shivering hard now, my legs and head becoming heavy, and I'm not sure how much further I can go.

'Young flesssssssshhhhhh.'

The voice completely freezes my already cold skin. Every system in my body responds like I'm under attack, and I whip around to see twenty Leeches coming towards me.

'Found you, we has. Yessssss. And dinner will not get away this time.' It's Black Tongue.

I lost my weapons in the river, so I literally have no defence. I don't even have any clothes, but I won't get taken without a fight.

I tense myself, ready for a final battle.

BANG.

The Leeches shout.

BANG. BANG. BANG.

Gunshots desecrate the air. I see several Leeches fall in the flurry of gunfire. They turn and run but more of them fall than escape. The shots come from behind me, so I can't see who it is, but I don't care anymore.

Every atom in me is hurting badly. They bit off some large chunks of flesh earlier.

Two shadows fly past me, pursuing the fleeing Leeches. They disappear beyond my vision and several hands land on my bare flesh.

I thrash hard. 'Get your scutting hands off me.'

'Hey, Seven. It's us.' Three's voice.

My heart slows, relief flooding in. But pain amplifies, like that part of my nervous system has just switched on, now the immediate danger has passed.

'Here.' Doc hands me a blanket and I quickly cover up. She kneels next to me, with fresh clothes on. She must have found the others and brought them after me. 'Anything serious hurt?'

'I'm so glad you got away,' I say.

She gives me a hard stare. 'Why didn't you run with me, like you promised. You look really beaten up.'

'Don't worry I won't die. Are you okay?'

She nods. 'I'm fine. It's you we need to help.'

The shock of what just happened, and what could have happened, are still too recent to do anything but be grateful we're alive and uneaten. Although now *everyone* has seen me naked. If Miller makes even one joke...

I hoped they might come back for me, but never dared believe it.

I place my hand on my glute, and I feel a chunk of flesh, still intact, but torn badly and bleeding.

'How did you find me?' I ask.

'Once we lost the Leeches, we decided we had to come and rescue you,' Three explains. 'We were almost at their camp when Doc came running right at us, followed by a couple of those Leeches. We got to their camp and most of them had gone after you. But the few that were left told us what happened and that they'd chased you downstream, so here we are.'

'They just told you where to find me?'

'Well, let's just say we were *very* persuasive.'

I don't want to ask them what they did to persuade them. All I care about is that Doc and me are alive.

'Doc told us you got her out of there. Very impressive,' says Three.

'Yeah, you're not totally useless,' adds Miller.

I shrug.

'You getting all humble on us, Chosen One?' Three says, laughing. Even Miller chuckles.

I lie on my back, and I thank them all in my head. As I press the loose flesh on my glute back into place, the pain, the terror, the ordeal, and the blood loss take their toll and my eyes slip shut.

FROM THE AUDIO DIARY OF
E820906. ENTRY 12.

Hail the Autokratōr. Serve the Realm. I must have said that thousands of times. Well, now I've met the Autokratōr, I say screw him and his Realm. I turned my back on them both when Seven was forced to shoot Cherish. When they held a gun to my head to make him do it. And yet again, they think they're going to use me to get him. But they won't. I'm too strong for them.

CHAPTER 25
THE STORM BEFORE THE CALM

For the first time in an eternity, I try to calm and clear my mind, as tut truck moves along towards Westmine.

Twelve hours have passed since I escaped the Leeches and my friends rescued me. Doc sewed my butt cheek, and that was scutting uncomfortable, in all sorts of ways. Then we slept for a bit, and got into the truck, ready to drive to our destinies.

I'm dressed in Guardian issue whites, stolen with the supplies from the truck we hijacked. This is not how I imagined it would be all those times I daydreamed. I study the uniform I once desired more than anything else and shake my head. I was so naïve then. I'm still naïve, charging after Leeches like I'm invincible. My tender body reminds me I'm not.

Most of my skin is purple, swollen, and sore to touch. My back has a fresh layer of antiseptic on it, and it stings worse than a hundred bees. But the external trauma is nothing compared with what I've just experienced. Doc has given me an IV drip, and says I'll be all right...physically. She rests her head on my shoulder. What must she be thinking after seeing all of that? I'll never forget it, so how will she?

So many questions go through my mind about the Leeches – how did they get like that? They must have just been normal Greenies like me at one time. And now they're cannibals who do all sorts of sick shit. The way they sucked blood and seemed to enjoy it so much, makes me think of that story Cherish told me about vampires and zombies, and how many books and films there were about them. Maybe they are real.

I don't like where my mind is going, so I use the old technique a Guru taught me back in camp. Breathe in, hold for three. Breathe out. Think only of your breathing and nothing else. Empty all thoughts.

My heart slows, chest swelling and falling, brain relaxing.

I refocus my thoughts to the tasks ahead. I can't keep looking back. We need to get to Westmine, we need to free and stir a rebellion in all those Nameless people who work for the Realm, in horrible conditions, mining their precious metals. But how do we do that?

But first things first – we need to get there. Safely. It's been a heck of a ride so far.

As our truck moves along, my mind fills again, and I think about Malt, Lasul and Cherish. About them, the good people they are. Were. And what each of them has sacrificed for me. They will never reach Westmine. They will never see the rise of the Orphans, standing up to the Realm they've plotted against for so long.

Cherish, watching over me during my childhood, putting up with an extremely stubborn, impulsive, and emotional kid. I was one of the worst and yet she always dealt with me with extreme patience. She gave up her life to act as my mother and paid the maximum price. For me.

Lasul, Malt and all those other Exiles who rescued us, took us in, even though it meant the destruction of their home and cost some of them their lives. The image of Lasul falling to the ground, as I watched and did nothing, flashes through my head as a constant reminder. My Realm instructors would have praised me for doing nothing, evading capture. But I know now that no Exile would have let him be shot. They would have shouted from the building. Sacrificed themselves to save the life of another. They are called the Nameless. Exiles. Outcasts of the Realm. But they are more human than any of the genetically advantaged citizens of the Realm. The encounter with the Leeches has shown me just how bad they could be. But they are not. They have an emotional understanding of what it is to be human and a greater grasp of the purpose of humanity than anyone within the Realm could ever understand.

I didn't understand. For a long time. I fought the instinct in my brain that told me this for so long. I nearly died trying to help Doc. Hell, I nearly got eaten, but at least I did the right thing. But I don't think that's what Cherish meant. A better tomorrow is about seeing past yourself and doing things for other people. It's what she did. It's a hard thing to accept, that there are bigger things in the world than yourself. That everything you do is insignificant, but that it's super important you do it, anyway. Cherish used to always say that to me, though until now I've never fully understood it.

But I think I'm there. I'm ready to be the strong person Cherish wanted me to be.

I will *live for a better tomorrow*.

'Hey, you okay?' asks Doc. She gives me a gentle shake.

'Yeah, sorry. Zoned out there.'

'How you feeling?'

'Pretty crunk.' I smile.

'No wonder. And now Westmine. It seems so unending.'

I nod. I wish I had more time to rest. My head is throbbing.

'You nervous?'

'No.' My stomach flips and I nearly vomit, but I swallow the small amount of liquid that comes up.

'Me neither.' She grabs my hand and holds it real tight.

I look at her, directly in the eyes this time. It's there, beyond the surface. That humanity, that compassion, that emotion that's missing from most of the people I'd known before.

'I know what I have to do,' I say, keeping my gaze fixed upon her.

She smiles. 'Good.' She squeezes tighter, and then sits back against the box behind us. 'I knew you'd get there.'

'How do you put up with me?'

'Seven, don't be so tough on yourself. You've been through some awful stuff in the last few days. I remember how tough it was for me to adjust after I was exiled. We all need a little time, and you never really got it.'

'Thanks.' I squeeze her hand back.

Then Six pops into my head, and my stomach does a triple somersault. No, I can't do this to myself. One thing at a time. Get through this rebellion, or whatever it is, then think about her. There's nothing I can do. It won't help to get killed because I'm thinking of her.

Bulk's reading his book again. 'Hey, Bulk. What you reading?'

'A book Lasul gave me.'

'What's it called?'

'You won't know it. It's very old.'

'Try me.'

'It's called the BFG. It was written by some dude called Roald Dahl.'

'Never heard of it.'

'Told you.'

'Well, what's it about?'

'I'll let you read it some time. Don't want to spoil it for you.'

Bulk hands out the weapons. 'It's time.'

Shiny, new Realm-issue rifles are held in the hands of everyone in the back of the truck.

'What's the plan?' I ask.

'No plan,' says Bulk. 'We have no idea what's happening there. We'll just have to think as we go. The key is to stick together. Fight

215

as a group. Together-like. There's a cloud of dark smoke in the sky ahead, so who knows what's going on.'

I climb into the front seat, beside Eagle, wincing with the pain. She nods and continues to look straight ahead. Through the muddy windscreen I can see the billowing stream of smoke coming from a point a couple of miles ahead. Not long now.

I press my right hand onto the dashboard to stop it shaking. I can't believe I spent all those hours daydreaming about fighting alongside Sharan on the Eurasian front. I clearly knew nothing of the real world back then.

Just ahead, a small wooden hut sits beside the rough road. A white barrier crosses our path, and two Guardians stand with their rifles on their shoulders, watching us approach. They'll think we're just bringing supplies.

'Eagle, slow down and approach normally,' I say. My voice is steady, somehow, hiding how I'm feeling inside. 'Then when I say, speed right up and drive straight through the barrier. We'll stay in the front here, so they don't suspect anything. The rest of you...' I turn to address those in the back. '...will jump out the back as we accelerate and take out those Guardians. Real slick-like, as Bulk would say.'

Bulk winks at me, but his hands also shake. This is what he was bred to do.

'I'm afraid it's now the time where we must start killing. All of us.' He looks to me and then disappears into the back.

I focus straight ahead, the Guardians move to the right of the barrier, but the guns are held loosely at their sides. They don't suspect anything. I hope they don't recognise us.

Eagle slows as we approach the Guardians. One of them moves closer to the road to speak to us. But just at the point where Eagle should stop, she hits the accelerator.

I hear shouts, then we smash through the wooden barrier. Then come gunshots. I look in the side mirror, trying to see, but they're all muddied.

BANG.

The front of the truck lifts into the air. Broken shards of glass fly into my face and I lurch backwards banging my skull off the headrest. The truck continues to flip. Time seems to slow, and we rotate while the truck also rises. We're upside down when we smash into the ground.

Another blow to the head.

On the edge of consciousness, I take a deep breath, trying to stay awake.

Blood runs up my face.

Petrol sprays in where the windscreen once was.

I smell smoke.

FROM THE AUDIO DIARY OF
E820906. ENTRY 13.

Torture is torture is torture is torture...

CHAPTER 26
CRASH

I wake up knowing two things.

My body is in widespread agony and I'm no longer in the truck.

The ground beneath me is damp and yielding. Before I try moving my aching body, I listen. The crackle of fire. Soft, squelching steps. The smell of petrol.

I open my eyes and see a dull sky, with drops of rain falling to the ground. One hits my forehead and runs into my right eye. The sting tells me my old cut has reopened.

'Ah, you're awake. Finally.'

I turn my head to the right, real slow, each inch hurting. Doc kneels next to Eagle, who lies on her back, unconscious.

She smiles at me as she places a bundle of rags under Eagle's head. 'You probably have a concussion. Some whiplash as well. Your neck's gonna hurt pretty bad for a few days, and you might feel sick for a while, but you'll live.'

I grimace when I try to smile. Too much. 'Ta.' It's all I manage.

I roll my eyes towards Eagle.

Doc looks down at our mute friend, taking a few seconds before answering. 'She's lost a bit of blood. I've patched her up and stopped the bleeding but she's so pale and cold. She's as tough as they come, though. If anyone could recover, it would be her.'

Doc pulls a sponge from a bucket and squeezes it gently over Eagle's mouth; small droplets of water rolling onto her cracked lips and into her partially open mouth. Her neck and cheek muscles move to swallow. That's a good sign.

A few moments pass, and I try to move my head a little more. *Bad idea,* my neck yells.

'Take it easy,' says Doc. 'Here, I'll help you sit up a little if you want. But take it slow and don't jerk.'

She places one hand on my back, the other on my head and slowly I use my arms to push myself up into a sitting position.

'There you go. Small movements only but keep it moving. It will recover quicker that way.'

'Thanks, Doc. Glad you're around. Seriously.' I finally manage a small smile.

'No problem. Didn't have much choice, did I? You guys decided to drive right over a land mine and nearly kill yourselves. Someone had to stay and take care of you.'

'Where are the others?'

'Gone to Westmine. They could all walk, so we figured they should go. Look, you can see the smoke is still rising. We're late, but they must still be fighting, even now.'

'How long was I out?' I ask.

'A few hours. You kind of woke up earlier, but you fell back asleep.'

'How did we get out the truck? I remember being upside down. The petrol was everywhere.'

'Bulk and Three got you both out. And only just in time. The truck exploded not long after. You were very lucky.'

'Yeah, lucky we hang around with a freakishly strong guy. I'll give the big man a kiss next time I see him.'

'How about giving me one?' She leans in close, her eyes partly closed, like she isn't sure if I'll kiss back.

But I do. For a while. It's not the most comfortable kiss ever. Hardly passionate, but I'm not even sure how that would go. After about twenty seconds, Doc pulls away, a huge smile on her beautiful face.

'You're welcome,' she says, before scurrying back over to Eagle.

I lie back for a moment, enjoying the feeling of being alive. I was close to being a goner. So close. Several times. But I'm still here and I had better appreciate these small moments, because with all that other scary crunk going on around us, I might not be in peace for very long.

I turn to check on Eagle. Still pale. Still asleep. Her clothes are covered in darkened blood. Her bare arms are exposed, and I see goose bumps on her skin. I slowly get up and walk over to the remains of the truck. Flames still flicker from the cabin at the front.

'Hey, get back down and rest.'

'I'm fine,' I call over my shoulder.

'Careful, then.'

Every step feels like I'm using my bruised muscles for the first time in weeks. I nearly stop at one point but force myself through it. Concussion and whiplash are nothing, really. Not compared to what happened to Eagle.

I get to the burnt-out truck and look at the remains of the cargo in the back. Most of it is burnt. I do manage to find one large blanket, dull grey and itchy looking, but it'll be warm.

I amble back to Eagle and place the blanket over her frail, cold body. Doc gives me a smile that warms me all over, despite the temperature. I sit back down, right next to her and Eagle.

'So, I guess we're to wait here, then?' I ask.

'No, we are to wait as long as is necessary and then get the hell out of here. Find some cover and wait.'

'Why? The fighting is kilometres away, we'll be safe here, wont we?'

'Only if we win. If not, Guardians will be coming back along this road in large numbers. Or even worse, perhaps more Guardians will arrive from New London. I'm not sure where their nearest rural base is, or whether they will even send anyone, but we can't take any risks. And there might be Leeches out here for all I know.'

I nod. That makes sense. We are pretty exposed, sitting here at the side of a main road into the Westmine district. And I never want to see another Leech in my life. If I do, my no-kill rule is done.

'How long before we can move her?' I ask.

'Well, *you* certainly can't move her yet, even if she wasn't so weak.'

I raise my eyebrows. 'Wanna bet?'

'Anyway, we need to wait a few hours. You'll be stronger by then. And so will Eagle, hopefully.'

She gives me a lifeless smile. 'You had better get some food in you and get your strength up. I will need you to help with Eagle, in all seriousness. It's over there.' She points to a blackened box.

I find many burnt packets, most of which contain inedible food. But some of the ones at the bottom are okay inside, so I pick out the best ones and return to Doc's side.

'Here you go.' I hand her some dried fruit. I put some of the stuff into my mouth. It's like heaven compared to our old camp gruel and the awful mushrooms we've been eating since we've been on the run. The sugar inside almost immediately has an effect on me. I feel stronger and more alert. The pain dulls slightly.

I eat three packs before I feel queasy and stop, taking on some water to wash it down. I go back to the truck and bring over two more blankets. If I'd been clever, I'd have just brought one back, but I give her one and wrap my own around my shoulders and sit in the rain watching her tend to Eagle.

My stomach is heavy and bloated, my throbbing body glad of the rest. I pull my blanket over me. The surface is wet, but it's waterproof, unlike my clothes.

As the night passes, I stare down at the one spot of light in the periphery, where Doc sits treating Eagle. I've been through so much with them. Eagle has saved me. Doc, too. I hope I will get the chance to repay them.

Sated and sleepy, I drift off in the damp grass.

'Get up.'

I open my eyes. Doc. Eagle. Smiles.

I get to my feet; Bulk would say slow-like. I rub my face and try to wake up.

'Nice sleep?' Doc asks.

'Oh, I just closed my eyes for a moment,' I keep my head down.

'Whatever. Lucky for you, nobody passed in the night. And Eagle is much better, but still needs to take it easy.' Doc gives Eagle wide eyes.

'You can't half recover quickly, Eagle,' I say, rubbing her bare, cold arm. 'And even if Doc has already said it, I want to say thanks for saving us. Again.'

She nods and walks towards the road.

'You okay?' Doc asks me.

'Yeah, I feel great. Well not great, but better. My headache has gone. I slept for quite a while to be honest.'

'Lucky you, I didn't sleep a wink. But Eagle is much better, which is the main thing. She heals like no one I've ever seen before. It's crazy, almost unreal.'

'Do you think it's a genetic enhancement?'

'I don't know. It's like all her body processes are accelerated, her metabolism and healing, especially. I've never had to treat her before, so I never quite realised.'

'Well, whatever it is, I am glad she's on our side,' I say. 'Imagine if all Guardians were like her. We'd be long dead.'

We start walking after Eagle, who's already put some distance between us. The pre-dawn glow illuminates the landscape, small crystals of dew covering the countryside. It's strange to think that such a beautiful day could occur after all the awfulness that has come before.

'Where are we going?' Doc asks.

'Westmine. We need to see what has happened, even if we are too late to help,' I reply. 'Hopefully there's still something to fight for.'

She clasps my hand as we walk on, and I warm a little inside. Her touch is energising. It makes all the crunk that's happened seem a little more bearable. The warmth will never fully return. Not without Cherish, but it will help me move on. And the guilty hole in my chest, where the deaths of Malt and Lasul sit, will never be filled, but maybe I can help the others. If we can help with something big here, maybe, just maybe, that will make sure their deaths were not for nothing.

Then an image of Six pops into my head. Who knows what's happening to her, back in Circle City. Who knows if she's even still alive. The thought crumbles my clarity again.

'What you thinking about?' Doc asks.

'Erm...' I let go of her hand. 'Nothing. Just hoping the rain stays off. It's nice to walk in the sunshine.'

'Rubbish. You had a big grin on your face. What was it?'

'Seriously, it was the sun.'

'I like you, Seven, but you're a rubbish liar. And you will never let anyone get close, will you? I understand, by the way. You've lost the person closest to you and you don't want to feel that pain again. But you can't stay closed off forever either.' She increases her speed and catches up with Eagle, who has started to slow.

I stop for a moment, confused. Is she right?

Around midday we reach the outer fences that surround Westmine. Eagle has us approach a point in the boundary where there are no Guardian towers or stations near. The only thing separating us from the mines beyond is this fence.

'So how are we doing this? Can you climb, Eagle?' I ask.

Eagle nods.

But Doc shakes her head. 'Hmmm, are you sure? I think you should climb over beside her, Seven. Then you can help if she's struggling.'

Eagle pouts her lips and shakes her head, but Doc is insistent. 'No, I'm the physician and I say you should have Seven there, just in case.'

'Yeah, Doc's right. We'll go together.' I start climbing the twenty-foot, crosswire fence, just after Eagle.

I watch her carefully and she's strained and tense. It's an easy climb, so she must be in trouble. I place my arm around her and pull her closer to help take some of her weight off.

She wriggles and tries to push me off.

'Stop it, Eagle. I'm trying to help.'

She shakes her head and pushes me so hard, my arm slips away. I almost fall to the ground, but I manage to grab the fence again and readjust.

'Come on. Be sensible. Everyone needs help sometimes.'

She shakes her head again.

'Fine, but accepting help is okay. I'm your friend.'

She stares at me, a fierce scald in her gaze, before she climbs the rest of the fence and down the opposite side. I follow and I'm grateful to hit the ground on the other side.

We wait for Doc who climbs down from just above me. I help her when she's close enough and hold her for a second more than I need to, just as I set her down.

Eagle tuts and strides off. I turn from Doc and follow, fighting an urge to say something. I want to tell her that I am open to letting people in, but I don't. I can't.

We walk, hunkered down low the whole time, until we're about two hundred metres from the edge of the fence. An alarm sounds in the distance, from the direction of the mines. Eagle quickly falls into the long grass and disappears. Doc and I do the same, twenty metres behind.

'What do we do?' Doc asks.

'Crawl forward. Being near Eagle at times like this is always the best idea,' I reply.

She agrees and we move through the unkempt grass towards the spot where we last saw our friend.

We find her quickly and she indicates that we should flank her. Me to the right, Doc to the left.

'Are you okay on your own?' I ask Doc.

'Seven, you're not my bodyguard. I survived long enough before you came along. I'll be fine. I have this pistol.' She shows me her weapon and crawls left.

I move through the increasingly damp ground and settle on a spot about twenty metres from Eagle. The grass here is tall, but not as thick, so I can see through it and make out anyone approaching.

We wait.

I'm soaked, my knees are numb and frozen, and the alarm still sounds in the distance, but no one has come. I'm just about to crawl back to Eagle when a truck engine sounds. I pop my head a little higher above the grass and see it approach. A Realm emblem on the front, it speeds towards us.

They must still have control of the mines. Which means the Exiles have lost their battle. The rebellion is over. The Orphans of Thasos have failed. And now we are trapped, hiding in the grass, and will have to fight our way back out of here.

This has all been for nothing. All we've given up. Good people's lives. Six being taken. All for this one goal, and now it's over. What can so few of us do if a whole mining population have failed?

I look through my rifle sights, waiting for the truck to get close enough. I can't just expect that Eagle will get them this time; I'm going to shoot. I reckon if I get the driver, the truck might crash or tumble and that will give us an edge.

The engine gets louder, and the white truck gets bigger in my sight. I aim for the shape on the driver's side. I wait, knowing my aim is not great, not wanting to miss. I'll give away my position if I shoot and fail.

But the truck slows and finally stops. It's still too far for me. It's well within Eagle's range. I wonder why she hasn't shot.

The driver's door opens and then the passenger side as well. I watch them approach us, armed and tense. I move my finger closer to the trigger. Why hasn't Eagle shot yet? They must be less than fifty metres away.

My right index finger caresses the trigger, ready to fire. I keep my arms steady; I focus upon the closest target. I can't miss. There are at least five of them, perhaps more in the truck.

'Show yourselves,' shouts a loud voice, which carries above the alarm. 'We mean no harm. Please, come out.'

I squint to identify the speaker, but I don't recognise her. She is too shabbily dressed to be a Guardian, though. Perhaps she is an exile. Or perhaps it's a trap to get us. I remain hidden, finger on trigger.

'We are friends. Do not shoot.' Doc rises from her position to my right. She puts her gun on the ground. 'Are you Exiles? Have we won the mines?'

I turn back to the speaker.

'Yes, we have won. Just about. There is only a small number resisting. We have many prisoners, but most of them died rather than submit. There's bound to be more reinforcements, though. That is why we have kept the alarms active. Come now, are you on your own?'

'No, I have two with me. Eagle. Seven. It's okay.' Doc looks over to our approximate positions, but neither of us rises.

That makes up my mind. If Eagle doesn't trust this, then neither do I.

'Why do your friends not answer? You don't have to lie to us to appear in a stronger position. If you're on your own, that's fine.'

'No, honestly, they're here. Seven, why don't you answer?'

I'm tempted to stand, but something feels wrong.

'Why lie to us?' asks the original speaker.

'I am not,' says Doc, a little desperate squeak in her voice.

'One sure way to find out. Bring her.'

Two of the other people behind the speaker raise their guns and aim them at Doc, slowly approaching her.

I leap to my feet, my own rifle aimed at the speaker.

I see movement to my right, and guess that Eagle is up, too.

'Drop your guns or we will shoot you,' I shout. 'And I guarantee you, Eagle doesn't miss.'

**FROM THE AUDIO DIARY OF
E820906. ENTRY 14.**

Help me...someone. Please...

CHAPTER 27
THE BLACK KNIGHT

Everyone stands tense, guns aimed. Several seconds pass.

'This is pointless,' shouts the first speaker. 'We have just lost hundreds of Exiles. I will not lose any more. Lower your guns.' She puts her gun down and indicates to her fellows to do the same.

I look across at Eagle, who doesn't budge. Doc nods to me. I put my rifle down. I'm a lousy shot anyway.

'And you.' Their speaker points at Eagle. 'Put your gun down, so we can take you in. I promise we will cause you no harm if you bring none yourselves.'

I turn back to Eagle. She is sweating and her arms are starting to shake. 'Come on, Eagle. I think we can trust them. And you need treatment.'

She scowls at me but lowers her rifle. She doesn't ground it, but they seem to consider this a good enough sign. The lady who spoke ushers us towards the truck.

'I'm Hess,' she says, as we arrive at the side of the vehicle. 'We will chat when we are moving, but let's get away from the fence first. There could be escaped Guardians anywhere out here. We don't have the people power to guard the whole complex.'

We follow her inside. It's a standard Military truck, like the one we stole yesterday. Like the one I got blown up in.

I sit beside Doc and a rather grumpy-looking young Exile. He's much bigger than me, so I say nothing. Eagle sits in the corner seat at the back, turning to face the wall.

'So, who are you folks?' asks Hess. The other Exiles listen but pretend to look away.

'We were with Lasul,' answers Doc. I'm glad she's talking. I turn to her and listen as she tells Hess our names and recounts our journey and the events of the last few days. Once she finishes, I look back to Hess, who looks sad.

'I knew Lasul, well. He was a good man. Had great ideas. The whole rebellion was his idea. He drew up the attack plan and gave me all the information we needed. I'm sorry he won't be here to witness our success.'

'So, you have taken over Westmine? You defeated the Guardians?' I ask, trying to speak up, like a leader should.

'Yes, as I said, many people died. Good Exiles. Good friends. We should be happy, and we will celebrate this day. But this is only a small wound for the Realm. Once they assemble a large enough force, they will strike here and take control of the mines, again.'

'Then why did you bother?' I ask. 'All those people killed, and the Guardians are just going to come back, and they'll be slaves again.'

'It's about power. Everyone thinks the Realm has an authority that's untouchable. That we can do nothing but accept our role as Exiles. But something like this, it gives people hope. We want a world where we are not slaves, where we do not have to live by the sick code of a dictator. Lasul has given us that. Today will give us that.'

'Wait, you said there was still some resistance? Guardians who didn't surrender?'

'Yes, but very few of them. An incredible fighter called Bulk was leading more than a hundred Exiles to capture them. You know I watched him take out a dozen Guardians over the course of the fight. There's a Black Knight among them that we'd like alive, so Bulk is seeing to it. You probably know him. He was one of Lasul's men.'

Doc nods.

'But what's next? How do you plan to keep that hope alive beyond the next few days? Surely once the Autokratōr sends a larger force, we'll all be killed. He won't let us live.' I want to be hopeful, but I suspect the Autokratōr, my father, won't allow this.

'It's a little-known fact that the number of Exiles in the Realm now heavily outweighs the number of Realm citizens. The Military dwindles every day, due to the constant warring at the Realm borders. You can't have such a large kingdom, without having to spread the Military and the Autokratōr has spread himself thin.'

'How do you know all this?' My own knowledge extends to one Greenie camp, and whatever I didn't listen to, and Six told me later, in Realm Studies class. Plus, what I've picked up in the last few days.

'Lasul. He has spies everywhere. Had.'

'But how? And why would people want to help the Exiles? Why would they help Lasul?'

'He was one of them. Very influential at one time, too. Many people remained loyal to him after he was exiled, though they pretended to stay loyal to the Realm. This is a lifetime's work for Lasul. Don't underestimate its importance.'

I definitely underestimated Lasul. And how important his work was. It's only now we're here, and I see these people, that I'm beginning to think beyond my own very small, narrow world.

'This is crazy,' I say. 'How many people are here? Will it be easy for us to find our friends?'

Hess nods. 'Should be. Most people are in the Pit. We have a megaphone. I'll call them if you like once we arrive.'

I give her a warm smile, to show my appreciation. A part of me is glad that the fighting is over. I'm fine with fighting someone on a one-to-one basis. That's just like Greenie training all over again. But the thought of a huge battle scares the crunk out of me.

For a long time, I wanted war. I wanted to serve the Realm in battle. But I've seen too many good people die to want more death.

If only there was a way to overthrow the Realm without anyone getting hurt. But it seems like the only way to do it, is to also lose. No victory without sacrifice, the physical Guru's used to say. And that goes for both sides.

I try digesting the information-overload I've just received, but it's no good. I've too many questions and I'm not sure we have the time to go through it all. I'll ask later. We need to get Eagle to a bed, and then I need to see if Bulk is okay. Miller and Three, too, I suppose. I think about Mother, who's leading the rest of Lasul's settlement through the country right now. With all we encountered, I worry they won't make it. Seriously man, everything's a bit of a mess.

'You okay?' Doc asks.

'Define okay,' I reply. 'I'm alive and fairly well, if that's what you mean.'

'No, I mean where's your head at? It's all a bit overwhelming, huh?'

'You're tellin' me.'

She moves closer and rests her head on my shoulder.

The truck stops and Doc wakes.

'Time to get out. There is some Guardian resistance in our path. We can help. You stay here and look after her.' Hess indicates to Doc to stay behind with Eagle, and signals for me to follow her.

Smoke. So much smoke in the air, I choke and spit.

Ten metres ahead, five Exiles have surrounded one Guardian. A Black Knight.

One of the Exiles is Three. He is on one knee. Bulk stands over him, protecting him. The other three Exiles keep their distance, holding their rifles at the Black Knight. Stalemate.

'Let's give these guys some help,' says Hess, walking forward.

'They seem to have it under control. He's surrounded. They have guns, he does not.'

'It won't be enough. This is the one I told you about.' She strides towards Bulk.

I follow slowly, watching the Knight. All those years of daydreaming, but I'd never actually seen one. Until now. He looks massive, nearly as big as Bulk, but it might just be the uniform.

He takes small steps, always leaning slightly forward, ready to repel any attack. He's intimidating, even from this distance.

'Black Knight of the Realm. I am Hess. Leader of the Orphans of Thasos. Westmine is ours. There is no more resistance. Surrender and you can keep your life.'

A laugh emanates from the voice box in his mask. I remember learning that they're to help the Knight's keep anonymity.

'No surrender. We fight until the end. *Hail the Autokratōr.*'

He springs forward, leaping into the air, his fist coming down upon the skull of an armed Exile. His fist makes a crunching noise. The Exile falls, inert.

The other two Exiles launch a flurry of bullets at the Knight, but they bounce off his bulletproof exoArmour. They die before the echo of the bullets is gone.

'I hate guns,' says the Knight. 'You're next, big one.' He points to Bulk, who is hovering over Three, holding his arm. He can't be hurt. Bulk is pretty much indestructible.

The Knight approaches Bulk, slower than before. He moves from one side to the other, taking small, precise steps. Bulk sways back and forth, his teeth clenched.

I need to help.

'Knight, this is your last chance,' says Hess. 'Reinforcements are on the way. We have hundreds. We will overcome you. And you will die. Last chance.'

He ignores Hess, maintaining focus on Bulk.

'You come in from the left, I'll go right. We attack at the same time. It's our only chance,' I say.

She nods and I move swiftly to the right. I watch the movements of the others closely. The Knight is still trying to work out the best way to attack Bulk. Bulk remains between the Knight and Three. Hess mirrors my movement on the opposite flank. He's not looking my way, but I have a feeling the Knight can sense me, because when I move a little closer, he takes a few subtle steps away.

Now I'm closer, I can see Bulk is a mess. His face is swollen, his right arm is badly cut, and he seems to be putting all his weight through his right leg. I've no doubt the Knight has spotted this, too.

I try to steady my shaking hands, waiting to give Hess a sign to attack. Not yet, she moves into position.

Come on, Seven, this is just like training all over again. You've had plenty of action since, you'll be fine. Focus. Just focus.

I nod and move towards the Knight. She copies me, striding forward. He turns to Hess first and advances on her. She produces a claustroBlade from her waistband and holds it high above her head as she leaps through the air. She clashes with the Knight, and both fall to the ground, the collision giving off a soft crunch noise.

The Knight is on top, deflecting Hess's attacks with the blade. I catch movement to my right. Bulks flies past me and thumps the Knight off Hess. They roll around on the grass, the Knight somehow able to compete with Bulk in the wrestle.

I fall beside Hess. 'Are you okay?'

She nods but doesn't move. 'My leg is hurt. Can't move.'

I look down and see the end of the claustroBlade sticking out from the side of her leg.

'Take it out,' she instructs.

I raise my eyebrows and turn to the fight. Bulk is on the ground; the Knight is landing a series of punches to his face.

'Hurry,' she adds.

I take a long breathe, grasp the blade, and pull it.

Hess lets out a shrill hiss, but otherwise remains cool. 'Help Bulk.'

I stand, the bloody blade in my right hand.

'Let's get him together.'

I turn and Three is standing now, holding his ribs.

'Sit this one out, Three. You're hurt.'

'No, come on, let me show you what I can really do.'

He sprints towards the Knight before I can stop him. I follow, striding out, watching the fight. Bulk's beaten. His face is bloody, his body limp. The Knight stops punching Bulk as Three reaches him.

In one swift movement, he clutches Three by the throat and throws him ten feet away. His body thuds to the ground. No movement.

My muscles tense as I throw my shoulder into the Knight. We tumble to the earth, but he's on top of me before I re-open my eyes. He holds my right wrist. He twists. Burning agony fires up my arm. I drop the claustroBlade.

I thrash and thrash. I put every molecule of strength into moving the Knight, but his exoArmour makes him too heavy. I'm pinned.

He spins the blade in his hand. Blood builds in my mouth and I choke.

Ten breaths...why doesn't he finish me? Twenty breaths...I struggle again, but my body won't respond. Thirty breaths...

'Who are you?' he asks. 'Who the hell are you?' He drops the blade beside my head and releases the pressure on my body, sliding off me and kneeling next to my head.

As I remain immobile, wondering why the hell I'm still alive, I notice a small gap in his mask. Just above the voice box, on his right cheek, there is a hole. Bulk must have broken it. I keep trying to move, even though my brain knows I'm dead.

The Knight's hand becomes still, the blade held loosely over my throat.

His breathing comes through his voice box. Ragged.

Slowly, I move my right arm towards the claustroBlade, watching the Knight. He continues to mutter. 'How is this possible? How can this be?'

I wrap my fingers round the handle and tighten my grip on the blade.

'Seven?' It's Hess. 'Seven, are you okay?'

The Knight turns his head towards Hess. As he does, I see flesh. His cheek. I jab the blade into the gap and twist. The Knight's grunts come through the voice box like a distorted wox howl. I pull the blade out and spring to my feet, putting distance between the Knight and me.

'Why? How?' The Knight murmurs. The fight has left him. He sits on the ground, his head lowered, blood leaking from his helmet.

The sound of truck engines drift closer. Reinforcements. I leave the Knight, he's no threat now, and run to Three. He's still and pale. I press his neck. A pulse. Weak, but he's alive.

'Medic,' I shout to the first truck. 'We need medics.'

I run to Bulk, whose face is a mess. But again, he's breathing. I can't believe anybody could take that beating and still be alive, but somehow, he is.

My muscles relax, the pain returns, and I flop onto the grass.

CHAPTER 28
WESTMINE

We stand at the top of the hill leading into the Pit. Hundreds of Exiles are crowded into it. At least a hundred more are spread around the lip of the raised ring, looking down at their fellow Exiles. It's like one of those old stadiums they used to play sports at. I think they still use them in the cities.

One man holds a long pole with a huge flag on it. A flaming phoenix on a black background.

The symbol of the Orphans.

I stand with Doc, waiting for Hess to speak on the megaphone. She sits on a wheelchair. Her leg wound was deep and required many stiches. Eagle is in the medical building, sleeping. We thought it best to leave her to rest. Miller's in there, too.

Hess holds up the megaphone to her mouth.

'Good people, I have a small announcement to make. Congratulations on our victory. We have struck a deep blow in the heart of the Realm.'

The crowd cheers, the pit amplifying and echoing the roars. It's magnificent.

Hess resumes. 'Second, one of the newcomers here is a fugitive of the Realm. He is the E820907 we've all been getting bugged about. Can I call forward all the leaders of the different mining groups, so that we can discuss what is to be done with him?'

Hess turns to me, her eyes narrowed, lowering the megaphone. 'Failed to tell me that little bit of information, didn't you?' She looks at Doc, then me. She moves closer. 'So, before we have our meeting, give me a good reason why we shouldn't hand you over in exchange for something *beneficial* to us.'

'Why would you do that? I thought you hated the Realm?' I ask.

'Yes, but what a bargaining chip you might be, to help us negotiate some kind of agreement going forward. We need to ensure a future for ourselves, and fighting is one way, but this way could mean that no one gets killed. Except for you, perhaps. I have no idea why you're wanted, but they want you bad. The word is that they'll do almost anything. Maybe they'll grant us some land where we can live, free from Realm Rules and slavery. I must consider every advantage we can get. So, tell me, why not hand you over?'

The leaders of the mining groups are approaching. Some have already arrived and are standing with their arms crossed. What do I say to that? Why shouldn't they hand me over? I wish I could tell them something. Anything.

'Lasul said I was important to the cause,' I say, blurting out something without telling her who I truly am. Would they accept me if they knew who my father is.

'What did he say?' asks Hess, crossing her arms.

But Doc answers for me. 'That he would be the one to lead us. That people will follow him. He could be the one to bring an end to the Autokratōr and free the Exiles.'

Hess laughs. 'This boy?' She turns to me. 'Sorry, kid but you don't look like a leader to me. Can't even say something good about yourself when your life depends on it.'

'Stopped that Knight, didn't I? You couldn't do that,' I say, crossing my arms. 'Even Bulk couldn't.'

'Fine, take him to the medical building and keep him there until we decide what to do.' Hess waves her hand at the Exile to her left, who signals to others. Six of them approach me, and two grab my arms. I don't resist.

'Take your hands off the boy, or I'll break 'em.' It's Bulk, running up the hill, followed by Three.

The two who hold me, turn to Hess who shakes her head. 'Do as I say.'

They start to pull me towards the medical building.

Four thumping strides later and Bulk is next to me, knocking both Exiles to the ground. 'The boy doesn't get harmed. He will not be getting handed over. And if anyone has a problem with that, they can deal with me.'

Bulk stares at Hess with his eyes narrowed, his brow furrowed and his body tense. Combined with his stitched, bruised, and bloody face, he is one scary prospect.

After several seconds, she shrugs.

'Fine, I'll have no infighting. But you better back Phase 2. We will need people like you.' She nods to Bulk. 'I assume that's why Lasul always had you at his side.'

'As long as the boy remains with us, I'll do whatever is needed.' The big man gives me a tight squeeze. I suppose it's a hug but it's friggin' sore. I can't believe he stood up for me like that.

Doc also joins in, squeezing from the other side.

When they release, I see Hess has disappeared with the other leaders already. Three stands awkwardly a few metres away. He looks in a lot of pain.

'How's Eagle?' he asks.

'Okay, I think,' answers Doc. 'She is weak and needs time to recover.'

'Where is she?' asks Bulk.

'Medical tent.' Doc points the way.

Bulk sprints away, Three hobbling in his shadow.

Doc and I are left alone.

'What a guy, huh?' she asks.

'Yeah, but why did he do that? That could have gone completely differently.'

'He likes you, Seven. We all do.'

I tilt my head and narrow my eyes. 'Really? He did that because he likes me?'

'Well, that and because of Lasul. Whether you believe it or not, Lasul knew something about you, and he believed in you, so anyone loyal to Lasul also believes it. And you'll find fewer more loyal than Bulk. Plus, you kind of saved him and Three from that Knight. If you hadn't stopped him, he would have finished them both off.'

She moves close and gives me another longer, softer hug that lasts the perfect amount of time.

If they knew the real reason Lasul wanted me, if they knew where I came from, they wouldn't be so quick to embrace me as one of them.

We wander around Westmine, watching the Exiles both celebrating and burying their dead. It's a strange, mixed atmosphere. I get several funny stares, but most people are friendly and there is a real community spirit amongst them. They help each other with the earth ceremonies, with treating and feeding the weak and injured. Nobody is excluded. These are good people.

Hess approaches again, her wheelchair pushed by a young girl. Her face is deathly white.

'Changed your mind? Going to hand him over?' Doc asks, standing in front of me.

'No.' She looks past Doc. 'A prisoner is demanding to see you up close.'

'And why would he want to see me?' I ask. That's weird.

'It's the Black Knight you were fighting earlier. You'll understand when you see.'

I follow her about a hundred metres back towards the medical building. To the right are thick iron prison cages. I wonder if they used these for the Exile slaves before.

Hess points to one prisoner, who stands next to the bars, both arms hanging out. He wears the uniform of a Black Knight but has been unmasked and his exoArmour removed.

'Look closely,' Hess says to me.

I approach the bars; the Black Knight's face gets closer and clearer.

When I am a metre away, I stop. My brain stops. My heart stops. I can't speak. This can't be happening. I turn back to Doc, who moves beside me.

'What is it?' she asks.

I turn back round to face the Black Knight, unable to believe it. His cheek is sliced very bad; I really did some major damage. But my focus is everywhere else.

'How?' asks Doc. She turns from the Black Knight to me, then back to the Knight. 'How is this possible?'

I'm still frozen, unable to accept what my eyes are showing me. It's not until he speaks that I accept it's real and that I'm not looking into a mirror.

'Hello, E820907. Someone has a lot of explaining to do, because there must be a very good reason that you and I are identical.'

CHAPTER 29
THE ORPHANS OF THASOS

My first, and probably last, meeting with the leaders of the Orphans of Thasos is happening in a lavish room where the senior Guardians must have eaten. It has telescreens and a duelling circle, as well as a huge portrait of the Autokratōr.

I stare into his face, spotting small likenesses. It disgusts me, so I turn away.

It is luxury compared to every other part of the mine. The chairs have gold-lined frames. The Orphans could be funded for the next year just by selling them.

My eyes wander around the circular table. Hess is across from me, sitting silently, waiting for another person to arrive and fill the one empty seat.

The other seven rebellion leaders chat quietly amongst themselves as we wait. I catch pieces of their chat, mostly about the battle and what they should do next. I hear outrageous suggestions, from storming New London, to fleeing over the channel. Both would result in the death of every Exile here; I have no doubt. But they probably think I'm just a Greenie with no name. A nobody.

The last few hours have been full of sleep, food, and recovery.

Our entire group is recovering well. We needed a break after the long journey here.

But every second that has passed, where my mind is free to wander, it's returned to Six. I neglected going after her to lead our small group to Westmine, but since I got here, I've realised they don't need me. They've got all these leaders here already.

I'm sitting alone, with no-one I know around me. I wish they'd allowed someone in with me. I asked if Doc could sit in on the meeting, but Hess refused. Apparently if she made that one exception, she'd have to let everyone be involved, and that just wouldn't work. Even when Bulk threatened to knock her and the other seven leaders clean out, she didn't budge an iota. I respect her for that, at least.

Her eyes remain fixed on me, and I squirm around uncomfortably in this hard, wooden seat. I'm still colossally freaked out about meeting my clone, or twin, or whatever that genetic experiment is, sitting outside in that cage. I just couldn't believe that someone could look so like me. I get that it's possible, he's probably one of the other siblings Lasul mentioned in his letter, but just seeing him, right there, in front of me, it's shaken me big style. He even whistles his S's in the same way I sometimes do. My hands tremble beneath the table.

Maybe Lasul was right. Maybe I am one of four.

The last person arrives, but she looks different to the miners, much cleaner, and older, than everyone else. I recognise her.

'Sorry I'm late,' says Mother. 'I had to reunite a girl with her brother.' She looks round the table, pausing briefly at me, before smiling at the others.

'No problem, Mother, but we really must get started,' says Hess. 'We have some big decisions to make today and whatever we decide must be put into action immediately. The Realm could be here, in force, any moment.'

There are nods and murmurs of ascent all around the table.

'First item. Stay or go?' Hess asks. 'Mother, the proposed

options if we leave are Eastwich or Dover.'

'I assume the Eastwich option would be Phase Two?'

Hess nods.

'And Dover the evacuation option?'

'Yes, I don't know how much Lasul shared with you, but these were the two that were decided in the original plan. I see no reason to deviate.'

Heads around the table nod. Mother remains still.

Phase Two? Evacuation? I didn't even know about Phase One. And I still don't really know why I'm here.

'So, time to vote. Those in favour of Eastwich, raise your hand.'

Four hands go up.

'And Dover?'

Four different hands are raised.

'Mother, why did you not vote?' asks Hess, motioning to the raised hands of the other leaders.

'I don't have enough information to make a good decision. I wanted to wait and see if the decision was overwhelmingly in favour of one action before I commented.'

'It's split, and you have the casting vote.'

'It would appear so. But to help me fully understand the situation, and make an informed decision, I would like to ask a couple of things.'

Hess raises her eyebrows.

'I'll be brief,' she adds.

'Fine.'

'How many are we?'

'About three hundred. We lost a lot of people in the battle. There are at least a thousand at Eastwich.'

'Lasul's last report put the Military population across England at ten thousand. Two thousand of which are in New London. For Phase Two to work we needed at least two thousand of our own. With the number who have died here, that makes Phase Two a more optimistic option, now.'

'Yes, optimistic, but not impossible. And who knows how many Exiles will join us once they hear of what is happening.'

'Who knows, indeed?'

'So, what are you voting?'

'Fine, Eastwich.'

'What about option three?' I say, pushing my shoulders back and my chest out.

'And what would that be, Seven?' asks Mother.

'I will go to Circle City, I will infiltrate the Autokratōr's palace, get to the Hall of Records and steal as much information as I can. And if the opportunity arises, I will assassinate him.'

The table erupts with chatter and outrage. I hear some say it's idiocy, while others declare it a fine idea.

But, for me, if I do this, then I could get into the prisons in Circle City. I could find Six and help her escape. While I do hate the Autokratōr, and the Realm, priority one is to save my friend. And I can find out if the Autokratōr is truly my father, once and for all. If he's not my father, the Hall of Records will have my name, my real parents, everything I need to know. But if I'm not on the records, then I am his child. One of three hidden by Lasul at birth. Those are my priorities. And if I can help the rebellion while I'm doing those things, I shall.

'Okay, time to decide.' Hess holds up her hand and the table goes quiet. 'Those against Seven's proposal, raise your hand.'

Four hands are raised.

'Seven's option?'

Four hands go up. Mother abstains once again.

'Mother, are you deliberately holding us up? Why did you not vote?' asks Hess.

'How can I vote for either option? How we can even think about it, I don't know...you should be ashamed of yourselves.' She looks at the four who voted for me to do it. 'But there is a huge problem with that plan.'

'And what's that?' asks Hess.

'Seven is the most wanted person in the Realm, based on the all the reports. How exactly is he going to infiltrate New London and assassinate the Autokratōr?'

I lower my head, knowing the answer, but not quite believing it.

'He has a clone, or a twin or something. At least one that we know of. And that clone is a Black Knight. The boy will simply pretend to be the Knight. He will gain us valuable information and most importantly, when he kills the Autokratōr, he will send a message to the Realm that the Exile community is strong and willing to do anything to gain a stronger foothold in this world.'

'And what if he is found out?' asks Mother.

'Then he will die,' replies Hess.

Great.

My first task is to speak to my 'genetically identical counterpart'. Apparently, he won't speak to anyone. The only thing anyone knows is that he's a Black Knight, and he looks exactly like me. As I walk through Westmine towards where he's being held, I notice eyes daggering into me. If only they knew the whole truth, there might be real daggers in their hands.

I approach the bars and spot him sitting at the far side, knees pulled up to his chin. He eyes me like I'm something he shouldn't see, like a ghost. My heart thuds audibly in my chest.

'I need to talk to you.' My body is tense, and I stand straight to appear taller. But I'm not sure how easy it is to intimidate a copy of yourself. If anything, I'm the one intimidated. We appear to be the same, on the surface, but he's a Black Knight and I am just...well, I'm a wanted exile. That makes us opposites in the eyes of the Realm.

He stands and moves slowly across the prison, a slight limp in his right leg. When he reaches the bars, he moves his face right between two of them, so I can see my own features staring back at me. His hair is shorter, his cheek carved, and the top of his right ear has been sliced off.

'Who are you?' he asks me.

He's not spoken to anyone else, so this is progress.

'I am an Exile of the Realm. E820907. I have no name.'

He arches one of his eyebrows. I don't think he believes me.

'Clearly you only share my appearance and not my *other*... abilities. Failed your Test, did you?' He smiles, but shows his right canine, turning it into a nasty leer.

'I have ability, I promise you. But your abilities are clearly not all that, if you find yourself behind bars, defeated by a bunch of Exile rejects.'

He smashes his hands onto the bars and starts to shake them. 'Exile scum. You have no idea how powerful I am. I could have killed you, but I spared you. You have no idea who I am. And it will stay that way. You will all be dead in a day. They will come for me. Soon.'

'Oh, really? Why are you so important?' I ask.

He relaxes and falls back from the bars. 'I am not.' He slides back into the shadows at the back of the prison.

'Tell me more about you?' I ask, moving close to see beyond the bars. 'I want to know where you came from. And why you are...so like me?'

'We are not alike, save in appearance. I graduated early and earned my name before you even reached puberty, no doubt. I am the youngest person in the Realm to ever achieve the rank of Black Knight. You have achieved nothing.' He sits back down and pulls his knees back to his chin, ignoring me. 'You are a disappointment,' he adds, before falling silent.

'We'll see about that.' It's a weak comeback, but I can see there's nothing else to be gained, for now.

I walk back to the medical building. Doc is sitting next to a fully upright and conscious Eagle. Miller is asleep on a bed near the other end.

Eagle gives me a wide smile and nods. I nod back.

'Well, did he say anything?' Doc asks, moving towards me.

'No, he just asked questions about me. Wouldn't say anything about himself really. Seems to reckon he's a big shot, though. Reminded me a lot of that Rex sog I was in camp with.'

'Well, did you get a good look at him? Any features, scars, or other differences?'

'Yes,' I gulp, thinking about what's to come. 'He obviously has the knife cut on his cheek and the top of his right ear is cut off. He also has a limp, but I can fake that. No need to break my leg or anything.'

'I'm sure Hess is crazy enough to try.'

'Well, you need to stop her,' I say. 'I want to do this, but not enough to get my legs broken.'

'I'll do the ear if you want. And I can cut in a nice cheek scar as well. I'll try to be gentle.'

'Ha, gently cut my ear off and slice my cheek? Gee, thanks. But I don't think we need to do the cheek as he didn't have that when he left.'

Doc moves close and gives me a long, tight hug. 'It's okay,' she whispers. 'All of this will be worth it, if you get to see Six again.' She gives me one last look and then disappears out of the door.

I stand for several seconds, thinking about it. I hope she doesn't think Six is the only reason I'm going. I know it's the main reason...but I'd rather other people thought I was doing it for some higher, nobler reason.

I think a part of me wants to play a part for the rebellion. To be strong, like Cherish wanted. And I will but saving Six is the priority now.

I give Eagle a thumbs up and leave.

If I need to get my face cut to pieces, I guess it's better just to get it over with now.

When I step outside, Hess confronts me.

'We need to move now. We can do the alterations on the way. Doc has agreed to do it. Last chance to back out?'

'No, I'll do it.'

'Seems I may have underestimated you. Still, I'll reserve my judgement until you actually achieve something.'

She strides away, followed by several Exiles that seem to be her personal entourage.

I stare all around the mine, taking in the hundreds of Exiles, all now moving with swiftness and a purpose, like hundreds of worker ants. This was Lasul's vision. He might even have approved this next plan, involving me. He always did rate me highly, even if he never explained why.

This is my time to prove him right, to do something of worth.

To give every Exile a reason to *live for a better tomorrow*.

I'll show that copy that I'm the better one.

I'll infiltrate his Realm and I'll bring the whole thing down from the inside if I can.

If not, I'll do as Hess says.

I'll kill the Autokratōr, father or not.

If not for me, then for Lasul, Malt and especially for Cherish.

But only when Six is safe.

'I need to speak with you.' I rattle the bars to get his attention. But he is unmoved, his back to me, in a corner of his cell.

I need to try and reason with him before I get my reconstructive surgery. He must be as intrigued as I am. He must want to know more.

'You need to tell me some things.'

He laughs, his shoulders bouncing.

Good. That might open him up a little.

'Someone I...I like is being held prisoner in Circle City. I need to know how I can get to her. To rescue her.'

He laughs again, this time turning his head. 'And why the heck would I tell a scut like you? You hold me prisoner after I spared your life. I'm not doing you, or any exile scum, any more favours.' He turns his back to me. It's weird to think I'd always wanted a brother and this scut could be it.

'I don't just like her...I love her. I can't lose her.'

I've no idea where that came from. I said it for impact, for maximum effect. Maybe he can relate, maybe not. But maybe there's some truth in what I said. Perhaps more than some.

He stands up and moves closer to me.

Instinctively, I take a small step away from the bars. That makes him smile. I don't want to show any weakness, any sign of inferiority. We are the same, so I must act like it. I take a large step forward, my face an inch from the bars.

He nods. 'Alright. How about this: you tell me some stuff and I *might* tell you some things. If what you tell me is interesting.'

I think about the letter that Lasul left me. How much can I afford to reveal, but still keep my secret? I'm about to find out.

'What do you want to know?'

'You? Why do you look just like me?' And something changes behind those eyes, identical to mine.

I recognise his expression, his eagerness for this knowledge. I recognise it because it's the same one, the same feeling, I've had my whole life. I wonder if he was an orphan, too. If he had a foster-mother, like Cherish. If he had to kill his Cherish, too. To live with that action, to show loyalty, to become a Black Knight.

'I don't know...' I can't tell him about the letter. About who my father was. But if he is my twin. If he is one of the four that Lasul delivered, then he could be the one who was raised by the Autokratōr. His father is my father. His mother mine.

'Of course, you don't...how could you.' He walks away, his head lowered.

'Wait...' I don't know why, but I tell him everything. I start with Cherish and the camp. Then about how I had to kill her. Then I get to the escape, the exiles, the Orphans, Lasul's death, even the Leeches.

But I skip one part. The letter.

He listens, to be fair to him. He doesn't scoff or shake his head. He is eager to hear about my life. About a life he clearly did not experience. His facial expression is a spectrum of otherwise unrevealed emotion.

'So, that's how I came to be here. That is all I have to tell. I can't answer your questions.'

He paces. Some kind of inner struggle seems to be happening. Maybe he's heard enough to want to help me. Maybe he's thinking about his own story. Maybe he's just frustrated about how little I told him.

'So, you never met your parents?'

I shake my head. Not a lie.

'Do you know your date of birth? Your parents' names? Anything?' He clutches the bars, peering through.

'No. I wish I could tell you more.' Lie.

He lowers his head. 'You are either lying...' He looks up at me. 'Or you are telling the truth and other people have lied to me.'

He slumps to the ground, picking up small shards of stone from the mine. And starts throwing them into his small bucket, presumably his toilet. He doesn't miss.

I want to ask him so much. I have an infinite list of questions, but I've got to be patient. Gain his trust. Let him offer first. Like Six would do. If I'm going to save her, I must be much more like her. Smarter, patient but never, ever giving up on something. Or someone. She never gave up on me.

'What do you want to know?' He doesn't look at me, just continues to chuck the rocks into the bucket. His words catch me off guard. I've no idea what to ask him first.

Stick to information that will help you rescue her.

'Where would they...you...hold her prisoner?'

'Depends on priority. But if she's important, and I'm guessing by how desperate you are, that she is, then she'll be in the Tube Prison. Beneath the Palace.'

'And how would I get in there?'

'Ha.' He smiles. 'You don't...unless...'

Now I clutch the bars. 'How?'

He stays silent for so long. I don't dare interrupt, even though I'm bursting to ask.

'Nah, it wouldn't work. She wouldn't trust you.'

'Who?' The dam holding me back has exploded.

'Someone I love. But I won't risk her. You're on your own, scut.'

I'm about to pursue it, to keep digging. But Six wouldn't do that. She'd wait, give him a few moments of thought and change tack.

The only way I can get to him is to use the person he loves as a bargaining tool. I could threaten them, but I doubt that would work. And I'm not even sure I'd be able to anyway. Cherish said that love always wins over hate. So, I'll use his love, rather than his hate of us, to get him to help me.

'Maybe I can get her out?' I say, not sure exactly what I'm proposing. I'm fishing into an abyss. The Orphans would never agree to this deal, but they don't need to know.

'Don't be ridiculous. You couldn't even defeat me on the battle-field. You'd never be able to get her, and your girlfriend, out.'

'Are you willing to risk it?' I edge close to the bars again.

'Risk what?' He stands.

Then I hit him with my strongest reason, the one I'm sure that will work. Or nothing will. 'Never seeing her again?'

'I'll be out of here soon enough. They'll send more Guardians down here and take the mine again. And I'll be free to go home.'

'But, what if they don't? What if we move you? What if you're killed?'

He picks at his scarred ear. Silent, eyes closed.

'No. No.' He turns away. '*Hail the Autokratōr. Serve the Realm.*'

I tried.

CHAPTER 30
GOODBYE SPY

My freshly cut ear hurts worse than I expected. The constant throb feels like a fountain of blood is pouring out, once a second, every second.

It had to be immediately stitched and covered in bandages to absorb the leakage. Doc has ordered me not to move my ears much, which made me laugh. She also said to rest my head on the good ear when sleeping, which totally makes sense.

'Hang in there,' Bulk says.

I wince for the hundredth time as we pass over another bump. The truck is full, and I don't even have any space to myself. We are crammed in because we needed to move fast and there were too many Exiles for the number of salvageable trucks. A scout had seen a whole hoard of Realm trucks approaching and we scarpered.

We are going to the same settlement that Mother led the other Exiles to. Mother said they'd help us with supplies and whatever help they could offer. But we'll need to move on quickly from there.

Well, not me. This next settlement is where I leave the Exiles. Where I begin my solitary journey to New London, in the guise of this Black Knight. I'll have to work super hard to pull this off. The

Exiles are going to keep him locked up and out of sight. If he escapes and gets word back to New London, it's all over. Every second I perform this charade, I'll be at the mercy of their ability to keep him inaccessible.

I wear the uniform of the Black Knight, a little battered and dirtied from the battle, but that will help with the deception and hopefully make it more likely I'll be taken in. It's not comfortable in the exoArmour and the broken mask, but I need to play the part. And he speaks in a deeper voice, so I practised that before Doc sliced my ear off. I asked her if that made me a famous artist, but she didn't enjoy the joke.

I think his name is Pol. It's inked onto the inside of the helmet. And I need to remember the limp, too. Hess was all for smashing my knee, as I thought, but most of the others saw it as pointless, and so I was saved that little bit of agony. I've enough to deal with as it is.

I try closing my eyes, to sleep thorough some of this torturous journey, but it's not happening. The road is way too bumpy. The thought of revenge for Cherish, and the outside chance I could rescue Six are the little bubbles that keep me afloat. Otherwise, I'd drown. I run my fingers through my new, short, short haircut. It's the weirdest feeling.

'Nearly there,' announces Mother. 'Doc, it's time to give Seven any last-minute medical advice and any other...well, thing you might want to say.' She turns away, smiling.

Doc burns red next to me. 'Just do what I told you already. Bandages on until tomorrow. Use the cream to keep it clean and stay out of Realm hands for long enough to let the wound heal. If they are too fresh looking, it will raise suspicion. And keep your back covered. He doesn't have any lash scars.'

I nod, using my eyes to signal my appreciation, to show how much I'll miss her. She's been a pillar to me these last few days.

The truck stops and the door slides open. I unbuckle and move out.

Mother, Bulk, Eagle, Doc, Miller, Three, and Hess all follow me out. We're in a desolate piece of the country. Nothing but flat ground for miles all around.

One by one, I say goodbye. My hugs speak the words, as I hold these Exiles, my new friends, as tightly as I ever held anyone, except Cherish. It hurts my chest to say goodbye after all that's happened.

Bulk squeezes me so hard, crushing me even through the exoArmour. So I'm short of breath as Hess comes close. She doesn't hug me, but just says one thing.

'We're relying on you, Seven. You could be the difference. Prove me wrong.' She nearly smiles as she hands me the Black Knight's rifle. Bulk gives me a huge, stretched backpack as well, full of supplies. He also hands me his book. The BFG. 'For the road,' he says.

They all move back inside the truck, leaving me alone with Doc.

She stands silent for quite a while. I see Hess is impatient in the truck, but Mother growls at her when she tuts.

I want to break the silence but can't. I grab her instead and squeeze her. It could be the last time. I inhale the scent of her hair. I caress her neck with my fingertips. I feel a small tear sliding down my face.

'I'll be seeing you, Seven. You hear me? If anyone can do this, it's you. I know it.'

A mammoth bubble swells in my chest, and I feel like I can take on the whole Realm myself, right here and now.

Then she slides the door of the truck shut and it drives off.

I watch, until it goes beyond my vision.

Then I turn slowly, using Mother's pocket compass, an antique, to direct me to the North.

This is the moment my life as Seven ends.

I am now a Black Knight of the Realm.

And I have a new name.

PART IV

SIX

I lie in foetal position.

The box is tiny, even for me (Seven wouldn't fit, never mind One!), and I lost all feeling in my limbs a long time ago. The air contains some fresh oxygen, provided by the little hole just above my head. The cool, narrow channel of air that flows in, also keeps a small patch of my cheek cool. The rest of me is soaked.

When I was put in the Cage of Solace last year, I thought it was just awful, but at least I could sit upright, and the bars let in air and light. I would rather the Cage right now.

I really hope they didn't hurt the others. If they let them go, unharmed, then I'd be able to live with this, horrible as it is.

Every so often the box jumps as the vehicle we're in hits a bump in the road, and the momentary feeling of weightlessness takes away the constantly squashed feeling.

My heart contracts faster. My head lacks oxygen. I bang on the wooden box. And again. I repeatedly hit the inside. This is like the worst nightmare.

'Stop it or you'll get a lashing.'

'I'd rather that.' I hit the inside, even quicker and harder than before.

A high-pitched noise, piercing and penetrating, slices into the box and causes a wave of nausea. I stop thrashing. I stay completely still, trying to fight down the vomit. My head thumps and the noise still comes.

I can't take it anymore and I vomit. The smell makes me bring up more. Each time I convulse and bang my head against the side of the box.

The sound stops and I instantly relax. My breathing and heartbeat slow. The smell is awful, and my mouth feels disgusting, my tongue furry, as I spit out remaining bits of sick.

I close my eyes tight and hold my nose. I try to think of a time before all this.

The memory that drifts in is a recent one. The river and splashing around with Seven. We were in danger, then. But a different kind. More distant, less real. I wonder where he is. When I last saw him, he was running off to rescue people. I hope he'll do the same for me, but that's ridiculous. I'm smart enough to get myself out of this. I don't need him.

Still, the thought lingers in the back of my brain. It's selfish of me to think it. He needs to avoid getting caught, but I fill my mind with daydreams of rescues, all involving the boy labelled E820907.

Three times they've sent that noise into the box. Each time I've retched. There's nothing left in my stomach to bring up. My throat is swollen, raw and aching. The smell from the previous vomit hits me and I gag. And again. I twist my head closer to the small air hole and get a waft of delicious clean air. My thoughts clear a little, but my head still pounds, smashing my brain repeatedly into the walls of my skull, like my head and the sides of this box.

The road is now smoother, less bumpy – what a relief. I reckon it means we're closer to the Circle City. Whatever they have planned for me, whatever imprisonment, or torture, I'd almost welcome it at this stage.

I position my head furthest from the side where most of the vomit sits. It runs back and forth with the motion of the truck and it's soaking into the back of my clothes. I close my eyes and force them shut, thinking of another time, of any other place.

The last day I saw Mum and Dad. My Eighth birthday party. I had earned a day away from camp. But something felt wrong. They were unusually quiet, asked me very little about my learning, and usually that's all they could talk about, so proud were they of my progress.

As we watched the telescreen, the Autokratōr was announcing new plans for going to war. Eurasian Guardians had come too far into our Realm. I remember it because Dad was supposed to be going. But he said he couldn't leave Mum, especially when I was away all the time.

I went to bed, but when I woke up, Guardians swarmed the house. Mum and Dad had been taken. I was returned to camp. I've never seen them since.

One day, shortly after, a woman came to speak to me. She said that they had been recruited in the war effort, but that they had died in duty, and I should be proud. I didn't understand because Dad had said he wasn't going to fight. It didn't make sense at the time. Since, I've pieced together the truth of it, or something close to the truth.

I think they were killed because they defied the wishes of the Realm. I've seen myself what happens to those who fall out of favour. I think about what life would be like if I hadn't left the Testing centre with Seven. If I had stayed, I would be working somewhere in the Realm right now, contributing to a society I don't believe in. Helping the same people who took my parents away from me, who tried to take Seven and who have taken me.

We go over a bump and my sick sodden hair falls near my mouth. I retch and retch, involuntary contractions shuddering violently through my stomach. My body is soaked in a cold sweat once more. When I recover, I push my hair back, close my eyes and try to lose myself again.

The truck stops and the engine dies. My emotions conflict: relief at the prospect of getting out of this box, but also the terror of getting out of this box and facing what's next.

The box is lifted off the truck, my body disoriented as I'm carried for over a minute, moving from side to side. I count the seconds, hoping each one brings me closer to getting out.

The box sways, sending the smalls pools of liquid back and forth. Much of it has soaked into the wood, creating a permanent scent of sickness.

My left calf cramps. Shoots of pain sprout up the back of my leg, the muscle in a state of unending contraction, my foot unable to stretch and alleviate it.

Please let me out. I'll take what comes next if they just let me out of here now.

Like he heard my thoughts, a Guardian pulls the lid off. I squint into the brightness that floods my captivity. Through my partly open right eye, I notice the Guardian take a step back as the newly released fragrance hits him. The accumulated aroma of hours, perhaps days, of stewing in my own excretory juices, can't be pleasant, but I've become partly immune to it. Partly.

A month ago, I'd have died if anyone saw me, or smelt me, like this. Now I don't care. I just want out. But I can't move. Every muscle so numb and cramped, I feel paralysed.

The Guardian pushes the box onto its side, and I roll out onto the wet grass. Bliss. I enjoy the dampness saturating my repulsive clothing and putrid skin.

I turn my left ankle upwards and relieve the cramp in my calf. I then try a big stretch, but my muscles fail me. I finally rest in a less squashed, foetal position. My body needs more time before I push it.

I start licking the grass, enjoying the moisture like it's a full glass of water.

'Stop that. Drink this.'

The Guardian forces his canteen to my mouth, and I guzzle it, not breathing. He pulls it away once I've downed half of it.

'Take it easy. That's plenty for now. You look like crunk.' He turns to two other Guardians. 'Privates, take the prisoner to the contamination station before she enters the city. And disinfect this canteen.'

Two female Guardians, one who looks not much older than me, take my arms and they lift me towards a tall, concrete building on our right. I can just about walk, but I'm real weak. My head spins as I check out the area.

Behind me, and to my right and my left, are fields full of workers, machines, and storehouses, stretching away as far as I can see. The harvest must be in full swing. The scale of the sight surprises me. But when I look beyond the building in front of me, I nearly pass out completely.

At least 1000 metres above me stands a massive wall, aluminium plated. The sun's reflection makes it impossible to look at it for too long. I spot many, many Guardians atop the walls, large weapons peering over the tops, like nosey birds, but only a few ground level entrances. A perfect protection. An unassailable defensive structure. Impossible to enter without permission, clearly. I wonder how Lasul ever thought we could break into this place. Its walls continue round to either side for many miles, well beyond my eyesight. I am here. A prisoner. The place I spent my childhood wishing to see, but the one place I don't want to be right now.

Our capital.

New London.

Circle City.

.   .   .

263

Square. White. Soft. One door. No windows.

This room is already driving me crazy. I've only been here for an hour, maybe two, but maybe it's much less time. This is the plainest, least comfortable room I've ever had the displeasure of finding myself in. But better than the box.

I'm currently lying flat on my back, hands behind my head, staring at the plain white ceiling. The roof panels are partly opaque, so some light filters in, but not much. Don't want to waste energy powering a bulb for a room like this. Realm efficiency at its finest.

At least I'm not lying in a pool of my own vomit and urine, wrapped in damp, stinking clothes. It's enough to keep me from crashing into a deep depression. But my situation is hopeless, right? They'll want to know everything, and I won't want to tell them. Then they'll probably do something pretty unpleasant, something that'll make the Cage seem like a cakewalk, or my box like a luxurious road trip.

A whizz of something mechanical makes me sit up. I spin round, searching the room for the source. A panel opens on the wall opposite the door. I stare as it slides backwards and disappears leaving a black square. Slowly, a telescreen moves into the gap and slots into the space, flush against the wall.

Great, what do they want me to watch, now? Better not be some high and mighty Military ad, showing the great and wonderful Sharan. Bet she doesn't even realise what the mighty Realm do to their unwanted. She probably just thinks of the Nameless like I once did. Lazy sogs who didn't work hard enough to pass their Tests.

The screen springs to life. Pixels illuminate the dull, white room, the colours flashing upon the walls.

'*Good morning, citizens. Welcome to Roundup, your latest Realm news*

*brought to you as it happens. It's Saturday 24th March 2091 and I am
Ged Geddes.*

*War continues at the Europa/Eurasian border. Eurasian Realm
casualties have reached the 1.1 million mark in Autokratōr Tyndareus'
latest campaign. Grand Guardian Sharan continues to inspire us all
with her efforts. Reports suggest she has led our Guardian Legion to
another great victory and forced the Eurasians back further into their
own territory. We are winning the war, but as always, we still need
more of our young Greenhorns to be assigned to the Military. Don't
delay, pass your Test today and you could be alongside Sharan, fighting
for our Realm, in no time at all.'*

What a pile of crunk. Can't believe I'd swallowed all that when I
was a Greenie. Although now I think of it, I'm not sure I ever did. I
was always going into Academics to work on something for the
greater good. To stop the food and energy shortages, to stop the
wars for territory and to stop all the needless killing of our already
depleted race. Thinking about my old crush on Sharan makes me
cringe. I'm glad I never told Seven.

The telescreen changes. Black, white, and grey static appears.
This happened all the time back in camp, but I'd have thought
they would have better aerials here in the city.

The screen reappears but it's not Ged Geddes who stares out
at me.

It's the Autokratōr.

The Autokratōr smiles.

I don't know what to do. Smile back? Or turn my friggin' back.

'E820906. You are imprisoned due to Realm Rule 16. For association with and assisting a known enemy of the Realm. The *normal*
punishment is termination.'

I'm silent, but I do look at the face on the screen. I spot a small camera just above the screen, which he must be using to see me. I try to keep my expression blank. It's not hard after all the training they gave us.

'You are disciplined and in control of your emotions. Good. I know you showed exceptional promise as a Greenhorn. In fact, I am informed that you scored most highly indeed. You were to be assigned to our very own genetic research Academics team, here in New London, until the...unfortunate incident.'

He intensifies his stare, searching for some kind of response, I assume. He won't get it. I process the information in a detached way, storing it for consideration later.

'So, with all that said, here is the very kind offer the Realm is willing to offer you. Fully paid, five-year position with our genetics research team, full pardon of all crimes committed, and full Naming ceremony, where your family will be waiting for you. Their criminal record will also...disappear.'

My family? No, he must be messing with me. I feel my mouth widening as the seconds of silence pass. As I process the Autokratōr's words, numbness flows from the tips of my hair to the end of my toes. Are they alive? Or is he tricking me?

'I see that this offer has some appeal to you. Think about it. A representative will be there to see you within the hour, expecting your answer.'

The screen turns black.

A tsunami of questions rips through me, building in intensity and volume.

They eventually dissipate until only a few remain, swimming around, insistent, and enduring.

When he said family, did he mean parents? Family suggests something more. Did they have more children after they left me? I'm probably just overthinking it. He probably just meant Mum and Dad. But if they were alive all these years, why did they not get in touch? Maybe they were imprisoned after they were taken that day. That's why he said he could reunite us. They might even be in this same prison.

But the longer I sit in the white room, my knees pulled up to my chin, the more I think it just can't be true. It's been too long to hear nothing. And what good is there in getting hopeful? I'll only be disappointed when I find out he's lying to me. This is all about getting info on Seven. They've clearly done their research on me, though. I'll give them that. They know exactly how to tempt me.

I chew my freshly washed hair. The little frayed blonde bits feeling smooth on my tongue. My tummy grumbles. It feels so tiny and shrunken that I'm not sure I could eat much anyway, but at least nothing's coming up anymore. My oesophagus still burns, my abs tender.

I spend a long time fantasising about the offer. Working in a real lab, with other Academics, trying to make the Realm a better place. Then returning home to my parents, where Dad would have cooked me a lovely dinner. The fire would be roaring, and we would chat about how our days had been, then Dad would tell funny stories about me as a young kid, and Mum would laugh and drink Ausmerican wine.

But for that to happen, and that's if I'm not being lied to, I'd have to tell them where Seven is. I'm sure that's their plan, and I won't betray him. I can't betray him. I know it's bigger than me or even him. It's about what his evasion means to the Exiles. The hope it gives them to have a symbol of rebellion, like Seven. He has no idea himself, of course, the big friggin' sog, but I know that whatever they have in mind for me, I won't crack. I won't give him up.

For a while, I think of him, and the time we spent together. I was happy, an emotion I'd been trained to squash. Real happy. And anyone who can make you feel like that is worth whatever they can throw at me.

A door slides open. It doesn't push in or out, just moves sideward into the wall, like the ones at the Testing centre. Two

Guardians, all in white, stride in with their rifles raised. They stop a metre beyond the doorway and remain static.

I hold my hands up to show them I'm no threat.

Several seconds pass in silence.

Then a tall lady, dressed all in black, enters the room and steps a little closer than the Guardians. She is unarmed, but I see a long sword at her side.

A Black Knight. I'm sure of it.

'Are you to accept our offer?' the Knight asks.

'I don't fully understand it. Are there conditions to it?' I ask, playing the game for a little longer.

'If you accept, you will divulge all known information on the wanted exile, E820907, and once he is recovered, you will receive that which was promised to you.'

'I thought you might say that. And while it's a tempting offer, and it really was alluring, I'm going to decline. I'm quite comfortable in my cell.'

The Black Knight takes a step closer and kneels.

'That is outstanding news for Reaper. He is waiting down in the Underground, licking his torture knife in anticipation. Take her away.'

I'm thrown down onto a metal table, real hard. They pull plastic cords round my wrists and ankles and secure me tight to the table.

The Guardians retreat to the bottom of the stairs. Rows of similar tables run the full length of the platform, many of them still stained with blood. The one next to me still drips.

On one side of the platform, there is nothing except the old, torn up tracks. On the other is a rusted train, three carriages long, each of its windows smashed and each of its doors open. Dull lights illuminate the inside of each carriage. We looked at transport mechanisms in Realm history, but the pictures didn't look like this. A worn sign on the wall says Canary Wharf.

The smell of rotting meat drifts into my scrunched nose, while I lie, breathing heavily, unable to control my emotions. I'm scared right now, real scared.

'Don't like the smell, huh?' says a woman, appearing from one of the train carriages. Reaper, I assume. 'You get used to it.'

The smell must be bodies. Dead people.

She approaches me, tilting her head and looking at me from different angles. I notice a lot of scarring on her face and part of her left ear is missing.

'Until she talks?' she asks the Guardians.

One of them nods.

'A pity to mutilate one so pretty,' she says quietly.

'Hand, get out here.' Her shout echoes through the dark tunnel.

A small man, with deathly white skin, emerges from another carriage. His gloves are smeared in red, and his apron is covered in flesh, tissue, and blood. 'Yeah?'

'We got a mute. Come help me loosen her lips.' Reaper pulls out a drawer from beneath the table and the clatter of metal followed by a sharp scrape makes me shiver.

Hand arrives and I get why he's called that. His right hand is huge, nearly twice the size of the other. I wonder if it's a genetically modified hand. Maybe he was one of the experiments. He holds a small black bag in his left hand, which he dumps at the foot of the table.

'Girl, I'd be speaking if I were you. Don't want this going no further.'

I stare at the sharp object in Reaper's hand. It is like a short, thin, and exceptionally sharp knife, but with three blades all sticking out at different angles. It hasn't been cleaned since it was last used and the blood that stains it is dark and dried.

The thought of *that* cutting me makes me almost vomit. I jerk my head to the right in case anything comes out, but luckily my stomach is empty. Who knows where that blade has been before? What if it has bacteria or some other horrible disease on it?

I close my eyes and try to slow my breathing. My heart's thundering rapid-fire. My thoughts turn to Seven for a microsecond. Would he want this? Is he worth it?

'Just in time, Frederick, we're about to start.'

I open my eyes and see the Black Knight approach and pull up a chair, ready to watch this. Sick sog. Reaper smiles at her, she looks at me, glee etched all over her scarred face.

'It's simple. Talk and I stop. Remain silent and I continue with my art.'

Did she just call it art? These people make me sick. No wonder they are down here doing this, hiding it from the citizens of the Realm. If only they knew. Maybe they should know.

My world stops, my body writhing in pain as the first incision slices the tissue of my right arm. I struggle against the cords tying me down and I get a lot of movement in my middle, but my limbs are pinned. I panic and open my mouth to speak, but it's just a garbled shout that comes out. She focuses on slicing near my wrist where my thrashing will disturb her work less.

I want to talk, to tell them every single thing I know about Seven, just to make it stop. But a stubborn part of my soul can't allow it.

As it continues, the pain changes from a tearing, agonising sensation to a numb feeling. I glance and see that I'm losing blood. Lots. And my brain is suffering, that's probably why I feel it less. Or am I in shock?

I'm focusing hard on controlling the pain, but it's so hard.

'Just start speaking and it stops.'

It could have been anyone who spoke; my brain just doesn't have any more room for anything else other than getting me through this. As Reaper moves up my arm, I stop resisting.

Finally, my thrashing stops. I can't stop my arm jerking every time she cuts, but I manage to master the terror a little better. I panicked but now I feel a strange sense of calm.

My whole forearm is cut open and I can see past tissues to something that looks like bone.

It's too much.

My eyes close, my body stills, and I feel no more.

In Human Biology, we learned that without water, we can die within 3 days.

It's been four days now.

I've been carefully pouring it out, down the hole for excretory waste.

Food, what little they give me, follows the water when it arrives.

I went into ketosis a few days ago, and I've just been drifting into and out of consciousness, or I guess it could be called sleep. But I know it's just my body's way of keeping me alive for longer. Lower metabolic rate, conserve lean tissue degradation.

In history, we used to learn about these people who would induce this starvation state voluntarily, to look better.

It's the biggest joke in our existence.

But this is no joke.

Humour left me when they took me.

And soon I will leave the Realm.

With nothing.

No information.

No Seven.

These may be my last thoughts.

I'm not awake much anymore.

Sleep consumes me for longer and longer.

My body less responsive, my brain less clear.

Occasionally I think of Seven.

But I try not to.

He keeps telling me to endure.

That he will come for me.

But he won't.

He can't.

This is the end.

PART V

THE INFILTRATION AND THE EXECUTION

CHAPTER 31
THE WATCHER

Someone is following me.

For three days, and nights, I've sensed someone close. The odd rustle of a bush, a branch breaking, even a cough once.

If it's a Leech, they'd surely have attacked, or got the rest of their clan. Actually, part of me has been wishing it was – in this armour, with these weapons, I'd love to take a few of them out. Repay them for my last experience.

If it's Guardians, they'd have revealed themselves by now, surely. I'm wearing a Black Knight's armour after all.

So, I'm guessing it's a solo friend or foe.

But all my friends left me just outside Westmine.

That leaves just one option.

The ear has a small infection, I think, as it's beginning to smell horribly inside this helmet. Although it could just be my funk after so many days without a proper wash.

I still haven't worked out how to get it to open, or come off, so I've been sleeping in it. Not much fun, but at least it's warm overnight.

I try to doze, the fire beside me burning low, when I spot movement in the trees. I leap to my feet, my claustroBlade drawn, ready to fight whoever my shadow is.

'Come out!' I shout, my voice sounding strange as it passes through my helmet's voicebox.

No response.

I walk around the circumference of the light circle formed by the glow of the fire. Nothing. Not a sound, or sign of movement.

Maybe I have been imagining it all this time. Maybe I'm just paranoid, and why wouldn't I be. But something in my gut tells me that there's someone there. Possibly just a few feet from me, staring back, invisible in the darkness.

I shiver.

But there's nothing I can do, except remain alert and take on this enemy when they finally show themselves.

I settle again, stoking the fire and adding wood. I won't let it die tonight. Or I might.

It's been five days and nights now since I left.

I've not slept for the last two nights. That horrible sense of being watched hasn't left me, and every time I close my eyes, I jerk awake almost immediately, like I'm being attacked. I shouted out once, and I heard a flutter of birds, possibly disturbed by the Watcher, whoever it is.

And I'm sure I heard something, like a bird call, but it sounded real human. And it happened three times in a row. Not natural at all. But I could easily have imagined it.

I spot a small river, at the bottom of a steep hill, and make my way towards it. I need to refill my water bottle and should try to clean my ear (and everywhere else if I can get the exoArmour off!).

I stumble down the steep decline, using tree stumps and bushes to help me down. But about halfway down it's becoming tricky. The distance between this tree stump and the next is too far. I'll have to jump and hope. If I miss, I'm sliding down a long way, but hopefully the suit will protect me.

As I spring for the next tree, something hit my helmet and I lose my focus and balance. The world somersaults as I tumble, over and over, and over again.

I finally stop with a splash, and I think I'm okay – there's no big pain and I think I can stand up. But the relief is immediately replaced by panic as I'm struck with something else, thrown from above. It smashes onto my right shoulder and takes me off my feet, deeper into the river.

Water begins to leak into my suit, covering my underclothes and soaking my skin with a cold layer. If I wasn't under attack, I'd enjoy the soak, but the Watcher has clearly decided to take me on here and I need to get up and fight back.

But it's not so easy to see with the helmet on.

As I push myself back up, much heavier, and clumsier for all the water I've taken on, I scan the hill I've just come down.

I can't see anyone. But I'm not surprised. This person is as stealthy as Eagle.

A brutal force goes through the back of my legs, and I fall forward, face first into the river. Someone is on my back instantly and is forcing my head down. Water flows in through the gaps in my helmet for breathing, seeing, and hearing.

I thrash as hard as I can, but I'm pinned, and the heavy suit and the water are combining to make it near impossible for me to shrug off the Watcher.

I take a moment to breathe deeply, to think of something to get this enemy off me. I reach for my claustroBlade, but it's wedged by my side. I go for the pistol on the other side, but the holder is empty. They must have taken it from me already.

My face is about to be submerged, so I take a final, long breath. And hold it.

I thrash around again, but I'm unable to move the Watcher. I have seconds of held air left, and instead of thinking of death, Six pops into my head. That day we were in the river, and I hid under the water holding my breath to jump out at her.

What would she do? Another few seconds pass and my lungs are close to bursting, desperate to release the caged air.

She'd outthink them. So, I remain still, releasing all the tension from my muscles, trying to mimic a dead person. Won't be hard in a few seconds.

But the Watcher does not relent. They must want to be sure, before releasing me.

I'm outta options, so I hold on, second by second, listening to my pulse slowing, the swoosh of water inside my helmet as it completely fills.

Then the pressure disappears. They've let me go.

But I hold on for another second or two. Let them relax.

And then I leap up, blindly swinging my arms, then clutching at my claustroBlade, unleashing it and jabbing where I think the enemy will be.

I still can't see through all the water in my helmet, the eyepieces still spewing out the collected water. I need a few seconds more. But I don't have it.

A thump to my helmet takes me off my feet again, but two lucky things happen. The blow has dislodged the helmet from my head, and after a few blinks and a splutter, I can see (vaguely) and breath (like a sprinter after a race). The other lucky thing is I'm now on the bank of the river, and above the Watcher, who is wading to me, with a quarterstaff in hand. I recognise a battered and discoloured Guardian uniform. It's stained with blood and mud, and who knows what else.

'Stop,' I say. 'I'm on your side. Look.' And I point to my helmet and exoArmour. 'I'm a Black Knight.'

'You're no Black Knight,' he shouts, pausing just a foot away from me. 'A Black Knight would have spotted me hours ago. They'd have responded to my signal. They'd have not been bested by me.'

As he speaks, I recognise the voice. Then it hits me. 'Thirteen?' As I say his name, I cough up more water.

'What?' he pauses, looking puzzled.

'You're E820913, right?'

He looks at me closer, then his eyes widen in recognition. 'E820907? Seven, you little scut! You're the most wanted person in the Realm. And I just caught you. If I brought you back, they'd reward me. Oh yes. Maybe I'd get to take that uniform right off your back!' He lifts his staff, ready to strike.

I could fight, and maybe win, but I'd have to kill him. And as much as I don't like him, he's only being a good little Realm Guardian. Doing exactly what I wanted to do for so many years. Plus, we were brought up together. 'Wait. You need me alive, and unharmed. I won't fight you, just take me quietly.' I lie to give myself more time to recover. I can always find a more opportune moment to escape him, or even capture him back.

He pauses, considering. 'This isn't a game, is it, Seven?'

I cross my fingers behind my back. 'No, I promise.'

He looks back up the steep slope, and then checks all around us.

'Who are you looking for?' I ask. 'Is there more of you?'

'No, no more Guardians,' he admits, carelessly. 'But there's someone, or something out there.'

I say nothing. I've sensed the same thing the last few days, but I assumed it was him. But now that I think about it, Thirteen is hardly skilled enough, or patient enough to do that.

'How did you find me?' I ask. 'What are you doing out here? There's no big settlements for miles.'

He continues to scan our surroundings, which is good. He's not focussed on what he's telling me.

'We got scattered as we retreated from Westmine. I was making my way back to our barracks, when I see your exoArmour this morning, and hailed you with our signal. When you didn't respond, but clearly heard it, I figured something was up and followed you.

I would have challenged you sooner, but this other person, or thing, has been pursuing me as I followed you.'

'So the hunter has become the hunted.' I smile, but Thirteen doesn't look impressed.

'Get up,' he says. 'Let's go.'

I decide to go along with him for now. There will be opportunities later. He'll have to sleep, for a start. And with him being so edgy about his Watcher, there's bound to a lapse in concentration. See Six, I'm learning.

I'm dry, but exhausted, as we stop to camp for the night. My hands are tied up in front of me, which is annoying to walk with, but I can put up with it. For now.

Thirteen is super alert, but not on me. I've done nothing but be compliant all day to lower his guard. He lights a small fire and even gives me some food.

'Thank you,' I say.

He grunts. 'Want you alive and healthy for the Autokratōr when we arrive. Nothing personal.'

'Fair enough. I'm going to sleep. I haven't slept in two days, and I know you're not going to kill me, so you can take watch.' And I mean it. He looks so edgy; I don't imagine he'll be sleeping. It's nice to have some company, even if it's the worst company ever.

And within seconds, I'm gone.

I wake to find Thirteen an inch from my face. I almost shout out, but his hand is on my mouth before I do.

'Don't make a sound,' he says. 'We're getting out of here. Real quiet. Don't try anything.' He holds a small knife to my throat. 'Got it?'

I nod.

He slowly packs up our things, and we're about to leave when a howl comes from the darkness. If it wasn't so close, I wouldn't be able to tell if it was a wox or not. But it's so loud, it's clear there's human in there.

The Watcher.

Thirteen jerks round, the pistol he took from me in one hand, my claustroBlade in the other. I'm defenceless, aside from my suit, so I'm kinda rooting for Thirteen here. At least with him, I know I'll live another day.

He moves to the edge of our firelight, but as he reaches it, the howl comes from the opposite direction. The Watcher is playing with us.

Thirteen turns and edges towards the latest howl, but again, when he reaches the opposite side, another howl comes from a new direction.

This game continues for three more rounds. I don't know who to cheer for anymore. Better the devil you know, I guess. This devil out in the dark could be anyone, with any intention.

But Thirteen has had enough. His nerves are clearly shredded. He's pouring with sweat, despite the cold night, and he's shaking, which makes me nervous as he's holding the pistol.

'Come out!' he screams into the night. 'Show you face. Fight with honour. Stop being a sneaky coward!'

Even I'm beginning to agree with Thirteen. It's surely time for the games to stop.

A loud bang rips through the air and my heart leaps. But my body does the opposite, as I hit the deck looking for cover.

Thirteen drops the pistol, and the blade. He stares at me with terrified eyes. Then falls to his knees. A large pool of fresh blood begins to grow from a small hole in his uniform. On the right side of his chest. Blood comes from his nose and mouth, illuminated by the fire he's so close to falling into.

I leap up, pushing him away from it.

Thirteen's awful, but he's a follower. A lemming who's so invested in a broken system and can't see it. His blind belief in the

Realm is a flaw, but it's not enough that he deserves to be burnt alive.

I stare out in the direction the shot came from, but I can't see anyone.

Then I hear a barrel click into place, right behind my head. I'm dead.

'The mighty Seven. Captured by Thirteen. Pathetic.'

I recognise the voice, and turn, hardly believing it.

But when I see his face, I believe. 'Three?'

He smiles.

'How? And why?'

'Let's deal with our friend first, then we can talk.' He moves over the still body of the fallen Guardian. Our old camp mate. He aims his rifle.

'Wait,' I say, hopping between the rifle and my captor.

Three frowns. 'He was literally about to hand you over to the Autokratōr – why wouldn't I kill him?'

'He's no danger to us now. Let's just tie him up and leave him. Give him a fair chance.'

'I thought you had some intelligence, Seven. That's a stupid idea. If he gets word out, it will blow your whole plan.'

I nod. 'I know, but are we any better than them if we kill unarmed, defenceless people just because they're on the "other side"?'

He pauses for a moment, as though frozen in time. Then his body relaxes, and he lowers his gun. 'Fine, have it your way Golden Balls. It's your mission.'

We tie Thirteen up in an old house, leaving him enough food water to last a few days. 'If you do somehow escape, do yourself a favour and don't come anywhere near us. Take off that uniform and run to the nearest settlement that will take you. If I ever see you again, I will kill you.' Three has never looked more serious about something in the whole time I've known him.

Even Thirteen doesn't say anything back, simply looking

furious at the situation he's now in. Last night he thought he'd won the best prize imaginable – presenting me to the Autokratōr – and now he's tied up, with no weapons, no allies, and nowhere to go. Well, until Three circles back round to pick him up on his way home.

We sit by the fire, the sun slowly setting behind the hills that surround us, chewing on some wox meat, freshly caught, and cooked by Three this afternoon.

'Why didn't you just offer to come along before I left? Why sneak around for days, following me?' I say, through a mouthful of meat. 'As much as I enjoyed you messing with Thirteen like that.'

'I knew you'd tell me to go away, and you'd puff out your chest be all Seven-like – "I need to do this alone. I, alone, can defeat the Realm..." Blah, blah, blah,' he laughs.

I smile. That's exactly what I'd have said.

'Why did you follow me, though? Like, at all?' I ask.

'You're going to save Six, and I want to help. She was always kind to me. And Cherish.' He puts his head down as he speaks, unable to look me in the eye.

'I'm sorry I wasn't more decent to you back in camp. I got so caught up in the whole system of doing well, and passing our test, and graduating and stuff. But I never understood why you didn't try. You've already shown you're capable of much more since we left the testing centre.'

'Smiler broke me.' He lifts his shirt to show me his body, covered in lash scars, like me. But so many more. 'I didn't want to be part of a world where that happens to kids. I knew I'd fail my test on purpose, and they'd exile me. I knew that whatever being Nameless was, it was better than having a name and being part of the Realm's system.'

'Well, you caught on quicker than me. I took all those lashings and still wanted to serve. Right until the end. Right until they made me...'

'You made the right decision,' Three says. 'Leaving the centre with the Orphans was the right call and that's all that matters. You did the right thing in the end.'

'Thanks, Three. You're not too bad, you know.'

He shrugs. 'Come on, we've got a lot of walking ahead of us, and a plan to come up with, to get you into the City with your cover intact.'

'Okay, let's go over my plan,' I say, pointing towards the small dot in the distance, which we think is New London. Circle City. Where Six is hopefully still alive.

'It was mostly my plan,' interrupts Three, grinning.

'Okay, let's go over *our* plan.'

He nods, satisfied.

I smile. 'I'll approach on foot and walk up to the patrol at one of the entrance gates. You'll be hidden within sniper distance, ready and waiting. I'll let you decide the best spot.'

'Why, thank you, Chosen One for allowing me to have some autonomy and not be micro-managed over where to sit.' He grins.

I narrow my eyes at him. 'Anyway, I'll start talking to them, and it's all going well, you can relax.'

'And if it's not?' Three asks.

'I'll give you a signal, and you can take a few shots. I'd rather you didn't kill anyone, but I'm not going to worry about that.'

'What's the signal?'

'I'll turn and point away from the city. I'll find a reason to do that. You just be ready and shoot if you see that signal. That means it's not going well at the gate, and I need a distraction.'

'That was my idea.'

'I remember.'

'Good. When they're worshipping you round the fire at the

next Orphan's "Ode to Seven" singsong, be sure to drop in that I did contribute.'

'Of course, I will.'

'Sure, Golden Balls. Sure.'

We both laugh.

'And what will you do?' I ask. 'After you've distracted them, and they come for you?'

'What I do best – shoot them if there's a few and hide if there's many.'

'You really are different, Three. Nothing like the kid I grew up with.'

'Maybe. I have learned a lot these last few weeks. Or maybe I'm just the same, which you'd have found out if you'd bothered with anyone else, except Six.' He winks at me.

I don't know much about Three, but if he's capable of so much change, then maybe I am too. Maybe I can rescue Six. And maybe, if I survive, I can become a leader one day. But for now, I must get back into Realm mode and do my best impression of a Black Knight.

Then the strangest thing happens. Three hugs me.

When we separate, there's a small nod of acknowledgement that we may never see each other again. I wish I'd gotten to know Three better sooner.

'Good luck,' he says, smiling. 'You're gonna need it!'

'Thanks, you too!'

And I turn and walk towards the Realm's capital.

CHAPTER 32
CIRCLE CITY

Circle City engulfs the landscape.

I walk towards the huge main gates. Two huge chunks of metal, hinged into even larger chunks of metal, which encompass the entire city. The Orphans have no chance of taking this city. Ever. But maybe one can sneak in.

I have the exoArmour and my helmet on, so no-one can see my face. Three helped me fix it back on after Thirteen removed it. I think it's pretty much broken now, there's no voicebox, and so my mouth is exposed, and my eyes, but it will mask some of my uncertainty. I hope.

I'm not even through the gates and I've passed at least a thousand Guardians, not to mention millions of workers in the factories, fields and farms that surround Circle City for hundreds of miles.

Its scale is beyond anything I had imagined.

'You look like you've never seen this place before.' The Guardian strides forward from the gate. He smiles, obviously seeing me as a friendly due to the Black Knight uniform.

I realise my mouth is wide open and I'm staring at everything.

'Yeah, no matter how many times you see it, it's still amazing, huh?'

'I guess. If you like steel fortresses.' The Guardian looks at me funny. Maybe my twin isn't usually as nice.

I stay silent. No slip ups. Say as little as possible to anyone. Listen. Find out where Six is. Get out. I'll get the Orphans some info, too, but it's not my priority.

As for assassinating the Autokratōr? It would be suicide. Even if someone got close, they could never get out. And I doubt I'll even see him.

Keep my head down. Get out with Six.

'So, what happened down there?' The same Guardian tries to chat to me again. 'You know, with the rebellion and all. How did you get away? We've had very few squads return.'

'There were too many of them. Barely got out myself.' Vague. Say little.

Another of the Gate Guardians pipes up. 'Thought you Black Knights fought to the death? How come you wimped out?'

The Gate Guardians around him gasp and take a step back.

I know what I should do. I should react angrily, beat him to a pulp. But I take a deep breath, pretending to compose myself.

'Mind your tongue, Guardian.' I edge towards him. 'Or I'll remove it.' I tap my hand on my claustroBlade.

His eyes focus on my hand. He swallows and holds his hand up. 'No offence meant.'

'None taken.' I sit back down and relax my hands. 'If you must know, I killed many of them, but they had GM's.'

The Guardians look at each other. 'Thought they were just rumours? You really saw some?' the one beside me asks.

'Several. The Orphans have many of them.' Ha, that ought to get the rumours going. Scare some of these guys into thinking the Orphans are stronger than they really are.

'I thought the Orphans were gone. It was just some rebel slaves, was it not?'

'It was the Orphans all right,' I say, enjoying the effect it has. About time they felt a little fear.

I look around again, beyond the gates, trying not to look too interested in the city. Buildings, tall as hills, large telescreens, every few hundred metres, people, scuttling around like worker bees, ordered and in unison.

'Then we must get to the Autokratōr right away. He must know this.'

I swallow, my wandering mind thrust back into the truck. 'The Autokratōr? No, I will just report to my captain.'

I consider giving Three the signal, and escaping inside in the carnage, but I shouldn't make a scene. I'm getting a free ride to exactly where I want to go. I just don't feel ready yet. I wanted a few days to get to know the city and the palace layout first.

Three will understand. He'll go back and re-join the Orphans. But part of me wishes he was doing this with me.

'No way. We'd be executed if we didn't get you straight to him. He needs to know this.' He shouts to the driver. 'Take us to the Palace, Duren. The Black Knight needs to see the Autokratōr, ASAP.'

We pass through the gates. The noise around us suddenly increases. People shouting orders, machines and generators humming. Electricity. Man, there's so much in this place.

I wonder if I could have lived here, a citizen of the Realm, and maybe I would have lived near Six. She would have done her research and I'd have defended the Realm.

But that life is over for us. We will never experience it. All I can do is try to extend it for us both for a while longer.

I have to rescue her, at all costs.

We walk the last part as no vehicles are allowed within a mile of the palace.

The Guardians flank me, like an honour guard, but I can't help feeling like a prisoner rather than a war hero. I must remember I'm a Black Knight. Almost untouchable in the Realm.

I stand up straighter and make my strides longer, racing towards Realm's dictator. The man whose rule forced me to kill

Cherish. The man whose system has oppressed so many people. The man who I have volunteered to assassinate. Every part of me wants to. But if I do, I can't save Six.

The road we walk down is smooth and red paved. I've never walked on anything like it. It's firm and even. I could walk on this, eyes closed, and never worry about tripping.

Either side we are flanked by large, green areas, with sporadic groups of trees. Several people are either trimming the bushes or cutting the grass short. Ahead of us, a circular monument stands high in front of the Palace gates. Water shoots from a huge fountain and a gold statue of the Autokratōr stands atop a stone monolith.

As we pass it, the sound of the water splashing makes me realise how quiet this part of the city is compared to the loud buzz of people and machines as I entered. Despite New London's overpopulation issues, it seems they can still give the Autokratōr a palace and large, peaceful grounds.

The gates rise fifty feet high, the surrounding fence only a little less. At least twenty Guardians watch us from a small outhouse, others posted just inside the gates themselves.

To the left, an enormous building rises higher and wider than most of those surrounding it.

I recognise it.

I've seen it a thousand times. In our books and in my dreams.

The Hall of Records.

My name is in there.

I've obsessed about this for so long, that I struggle to keep my feet moving away from it. It was a child's dream. Saving Six is the mission. But perhaps I can do both. Perhaps if I can save her, we can go that way. I can use my status to get access to the records. Just a peak...see if Lasul was telling me the truth.

I turn away.

We stop in front of the iron entrance, and I wait for the

Guardians to pull it open. They don't, instead they frown at me and look to one another.

'Retinal scan, remember.' The Guardian who sat beside me for twelve hours as we travelled to the city helps me out.

I nod to him and move to the metal box, fixed into the bars of the gate. Fortunately, I remember enough biology to know retina is in the eye. I move my head to align my eyes with the two holes.

A flash of light blinds me for a second. I clamp my eyes shut and take a step back. Then I remember I'm supposed to be used to this, so force them open again and cough a few times.

The gates swing open.

'Good luck, Pol.' I turn and the first Guardian salutes me. Then he and his men disappear back down the red-paved road.

I face the Palace, it's wide, white walls covered in many curtained windows.

I force my feet forward, following the strangely dressed Guardian who now escorts me. He has a red uniform, unlike the normal whites of the Guardians. He also walks funny. Long, deliberate strides, legs straight. But even funnier than his walk is his helmet. Or whatever it is. Tall, black, and fluffy. Rifle resting upon his shoulder.

When we reach the palace building, we pass under an arched tunnel and through into a large, open, square space. Many more Red Guardians are stationed, every one of them as still as the statue out at the fountain.

We turn left and reach a smaller door which leads into the actual Palace.

I recognise the circular bracelet they used back at the Testing centre. DNA sample. Here's where we find out just how identical Pol and I are.

I guide my hand into the device, and it clamps on my wrist. It stings. Then it releases me. We wait for a moment in silence, the Red Guardian still.

Then the small screen next to the device beeps. Green text appears.

Pol T. – Black Knight of the Realm
Access authorised

The door swings open.

Same eyes. Same genes.

Crunk, I really do have a twin brother.

'You know your way?'

I nod.

The Red Guardian probably isn't authorised to go inside, so marches back to his post.

My exoArmour struggles climbing the narrow, twisting stairs, or maybe I just struggle navigating it in such a tight space. All the training I did on my long walk here, and I didn't think to practice in tight spaces. Let's hope it doesn't come to that.

I exit to a large, circular room, the walls covered in ancient paintings.

And fifty or so Guardians.

Some in red, some in white.

And some in black.

'Pol, you made it back!' Twelve strides towards me.

CHAPTER 33
THE AUTOKRATŌR

My right fist balls and the exoArmour fist follows.

Twelve spots it and frowns, but I instantly release, smiling and reaching out the hand to shake.

He also smiles but takes a step back. 'Wow, I'm not shaking your hand while you're in that suit, man. You wanna crush my bones?' He turns to a few of the others, who laugh.

None of the other Knights have their exoArmour on. Nobody even has a weapon.

'Help me get out of this, man.' I address Twelve, calling him 'man' as I have no idea what his name is now. But he frowns at me again.

'They hit you hard on the head? Just press the unsuit button.' His right eyebrow arches.

All eyes in the room are still on me. I can't blow this. Think. Think.

'My suit has been playing up. Got damaged in the battle and not been serviced for a while.'

A few nods. 'Fair enough.' Twelve strides towards me and his right hand moves to my throat.

Instinctively, I jerk my head away.

'Hey man, take it easy. I'm just going to release you.' He presses the small black button beneath my helmet, and it flicks off, the rest of the suit sliding away from my body in a fluid and easy motion.

My body floats and every movement is easy. I've been hauling myself around in that suit for weeks and suddenly I only need to move my own weight.

I almost fall over as I step out of the suit, now opened like a funeral cask.

'You need some rest and some food I think.' Twelve puts his hand on my shoulder.

His touch repulses me and I want to end him. Right now. But that's not the mission. I see several of the others watching me closely. They've formed a subconscious circle around Twelve.

Nothing's changed.

He's still got followers. Just these ones are more powerful. And well trained.

So, I nod and smile. 'Thanks, that would be good.'

He leads me to a table, where several of the other Knights sit.

Plates of meat, vegetables, fruit, cereals, and jugs of juices, wines and beer lie half-consumed in the middle of the table.

I can't help myself and grab large portions of everything.

I glug down the juice, a tear into the meat, I bite greedily into an apple, the crunch and the juice hitting every sweet spot in me.

'How long were you out there, Pol?' It's Twelve again. The others watch and wait, eager to hear about my contribution to the war, no doubt.

'Weeks. The exile scum overran us in the battle. I had no choice. I took out as many of them as I could, but I was overcome and had to retreat.'

I take another few bites, buying time, and trying to avoid saying too much. I'm not sure I've nailed the accent, nor the pronunciation, which is definitely different here in the capital. Even Twelve is speaking a little differently from a few weeks ago.

'We heard that it was the Orphans.' Twelve drums his fingers on the wooden table.

Careful.

'Whoever it was, they had the numbers.'

Twelve continues to stare at me. He's not stupid. He might work out who I am. No slip ups. 'You know what, Pol. You look just like this scutting Greenie I grew up with. If it wasn't for that cut ear, I'd say he was your doppelgänger.' He smiles, but I can tell he's probing.

I just nod, trying to not do anything Seven-like. It's hard with his smug face right next to me.

'Pol. The Autokratōr will see you now.' A fully uniformed Red Guardian stands at the door. 'Follow me.'

I get up, stuffing some fruit in my pocket. I nod to Twelve and the other Knights, hoping I've not completely blown my cover.

The Red Guardian takes me down a corridor of varnished, gleaming wood. My boots almost slip a few times. The same fancy paintings hang on the walls. Lots of shiny metal on the tables at the side. Plenty of uniformed and upright Red Guardians.

My guide takes me a long way from the room where my exoArmour – my only real defence – sits empty.

'This way.' He opens enormous roof-high doors, which swing towards an equally colossal room.

But it's very different to the rest of the palace, which has an ancient feel. This room is covered in tech of every variety. Screens, flashing lights, computers. And other stuff I've never seen before.

Behind a semi-circle of telescreens, sits a man who I recognise.

'Hail the Autokratōr.' I play along nicely.

'Come, Pol. Come.' He leaps out of his chair and moves towards me, his arms wide.

The warmth catches me out and I only just manage to get my arms up in time for the tight hug.

When he lets go, he holds my elbows at arm's length and inspects me. He sees the scars, old and new...to him. They're all new to me.

'I am glad to see you alive. It worried me when I heard of the rebellion. It was a tough initiation. How did you manage to make it out alive?'

He indicates for us to sit.

I don't know what I expected – a throne, surrounded by hundreds of guards. A cold man, a dictator. Certainly, not this. He seems like a human, not the god-like ruler we're moulded into worshipping.

I sit beside him, and he gives me his full attention.

He is less than a metre from me. No armour. No weapon. Open and exposed.

The doors close.

Only me and him.

I could end it all right now.

It's what the Orphans wanted me to do.

I could kill him.

I should kill him.

But he might be my father.

I killed Cherish to prove loyalty to him. But can I kill him to gain revenge for her.

'Pol, are you okay?'

I nod.

'I see you've taken on some injuries – have you seen the doctor, yet?'

I shake my head.

'That's where you're going next.' And he edges a little closer. 'But first, tell me what happened down there. We've had very few come back. I need to know everything. How did they get so organised? Was it the Orphans? We must stomp this spark out before it becomes a fire.'

'It was the Orphans.'

'Did you see who was leading them?'

'No.'

'You didn't see anyone organising them?'

'It was so manic. I barely made it out alive.'

'Understandable. But I need to know. Were there GM's?'

'Yes. Several.' My heart smashes the inside of my chest. Keep the answers short.

'Okay. Okay. Perhaps you'll be able to tell me more later once you've had a medical check and some rest.'

I nod.

'Go for now. I will call for you later. Rest easy.' He turns immediately back to his computer, his warmth disappearing in an instant.

I stand up, uncertain if I've been dismissed but the door opens, so I take that as a cue to leave.

When I'm outside, a Black Knight meets me. 'Welcome back, Pol.' She takes my hand. 'I didn't think I'd see you again.'

'Didn't think I'd see this place again. Or you.'

'Follow me.' She takes me the opposite direction from where my exoArmour is. Further and further away from my weaponry. My defence. Great.

I follow her into a small room, with only one thing in it. A large, comfortable looking bed. And a small bathroom just off it.

She pushes me onto the bed.

And jumps on top of me.

'Oi.' I think she's attacking me, and I tense, ready to fight her off.

But then her lips grab me. Her tongue finds mine and she presses her body into me.

For a moment, I don't move, enjoying the close touch of someone after those cold, lonely nights as I marched up here. But then I remember Six. And Doc.

I push her up.

She frowns. 'Miss me?' She moves to kiss me again, but I slide out from under her.

'What's wrong?' She jumps to her feet.

'Nothing...I just...I'm just tired. Exhausted.'

'You haven't seen me in weeks...I thought you were dead...' She grabs me and this time pulls me into a close, warm hug.

Love replaces lust.

Great, this was Pol's girlfriend.

Just what I need to complicate things.

And I don't know her name. I'm bound to mess this up.

She beams at me. 'I'm not letting you out of my sight for at least a month!'

I've no idea how to deal with this.

I could stay with her but the longer I'm here the more chance I'll be found out.

I should leave, but if I do that, she might suspect something is up and tell someone.

'I'm dizzy...need to go for a walk.' I fake a sway.

She grabs me round the waist. 'Okay, I've got prison duty starting soon, so walk me there. It's just me tonight, so maybe you could just stay down there with me?'

Anywhere is better than being stuck in this girl's bedroom, especially when she thinks I'm my twin. 'Sure, let's go.'

And she's taking me right to where I want to go. To prison level. Six.

She holds my hand as we walk, which isn't so bad. She's about the same height as me, and her grip is strong but soft.

I glance at her face, and she gives me a peck on the cheek.

She seems so happy to see me.

Guilt has a riot inside me. I'm messing with people's emotions. With the people they love. It's not fair to this girl, who seems nice and madly in love with Pol.

Even the Autokratōr seemed decent.

I harden my thoughts, thinking of the moment I shot Cherish.

They are responsible. Don't get soft, Seven!

We descend a spiralling set of stairs – they love them in this place. It gets darker and colder at each level until finally we reach the bottom. Before she opens the door, she grabs me close, and we cuddle.

Much less passion this time, far more depth.

'I'm glad you're home.' She smiles and presses the combination into the pad, followed by a retinal scan.

The door beeps and the magnetic lock releases.

The dungeon beyond is cold, wet, and dark, lit only by the occasional red glow of halogen lamps. An endless corridor extends beyond sight, flanked either side by the rusted metal bars of hundreds of cells.

A central island desk, with telescreens and a computer, greets us. Behind the desk sits a tired Guardian.

'Gruff, I'll take over a little early tonight.'

Gruff looks at her, then at me and narrows his eyes. 'No, thanks. I will finish my shift. And *he* shouldn't be here.'

He turns back to the row of telescreens and runs his fingers across their surface. Cell after cell comes into view. All with miserable looking inhabitants.

'Come on, Gruff. I'll do your shift on Tuesday as well. Just forget you saw Pol come down here with me.' She plays with her hair and leans on one leg as she speaks. It makes her look very sexy.

He looks up briefly. 'No, thanks.' His eyes return to the monitors.

I've forgotten just how loyal some of these Realmers are.

It's crazy what people will do in the name of loyalty to the Realm.

Cherish. Gun. Blood.

'Okay, here's the deal Gruff. Disappear now...' she moves rapidly, grabs his arm, and twists it behind him. '...or I'll break this. You and I were Greenies together. You know what I can do.'

She lets go and his mouth moves but he doesn't dare speak.

'Thanks, Gruff.' She winks at him.

He gets up, narrows his eyes at me as he passes and exits, slamming the door closed behind him. The noise echoes for several seconds through the vast prison corridor.

'Won't he tell someone?' I ask.

'Nah. He acts all dutiful, but he knows the score. Nobody messes with my prison.' She smiles and slides her arms around my waist. She gently kisses me. I don't resist.

My mind is on those computers and telescreens.

If I can get access to them or manipulate her to show me who's in the cells, I might be able to find Six.

If she's in here.

If she's still alive...

CHAPTER 34
TUBE

'I'm just going to do my rounds; check they're all tucked in for the night.' She winks at me.

I still don't know her name.

Better this way.

Won't feel as bad about taking her out if I need to.

'Okay, I'll just wait here.'

I watch her pass through the first door. It's transparent and I can still see her after she closes and walks beyond. But she can see me, too.

She uses a retinal scanner at each door to pass beyond. I wonder if Pol has the clearance to pass. I'll check that out in a bit.

But first.

Find Six.

I type E820906 into the database search box.

One hit.

Cell H29

Subject has been subject to intense advanced interrogation techniques by our top specialists. Refuses to give information on the whereabouts of the traitor, E820907.

Scheduled for termination due to lack of cooperativity and treason.

Fuck.

I quickly flick through the cameras, arriving at H29 and I zoom in.

Curled up in a corner, covered in half-healed scars, and very little else is Six.

Her arms are curled around her shoulders. She looks cold. And sad.

I zoom the camera further in.

Her face is gaunt, her eyes are sunken. Her cheekbones are prominent, and her hair is patchy and matted. It's unclear if she's breathing.

My fist goes through the telescreen.

Shards of glass protrude from my knuckles and streams of blood flow down my arm as I lift it away from the shattered computer.

A voice comes over the comms. 'Pol, you okay? I got a malfunction warning from one of the monitors.'

'Fine. I'm coming to see you.' I stride towards the first door.

'Hold on, I might need to scan you through.' Her voice is background.

The scanner flicks over my eyes.

The door opens.

This guy Pol is a big deal! All the better for me.

'Hey, how did you get through?'

I shrug.

She shakes her head, smiling. Then the smile dies as she sees my bloody hand.

There are two clear doors separating me from her.

We both stride towards each other, faces hardening. Muscles tensing.

I recognise the movements.

We're going to fight.

And I can't win.

Even if I win the fight.

I must talk to her.

What can I say to her to make her help me? She seems reasonable. Decent, even. She even said it herself, she was a Greenie, too.

'You're not Pol, are you?' She opens the last door separating us.

Prisoners rise from their dark corners and lean against the bars of their cells.

'I am not. But let me explain...'

She doesn't let me.

Instead, a flurry of powerful strikes come down upon me.

I go limp.

I won't fight her.

The only way to get out of this alive is to let her beat me.

And she does.

Blow after blow thunder down upon my head and my body.

Okay, maybe I need to do something. She ain't stopping. 'I didn't kill him. He's alive.'

My words act as a momentary buffer.

Her fists are still curled up, covered in my blood. And possibly hers.

Her breathing is ragged, feral and uncontrolled. She lost it. But I can see she's trying to recover herself. She wants to know more.

'We have him. I can take you to him.'

'Is he...hurt?'

I nod. 'But he's being well treated. I assure you.'

She sits back on her bum, her shaking arms either side of her. They wrap across her chest, trying to steady herself.

It reminds me of the image of Six in her cell.

'I'm sorry, but if you want to see him again, you must help me do something. Now.' I stand up, unsteady and sore.

'What do you want from me?' Anger diffuses from her eyes to mine.

'Help me get my friend out of here. Out of the city.'

'Your friend is in here?' She laughs, but with no joy. 'Then she may as well be dead. And so is Pol.'

'No.' I pull her up to stand. 'We have to get her out. She's in H29. Help me, and I can help you. I promise if you get us out, you will see Pol again.'

She bites her lip for a moment, silent.

'How? How will I see him again? I'd be surprised if the Orphans haven't killed him already.'

'Trust me, they haven't.'

'Well, if I'm relying on trusting you, a stranger who has already lied to me, and deceived me into thinking you were my...my Pol...'

She's silent again.

'He spoke of you. Back at the mine. It was the one thing that almost made him help me. The thought of never seeing you again almost made him betray the Realm.'

I leave that comment to settle. If that doesn't do it, I'll have to do this without her.

Finally, she nods. 'Okay. But if they catch us, we're dead. No messing around. Get her, then get out.'

'Got it.' I nod.

'It's so weird...you look just like him. How? Are you twins? Is he your brother? He never mentioned any siblings to me.'

'I honestly don't know either. I didn't expect to get the chance to rescue Six so quickly. I had planned to go to the Hall of Records and find out more.'

'So, let's be clear. I get you and your friend out; you take me to Pol, and he gets released and we both walk?'

I pause for a milli-second. The Orphans would not approve of this plan. None of it. They'd want me to get back in with the Autokratōr and assassinate him. Six is secondary to their plans and they definitely won't give up Pol. Even Six herself wouldn't agree to this.

'Yes, absolutely. I promise.' I hold out my open hand.

She takes it and nods. 'Follow me.'

We advance further into the cell block, passing through several clear doors.

H-Block.

'Your friend is in the cell at the end. But when we open these cells, they send a message to the duty Black Knight. It's protocol because all H-Block prisoners are high priority for the Autokratōr.'

'Okay, so how do we do this?'

'You need to go through that door at the end and hide in the corridor beyond.'

'Why?'

'There's a camera that the Knight will check when I open the cell. If they see me escorting a prisoner out, they won't be suspicious. If they see us both, they will. You're well known around here.'

'I'm supposed to go and wait? What if something goes wrong and I can't get back in?'

'Then we're both dead.'

'Reassuring.' I shake my head.

She moves to the retinal scanner at the prison block exit. It opens and I move through. My eyes linger on H29.

This new corridor is much older, clearly little used. It has several junctions and turnings. If she's screwing me over, there would be nowhere better. I'd be lost in minutes.

A small booth, with all its glass windows long gone, sits dusty to my right. A sign at the top says 'tickets'.

On the wall beside it is a barely comprehensible tangle of coloured lines, all crossing over each other, each one with a series of connected dots. The dots are named.

St James Park

Hyde Park Corner

Green Park

Victoria

And hundreds of others.

I turn away from the maze of transecting lines and read the signs above each potential exit.

And then I realise I know where I am, though I've never been here.

The map.

The one Cherish made me memorise. It's this grid of coloured lines. But as I have no clue where to go, it doesn't help us much right now. This girl better be for real. I'm putting my life, and Six's, in the hands of the nameless girlfriend of a known enemy.

Nameless.

Just like me, I guess. And Six. And many other people I know and like.

It used to be all that mattered to me. And it still does.

But for different reasons now.

The door slides open and the Knight, my new ally, appears, cradling Six. 'Here, you take her. I'll need to focus on the way.'

My heart skips so many beats, seeing her again. But it's also crumbling seeing her like this. So tortured and weak. Because of me.

'You do know the way?' I ask, taking Six into my arms. She's so light.

'Sort of. I've seen it on maps.'

I shake my head. Our chances of escape have just plummeted, along with that small swell of hope.

'No time for doubts. They know I'm up to something. The alarm was triggered. They're coming for us. Follow me.' She sprints down the corridor marked *Green Park*.

I run after her, wishing I could take some time to check Six. She weighs nothing, she's hardly breathing. She needs a medic ASAP.

The corridor is dully lit, automatic lamps flicking on as we approach.

'Will they be able to track those light sensors?' I shout.

'Not sure. Let's hope not or they'll know exactly where we are.' She replies without even turning, her focus on the dark corridor ahead.

We ignore several side doors and keep on the main route. After a couple of minutes, we stop.

Two choices on the wall.

'I think we take the Southbound...'

'Think?'

Every light in the corridor and beyond suddenly erupts into full brightness.

'They've redirected the power to this place. They know we're here.' She runs towards a dark shaft.

'Where now?'

'We need to climb. Can you carry her as well?'

Six is stirring, but even when her eyes flicker open, they're not here.

'I can. Tie her arms together round my neck.'

She grabs her cuffs from her belt and secures Six's arms with them. I swing her around behind me, so that she's on my back. I secure her legs with my arms.

'How are you supposed to climb like that?' the Knight asks me.

'I'll be fine. You go first.'

'No, you first. I might need to fend off our pursuers. You can hardly do that right now.'

She pulls the doors to the shaft apart and I step through and begin climbing the metal-rung ladder. I climb, glancing down to see the girl closing the shaft behind us, bringing us into near darkness.

'I can't see.' I say, the echo reverberating throughout the tight shaft.

'It's even rungs all the way to the top. Just keep going. If I left it open, it would be obvious where we went.'

I continue to climb, my arms already aching. Sweat drenches me very quickly, the darkness making the journey seem endless, like climbing up into a reverse-abyss.

A small light at the very top of the shaft is now visible and I reckon we're less than half-way up.

Shouts come from below, beyond the doors of the shaft. Probably in the very corridor we just vacated. Any second, they'll bust open those doors and see us.

I climb faster, ignoring the ripping pain in my arms and upper back.

The doors clang open beneath us.

Streams of light flash up from multiple torches.

They find us and focus.

Thin, red lines of infrared light target us.

Several red dots fall on my back and on Six, who hangs lifeless behind me.

I turn my body, so that Six is pressed against the ladder and my body is now covered in the red dots. I hold on with one shaking arm.

'What are you doing?' hisses the girl below me. 'Keep climbing. They won't shoot. We're Black Knights. And you're the heir to the Realm. Well, they think you are.'

I hesitate but after a few seconds, they haven't shot. But the dots are still there.

'Fine.' I haul myself back round to face the ladder, Six behind me again. Her cuffs are really cutting into my neck. I'm sure they are cutting into her wrists, too. We need to get up there quicker.

The ladder vibrates with the additional weight of several more people in pursuit.

I keep going, my body close to complete exhaustion.

My sweating hand slips, but I hold on, wrapping a leg around the ladder on that side to hold the weight. I take a second or two to compose. To recover.

'Hurry.'

I ignore her, take another breath, and then climb once more.

Less than ten metres to the top.

The light shines through the closed shaft doors above us. I hope no-one is waiting for us, but I see no shadows, nothing blocking the dull light shining through. They haven't redirected the power up here, so perhaps we've got a chance still.

Five metres.

BANG.

The bullet clangs on the metal and echoes for several seconds.

I glance down, unable to help myself. Red dots swim over Six and me.

I grab the next rung, pulling with everything I have left.

BANG.

My right arm erupts with agony.

It can't hold on and it falls to my side.

I curl my left arm through the rungs and loop my legs through as well.

I'm roaring into the darkness, the pain taking over.

My neck is being pulled backwards.

Six hangs limp behind me stretching me towards the abyss.

My back is arched as far is it can go.

My left arm is slipping.

'Cut her loose,' says the girl below me.

'No.'

'I'm not getting caught. I'm getting out of here. I must see Pol. But she's in my way.'

'I won't cut her loose.'

'Then I will.' She climbs towards me, pulling her keys from her belt.

My arm can't hold our combined weight.

Either Six falls.

Or we both do.

CHAPTER 35
THE HALL OF RECORDS

'If you let her fall, then I will go after her. You will not escape, and you will not see Pol.' My teeth grit together as I speak.

The girl is directly below me. The ladder vibrates from the approaching Knights beneath her.

'No. Drop her.' She moves to put the key into the cuffs.

'Don't you dare.' My left arm shakes. A chorus of lactic acid screams at me to let go.

She glares at me. 'Fine. Don't have much choice, do I?'

As she climbs next to me, her body gets close.

She hauls Six up and away from my neck, onto hers. She does it in one easy movement. She's strong. Too strong perhaps. Only person I know who could do that is Bulk. Or Eagle.

I watch her haul Six up the last few rungs with ease and open the shaft above. A wide chunk of light illuminates the top of the shaft, but no more shots come up, despite how easily they must be able to see us.

I scramble up after her, so slowly that the chasing Knights are only about twenty metres below when I exit the shaft.

My arm has an inferno burning inside it, but I try to close it out. Greenie training coming into use again.

Around us, a labyrinth of corridors and doorways bamboozle.

I'm a passenger in this runaway train ride, one of my enemies steering us away from more of my enemies.

With Six still cuffed round her neck, the Knight moves to a fuse box. She opens it and slashes the wires with her small knife. The main corridor plunges into darkness. The elevator shaft is also dark.

'That'll slow them for a bit,' she says. I hear her footsteps move into the corridor next to the box and I follow.

The lights in here are still on but burn delicately. And I see immediately why.

Books.

Aisles and aisles of books. Stacked high on huge shelves.

'Is this a library?' I ask.

'Hall of Records. There's an active underground rail line beneath the Hall. It's used for transporting in books from all around the Realm. But discretely. The Autokratōr doesn't want everyone knowing about these.'

'Why not?'

'He doesn't want too many people to read all those classics. The books of the past, depicting the rebellion and uprising of groups, just like your Orphans. He wants to keep those ideas away from the minds of those who might try and overthrow him. Wise, in my opinion.'

'You would think that.'

'Listen, I don't like you or what you stand for. And you don't like me. I get it. But we both want something the other can get. So, let's just get on with this. No more talking or questions.' She gets close as she says it. Obviously used to intimidating younger Guardians and citizens. And considering how strong she is, I can see why.

If we do escape, I need to lose her. She can't go anywhere near the Orphans. She's too loyal and would take out too many of us. Guilt wriggles as I think it. But I've done worse.

Six. I left her here and went off to Westmine. Everything that's happened to her is my fault. It's all on me. I need to fix it.

'Fine, let's just go.'

We glide through the rows and rows of books, all stacked neatly and categorised alphabetically and chronologically. If you knew what you were looking for, it would be easy to find.

We pass a bank of computers. Above them is a sign.

Hall of Records – electronic database.

The screen has a flashing prompt.

Type in keyword.

I could find out anything on there.

My name.

My family.

'Move it.'

I continue to stare at the screen and find myself sitting down.

The Knight grabs my arm. 'Move. Now. The entrance down to the track is just ahead. They haven't found us yet, but if you continue to mess around, they will.'

'Just a moment. I need to check something.'

'No.' She thumps the keyboard, and it skids across the floor, beneath a bookshelf.

I slide along to the next computer.

She does the same.

I stand up, getting close to her face. 'Stop it. It will just take a second.'

'Fine.' She unhooks Six from around her neck and sits her in a chair. 'You carry your friend. I'm going.' She strides away towards the green glowing exit sign, just fifty metres away.

Six is still unconscious.

'Sorry, this will just take a second.'

I start typing.

E820907

I hit search.

CHAPTER 36
HEIR

'Seven?' Six's croaky voice startles me.

I whip round and fall to my knees in front of her.

I cup her frail hands in mine and smile wider than I've done in a long, long time.

'Hey.'

'Where are we? How?' She tenses.

I stroke her hair. 'Relax. I'm here to rescue you.'

Her muscles relax a little, but her head spins around. 'Where is this? Is it the Hall of Records?'

Even in this state, she can surprise me. I smile. 'Yes. But we're leaving.'

She turns to the screen. 'Wait, Seven. That's your number on screen.'

I turn away, lifting Six into my arms. 'I've just been reminded what's important to me. And it's not a name.'

It takes every ounce of my strength and willpower to jog down the aisle towards the green exit light. I hope the girl hasn't gotten too far ahead of us.

'Seven, I thought I was going to die in that cell.'

'Shhh, rest. Take it easy. We can talk later.'

'Thank you.' She strokes my cheek.

I nod.

As I reach the door handle, I sense movement in the open space behind us.

BANG.

The bullet hits the wall above. Clearly not meant to hit us.

I lower Six to the ground and turn slowly, hiding her.

Striding towards us are twenty Black Knights, each in an exoArmour with large pulseRifles in one hand and claustroBlades in the other. They take up a regimented, rehearsed formation around us. Semi-circle. All exits cut-off except the one behind me, but if I even twitched towards that handle, twenty rapid-fire shots would rip through me and Six.

Then silence.

'What are you waiting for?' I say it loudly, trying to force out some of the fear that floods me.

None of them respond.

'Fine, I'm leaving.'

But before I even have a chance to move, a single shot thuds into the wall again.

'Okay, I get it. But what are we waiting for?'

No response.

I scan the aisles and aisles of tall bookshelves, looking for a reason that they wait.

Then I spot my new ally.

Crouched at the base of a nearby bookshelf, her finger on her lip.

I turn away, fixing my eyes anywhere but towards that spot.

The Black Knights stiffen as footsteps come quickly towards us.

'*Hail the Autokratōr. Serve the Realm.*'

The Black Knights each repeat the word, lifting their claustroBlade hands to their chests and then resuming military stance.

Marching between the two Knights in front of me is Autokratōr Tyndareus. He has changed and looks much more formal than earlier, like he does each time he appears on the tele-screen to give a speech. His red, medalled suit is the brightest thing in the room and my eyes are drawn to this man, who now looks much more like a powerful dictator than before.

'Imposter. Come forward.' His voice has also changed. Before it was fatherly and encouraging. Now it's commanding and lordly.

I plant my feet. My knees wobble. 'I shall not. I came here to free my wrongly imprisoned friend. That I will do. Or die.'

'You will not free her. And you will not die.' He steps forward, his Knights flanking him. He waves them back. 'It's fine.'

He gets to within lunging distance, then stops, crossing his arms and leaning to the right. Then smiles.

'You do look so much like him.'

'I am nothing like him. I'd never serve you. Or your Realm.'

'But you have before. And I suspect you will in the future. Once I've had my say.'

'I will not.'

'We shall see.'

He takes another step forward, one hand moving to his chin. Twice he begins to speak, then stops.

'Before we discuss your options...confirm to me your Realm designation number.'

'I'm not playing this game.' My lips struggle to form the words, but I force them out. 'You forced me to kill my mother.'

'That's confirmation for me, E820907.' He smiles.

My hands coil into fists.

'Now, I have a deal for you. One where you will live.'

'I refuse. I hate you and won't do another thing this Realm asks me to.'

'You don't want to refuse this. Trust me.' He takes another step closer. 'The deal is this: serve me. You and your friend. You will become Realm citizens. There will be a Naming Ceremony and you can both finally learn who you are. Who your family are. You will have names.'

'Not interested.' I move even closer to Six, who I can feel moving around behind me.

'I'm giving you the best deal I could possibly give to two unco-operative traitors. Do you really want to pass this chance up?'

'What about all the other Nameless?' Six asks. 'What will happen to them?'

'The Orphans at Westmine? Don't worry about them. They've already been taken care of. Some of my best Legions have gone to retake the mine. Grand Guardian Sharan is there.'

My friends' faces whirl in my head, from Eagle to Bulk to Three to Mother.

To Doc.

'Have they been killed?'

'Not all of them. I am not so bad as that. We need people to work the mines.' He takes another step towards me.

I back away, keeping myself between him and Six.

'Relax, Seven. I will not harm you. These Black Knights have been ordered only to shoot if you attack me. You can untense.'

My arm throbs. 'Really?' I turn my arm to show him the bullet wound.

'An accident. You were trying to escape. I did not want you to.'

Then I ask the thing I've been wondering for weeks and weeks. 'Why me? Why make me do...what I did? Why hunt me? Why not just kill me now? You have plenty of reason to.'

'Ah, at last you ask the right things.'

The Autokratōr turns to his Knights. 'You can all go. Except you two.' He points to the two who flanked him earlier.

The other eighteen Knights all retreat from the library, marching in sync, loyal and disciplined as always.

'Seven. I can see you will not bow to my will, using my role as Autokratōr. The Realm has mistreated you. The system failed you. But perhaps I can get through to you in a different way.' He turns to one of the Knights. 'Bring in his mother.'

CHAPTER 37
REJECTION

The lady the Autokratōr calls my mother stares at me. Her hands cover her mouth and she's starting to cry a little.

'Is it really him, Sparta?' she asks the Autokratōr.

'Yes, Leda. We are sure.' The dictator of the Realm suddenly looks human again, the love for his wife beaming from him. He puts an arm around her shoulders.

I'm struggling to breathe. I'm certain this is a trick. Some kind of mind game to mess me up, like they did with Cherish. I won't believe this.

Lasul told me in his letter, but I never wanted to believe it.

'Cas, come to me.' Her voice is soft but uncertain.

I thought Cas was the name Cherish gave to me. Not this stranger. Lasul said he took me at birth, so how could she have named me? A part of me wants to stay, to talk to her, to hear her call me her son and tell me why she chose that name. To be with a family, whatever their faults.

Her arms are wide, and for so many years I'd have run into them. But not now. It's too late. Even for this. Even for my real family.

I shake my head. 'I don't know you. You're not my mother... you're...you're not.'

'Sparta?' She turns to her husband, who seems more certain than her.

He nods. 'I assure you it's him. The Orphans tried to cover up his identity by messing with the DNA samples for a long time. But we finally got a true sample. And it's him. It is *our* son.'

'No...no...no...' Despite the letter, despite all that time thinking it over, coming to terms with what Lasul had written. I never wanted to believe it completely. And even now...it must be a trick. It can't be true...I can't be their son...

I turn to Six. She looks even paler, if possible. She shrugs.

There's nothing they can say. I'm not falling for anything he says ever again. I cannot let the Realm get any hold on me. Ever, ever.

I turn to the door, grab the handle and another shot thumps into the wall.

'If I am your son, you wouldn't kill me, right?'

Leda. My mother. Apparently. Sick game.

'No, but we also can't let you leave here and return to the Orphans.' The Autokratōr voice returns. 'Do not be silly about this. It's not too late for either of you. Please, for your mother's sake, come to us willingly. You will have a place at my side. My heir. You can replace your brother if he fails to return to me. You can have anything you want, my son.'

I turn again to Six, looking at her as I speak. 'I will not be your pawn. Nor the Orphans. I've spent my whole life wondering who I am. But now I know. I am not your son, nor am I an Orphan. I will die rather than bend my knee to you.'

A long silence follows. I know these could be the last few seconds of my life. But if I die, at least I do it knowing who I am and what matters to me. I look again at Six, barely conscious.

Before the Autokratōr can respond, several things happen.

The bookcase to my left falls in slow motion, books spilling from the shelves and thumping the heads of the two Knights, the Autokratōr and his wife.

I spot the girl who's escaping with us, the girl whose name I don't know, skip around the falling rubble towards us.

For a second, I hesitate, watching the books and the bookcase itself, fall upon the leader of our Realm, and his wife. What if she is my mother? She seemed so genuine.

And if she's my mother, then is the Autokratōr my father?

But I don't wait to see if they survive the fallen bookcase.

I can't afford these sentiments right now.

I came here to save Six.

Finally, I recover my focus, and pull Six and me through the door behind us.

Followed by our saviour, we stumble down a dark, winding staircase.

CHAPTER 38
FINAL FIGHT

We dive on board the postal train. A few confused workers stare at us, but when they see the Knight, they step away and don't argue. Most of them look like Nameless slaves anyway.

I should invite them on board. Try to save them, too. But the time will come for that later. I need to do one thing right now. Save Six.

I put her down on the floor of the train carriage and stand next to the open door.

'How do I shut this?' I ask the Knight.

'Pull that red lever. I'm going up front to drive us out of here.'

I nod and she disappears into a small box room at the front of the train.

As I pull down the lever, a black blur drives into me.

The wind is completely ruptured from me as I'm thrown across the carriage, and the back of my head thumps against the opposite door.

My head spins as I try to focus upon the attacker.

'You, Seven, have made my day.' Twelve's fists come raining down on me. His early Military training is evident very quickly as I take blow after blow.

I throw a couple of feral swipes, but I'm beaten. My right arm is blazing from the bullet and my ribs and head are thumping so hard I want to both pass out and vomit.

Finally, he stops.

The train is now moving. Perhaps it has been for a while, but the rapid blows from Twelve are wrecking me. Dulling all my senses.

I can't let him win now. Not after all I've been through to save Six.

'He needs you alive, otherwise I'd end you right now, Seven.' He kneels and comes close to my face. 'I thought it was you. When you came into the Guardian's room earlier. Pol wouldn't have given any of us the time of day. He's a horrible bugger, but you...' He spits on my face. 'Be back in a moment, let me just deal with your driver.'

I hear his steps moving up the carriage.

'Watch out!' It's all I have left.

A scuffle follows and I push myself up, useless to help.

Six is still on the ground, but her eyes are now open. She nods to my belt.

My claustroBlade.

I glance at the fight at the front of the carriage. Both Knights are scrambling on the ground, thrusting kicks or punches between locks and grabs.

Six pulls herself up and takes my blade.

'I'll do it.'

'You don't have the strength,' I say.

'I have enough to end him.' She hobbles silently to the front of the carriage.

She stands, still as a statue, and waits.

Then, as Twelve gets the advantage and is jabbing the other Knight in the ribs, Six thrusts the blade deep into his back.

He collapses.

Then she crumples.

I crawl to her, my nose so clotted with blood I struggle to breathe.

The other Knight pulls the claustroBlade from Twelve's back and drives it into him several more times, including once to the head.

She looks at me and shrugs. 'I'm not taking any chances.' She chucks the bloody blade at my feet. 'Get some rest, we haven't got long until we need to change tracks.'

CHAPTER 39
NAMELESS

The train jumps every so often upon the tracks.

'They are old,' our Knight friend tells us. 'Not been used in a long time. You can feel the difference from the postal line to this one, no?'

I nod. Six lies across the seat, her head on my legs, fast asleep.

'Where will it take us?'

'Not completely sure, but outside the Wall. These old underground lines extended right out to the edges of Old London. This one goes to an airport. But we'll just go as far as we can.'

I nod. Now that we're safe, for the moment, I need to find out more about my newest companion. 'What's your name anyway?'

She smiles when she turns. 'I thought you Orphans didn't care about names.'

I smile back, a strange feeling after tonight.

'But if you really need to know, it's Helen.'

'Why did you help us, Helen? When the Autokratōr had us trapped in the Hall.'

'He said you could just take the place of Pol. My Pol. I just want to get to him. And you're my best bet to do that.' She turns back to the controls. 'Plus looks like *I'm the traitor* now, for helping you.'

We're in the front carriage of this train. It's my first time travelling in one. I'm sure it will probably be my last. I hope never to set foot inside Circle City again. But perhaps I won't get that choice.

I push Six's hair off her face, sweeping it straight back, over, and over. It's soothing, like it was back in camp, on those nights we'd lie out on the grass, staring up at the stars.

Back then, we only thought of our roles in the Realm. Speculated on what our names would be and what our futures would be like.

But none of that matters anymore.

I spent my childhood wanting to know my name.

To find out who my parents were.

And tonight, I found out both.

But I'm running from them, to save the person that matters to me most in this world. She means more to me than family. She always will.

And my name.

Well...I've yet to decide what it's going to be.

THE END

ACKNOWLEDGMENTS

To my wife, Helen, who has helped me shape my own identity and gave me the confidence, structure, and support to become a writer.

Without her, I wouldn't be Nameless, but I'd be pretty Aimless.

To my kids, E and X, always an inspiration for me on a daily basis, showing me love, and reminding me there's more to life than a screen, when I start to fail the Test as a father. But you're both far too young to read this book, so put it down now!

To all my writing friends, who continue to support me by shouting about, buying, or recommending my books. Thank you.

To Emma, for your Eagle-eyed edits.

Thank you to Tom, for your brilliant cover design, which really does make the book stand out, but also blend in with, books in the same genre.

To my beta readers, who did the Bulk of the developmental corrections that this novel needed: Natalia, Liz, Natasha, Rebecca, Jonny, Kate, Estelle, Richard, Carey, Kathryn, and Debbie.

I am writing this before the ARC's go out, but thank you to all of you who have read the book and are now here at the acknowledgements. Your support and reviews are greatly appreciated, and never taken for granted. I read every one.

And thank YOU, reader, for sticking with Seven through his struggles - this is only the start for him and his story. I hope you'll stick with us both.

ABOUT THE AUTHOR

Stuart is an award-winning author and secondary school teacher. He has a Masters Degree in Creative Writing and founded, and now runs, WriteMentor. In 2020 and 2022 he was placed on the SCBWI Undiscovered Voices longlist and named as an Hononary Mention for his novels 'Ghosts of Mars' and 'Astra FireStar and the Ripples of Time'. In 2023, he won the WriteBlend award for his middle grade debut, Ghosts of Mars.

Stuart was included in The Bookseller's 2021 list of Rising Stars in the publishing industry.

You can follow Stuart on his newsletter https://stuartwhite. substack.com/ or his website https://stuartwhiteauthor.co.uk/ or any of his social media channels.

Also by Stuart:
Ghosts of Mars: https://amzn.eu/d/d3YHR3A